Cave of the Wind

Avery Kloss

This is a work of fiction. Names, characters, places, and incidents either are the product of the author's imagination or are used fictitiously, and any resemblance to any persons, living or dead, business establishments, events, or locales is entirely coincidental.

CAVE OF THE WIND

All rights reserved.

Copyright © 2018 by Avery Kloss
ISBN: 1720464944
ISBN-13: 978-1720464945

Cover art by Avery Kloss

This book is protected under the copyright laws of the United States of America. Any reproductions or other unauthorized use of the material or artwork herein is prohibited without the express written permission of the author.

First Print Edition: May 2018

Chapter Twenty-Five	158
Chapter Twenty-Six	165
Chapter Twenty-Seven	173
Chapter Twenty-Eight	179
Chapter Twenty-Nine	185
Chapter Thirty	191
Chapter Thirty-One	198
Chapter Thirty-Two	204
Chapter Thirty-Three	210
Chapter Thirty-Four	216
Chapter Thirty-Five	222
Chapter Thirty-Six	227
Chapter Thirty-Seven	233
Chapter Thirty-Eight	239
Chapter Thirty-Nine	246
Chapter Forty	252
Chapter Forty-One	259
Chapter Forty-Two	265
Chapter Forty-Three	272
Chapter Forty-Four	278
Chapter Forty-Five	284
Chapter Forty-Six	290

"I am the bended, but not broken. I am the power of the thunderstorm. I am the beauty in the beast. I am the strength in weakness. I am the confidence in the midst of doubt. I am Her!" — Kierra C.T. Banks

CONTENTS

Chapter One	1
Chapter Two	9
Chapter Three	16
Chapter Four	22
Chapter Five	29
Chapter Six	36
Chapter Seven	42
Chapter Eight	49
Chapter Nine	55
Chapter Ten	61
Chapter Eleven	68
Chapter Twelve	74
Chapter Thirteen	81
Chapter Fourteen	88
Chapter Fifteen	94
Chapter Sixteen	101
Chapter Seventeen	107
Chapter Eighteen	113
Chapter Nineteen	120
Chapter Twenty	126
Chapter Twenty-One	132
Chapter Twenty-Two	139
Chapter Twenty-Three	146
Chapter Twenty-Four	152

One

You're safe here ...
Enwan's words drifted through my mind, but I knew the truth. Ronan and I and our son would not be safe at the cave of the wind, because a threat approached from the forest. I slept little, plagued by worry and restlessness that eventually drove me from the pelt where Ronan lay with Bannon; the two of them snuggled together. I added a thick branch to the fire, listening to the flames crackling around the wood, sparks flying.

Putty, a mangy camp dog, trotted over, licking my leg. "Hello," I whispered. I petted him, the animal sitting by my thigh.

Staring into the flames, I felt impatient for daybreak, knowing I had to speak to Ronan. I had confided to Enwan about Greggor, my friend having guessed my feelings, for which I felt a measure of alarm and shame. Greggor had held me hostage, the man my enemy, but my son considered him to be his father. I mustered up the courage to run away a few days ago, Shay and Wildre prodding me into escape. If they had not, I would still be with Greggor. I had grown soft as his captive, the man no longer the monster of my dreams; he was something else entirely now, but ... I could not stay with him.

Warmed by the fire, I sat with Putty, the dog curled up next to me. The blackness outside gradually lightened to grey, the sun rising. Soft snores filled the cave, people sleeping around the fire pit, while the smell of smoke and perspiration lingered. I waited for the men to rouse,

Bondo being the first up. He looked so odd with pale skin and flaxen hair, yet his face and build indicated he came from people like my mother's clan, his parents of mixed race.

"Good morning, Peta," he murmured, smiling. "You're awake early."

We talked in hushed tones. "I am."

"Excuse me. I'll be back." He left the cavern to relieve himself, the latrine at the side of the mountain. When he returned, he settled by the fire to chew on a strip of dried meat, the dog perking up at once. He fed him a small piece. "We hunt soon."

"There's plenty of meat still."

"I wish to smoke more. One can never have enough meat."

"True."

His attention lingered on me. "It's good to see you, Peta. I worried you might be gone forever."

I thought the same. "I … I had to come home."

"You do well for yourself."

"What do you mean?"

"You're skilled at survival. Most women don't travel alone."

"I hate it. It's not by choice." I thought about the past. "I'm forced to be alone when things go wrong, and things *always* go wrong." I stared sadly into the flames, knowing the difficult conversation I needed to have with Ronan. "I fear I won't be here long either."

"What? But, you only just arrived."

"Trouble comes. I brought it here." I nodded absently, unpleasant thoughts ruining what should be a perfect morning. "A man comes. He's looking for me. I don't know what he'll do when he finds me, but I can't risk it. I've angered him greatly."

I've cut him to the core, a wound that runs deeper than anger.

"I overheard some of what you said to Ronan. It's

this Greggor person."

"Yes, he's coming. He thinks I'm his wife. He sees Bannon as his own. It's best I leave at once."

"Ronan won't be happy. He's missed you greatly."

"We've been separated too often. We'll leave together. Then we'll return when it's safe." I had already settled on this. Now, I just had to convince Ronan.

"This Greggor person doesn't know where the cave is."

"No, but he's smart. He can follow a trail. I'm sure I've left something behind. I don't doubt that for a moment. I was careful, but he's an experienced hunter. He's on his way." A prickle of alarm drifted through me, confirming the suspicion I dared to voice. It made it real. "I have to wake Ronan. Is there enough dried meat for a long journey?"

"Plenty."

"Good. We'll need it."

Someone stirred, Enwan tossing back a pelt. "I can't sleep with this noise," he grumbled. Getting to his feet, he stretched arms over his head, his naked torso reflected in the firelight. "We might as well hunt soon. I shall nap the rest of the day." He strode to the entranceway, a thick barrier of thorny brambles blocking most of it to keep predators at bay.

The women continued to sleep, my son having spent the night without fussing, exhausted from traveling for days. I hardly desired another trek into the wilderness, but it could not be helped.

Bondo held out a piece of meat. "Eat."

I took it. "Thank you."

After Enwan returned, Ronan stirred, yawning loudly. He eventually stood, stretching and coughing, a series of groans escaping him. Bannon slept alone now, although Putty soon joined him, curling up next to the boy. I smiled fondly at the sight, wishing we did not have to leave. The cave provided a safe haven for everyone, the interior spacious, with enough room for even more people and another fire pit or two. With Saffron and Leota, it felt like a small tribe, the women accompanying Ronan and Enwan. I would not have time to get to know them, the need to flee once again a threat to clan harmony.

I waited for Ronan, his hair a riot of golden tangles down his back. He nodded at me, a tired smile softening his handsome face. We had not seen one another since before Bannon's birth, the reunion hardly complete, yet it would have to wait. I followed him out, as the grey of the day slowly transformed to a beautiful, deep blue, the sun not yet cresting the mountains in the distance.

"Good morning, Peta," he murmured. "I don't need a guide, but I'm pleased all the same."

I trod after him upon a small, rocky trail leading to the latrine, which I smelled on the wind. "I have to speak to you. It's important."

He urinated off the side of the mountain, his back to me. "You didn't sleep well, did you?"

"No. Trouble comes."

"This Greggor person?"

I sighed. "Yes. We're in grave danger."

"You believe he'll find you?"

"Yes."

"Despite being careful not to leave a trace?"

"It's impossible not to make a footprint or two here or there. I don't know." I ran fingers through my hair, feeling a growing sense of panic. "We need to go." I pointed to the mountains across the valley. "We must travel there. We can climb the mountain and watch the cave at a safe distance. Once he's gone, we come back."

He gazed at the treetops in the distance, pursing his lips. "I desired a better reunion with you than trekking across a river. You know it's a big river. It's wide and deep. There are shallow parts, but not many."

I had not realized that, frowning. "We have to cross or go some other way. It's urgent we set out at once. I'm sorry. I'm sorry to be so much trouble." Tears filled my eyes, my senses flooding with emotion and anxiety. "I had a bad dream. I know he comes. The last thing I want is for him to kill you or Enwan."

"Don't you think he'd do that anyhow?"

"Not if I'm not here. He'll just go on. He'll keep searching."

He scratched his head, frowning. "I'm happy to see you, Peta. I've missed you terribly. I'll do as you ask. You're not to travel alone again. We shall go together. If you feel strongly we're in danger, than so be it."

I flung myself at him, relief drifting through me. "Thank the gods. Yes, I feel strongly about it. We must pack and go as soon as possible."

***

Despite his agreeing to my plan, it took all morning to leave, Leota appearing aggrieved. She took Ronan aside, her eyes glistening. "Please, I don't understand. Why must you do this?"

I paced back and forth before the entranceway, Bannon secure in the leather carrier on my back, but he had not been all that happy to be put in it, fussing.

"We shall return when we're able. There's some trouble. Enwan and Bondo will see to you. You'll be taken care of, Leota."

"I consider you my husband. I feel like you're abandoning me. I'm carrying your child."

I could not pretend her words did not bother me. This would not have happened, if I had not been gone so long.

Ronan looked my way. "We'll come back soon. It's safer for everyone, if we leave until the threat passes."

"You say a man comes, and he means to kill us. By that reasoning, you're fleeing to safety, and we're staying to die."

"He wants Peta. He'll kill me, if he finds me here. He'll take Peta and my son away. He won't harm you. He has no quarrel with any of you. I must think of what's best for Bannon. I'm his father. I can't risk having him taken."

"What if we're all murdered? You brought me here promising a better life. It's beautiful, to be sure, but you never said you'd abandon me." She snaked her arms around his neck. "Please don't go. Take me with you. I can travel. I came here with you, and it wasn't easy, but I managed."

He worked to pry her arms from around his neck. "The less people, the better. We can disappear easier that way." Ronan glanced at Enwan, silently pleading for help.

"Let him go," said Enwan. "He won't be gone long."

"We'll cross the valley to the mountain. We need to leave now." Ronan stepped away from Leota, who pouted unhappily. "Bondo and Enwan will provide. You and Saffron are far better here than sleeping outside. You've everything you need in this cave." He kissed her cheek. "Take care, my sweet. I shall return."

I held a spear, with the bow around a shoulder, still waiting to leave. "Goodbye, Enwan. This won't be the last time you see me."

"You're always leaving, Peta."

"I'll be settled for good one day. I wish it more than anything." Although in that dream, I lived with my mother and sisters too, my family having scattered to whereabouts unknown.

"Goodbye then," said Ronan, smiling. "Fear not. We shall return."

"Safe travels," said Saffron.

Enwan murmured, "May the gods lead the way."

The dog followed us down the path, thinking we took

him to forage. I glanced at Ronan, feeling a measure of irritation over what I had just witnessed. "So, do you wish to tell me your true feelings? What is Leota to you?" Speaking of his paramour, she stood at the entrance of the cave with Enwan and Saffron. "What was that about?"

"I ... didn't know if I'd see you again."

"Do you consider her your wife?" From the odd expression on his face, I guessed this to be correct. Our relationship needed far more repair than I realized, my absence creating an opening for another woman to step in: a rival for his affection.

"I'm sorry about that." He touched my shoulder. "I knew you'd come back. We did speak of making the clan bigger." When I failed to look at him, he took my arm. "Stop, Peta."

A range of emotions from jealousy to shame and confusion battled within me. I faced him, meeting his gaze. "I shouldn't chide you for finding another wife. I shouldn't. I don't like it, but ... I'm in no position to judge."

"Because of Greggor." A hard gleam appeared in his eyes.

"Yes. You won't like this, but ... it wasn't my choice to leave."

"To leave *that* man?"

I nodded. "I was ... going to stay." It pained me to admit it, but I needed him to hear the truth. "His wife and her friend encouraged me to run. I wasn't so sure. I was ... torn. If I had stayed with him, he'd be my husband."

"He would've taken care of you."

"Indeed. He loved Bannon as his own." We began to walk, some of the tension having shifted. The dog stopped at a distance, watching us.

"I can forgive you for Greggor."

That sat ill with me, as did the entire conversation. "And you want me to forgive you for Leota?"

"I do feel a little guilty."

"That you left her?"

"That I brought her here in the first place. She needed protection. We wanted a bigger clan. I didn't stop to think how you might feel."

Before we stepped into the woods, I turned to face him. "I'm grateful now. We need this time alone together. I can feel a rift, Ronan. I don't like it." I had to somehow remember all the things I loved about him, praying to forget Greggor in the process. Would that even be possible? "What do you think?"

"I agree. I can see you're hurt by this. I don't know if you're upset about Leota or if you're missing Greggor."

He sees right through me …

I thought this reunion would be different. We had not even mated last night. I hated the distance between us, truly worried that nothing would ever be the same again. "I can forgive you for Leota. I wish we didn't have to go. I would've liked to know her. I don't mean to cause her pain by taking you away."

He touched my face, smiling, but a hint of sadness lingered. "It's only for a few days. I doubt it's even needed anyhow. We'll climb the mountain over there and make camp for the night. I desire to spend time with you and my son. I love you both very much."

Tears filled my eyes, my throat swelling with emotion. "I love you."

Two

Having walked a while, I squinted in the sunlight, feeling warmth upon my shoulders. Bannon slept at my back, the boy a sweet burden to carry. When we stopped to rest, the sound of rushing water echoed all around, but I had not seen the river yet. I lifted my son from the leather carrier, the boy fussing.

"I know you're hungry." He suckled a nipple, while I ate a piece of dried meat, sitting with my legs crossed. Small bugs crawled through the blades of grass by my knee.

Ronan scanned the forest, acutely aware of everything, every sound. He smiled at me. "Gods' teeth," he murmured, his blue eyes softening. "You're truly beautiful. You're even more beautiful with my son in your arms." He approached, kneeling before us, a thin sheath of leather hiding his manhood. "You've done well, Peta."

I continued to feel twinges of guilt, hoping the sentiment would pass. "I had little choice. The gods were kind to me where Bannon's concerned. They blessed me with a strong, healthy boy."

He touched his head gently. "I never wish to be parted from you again. Ever."

"You won't. I've come home." Perhaps I would have returned anyhow, even without Wildre or Shay's prodding. "It's your son too. He's just like you, Ronan."

"I was terrified for you. I've never been so worried. When I saw the three dead men, I assumed you'd bested them. That's when I realized you could protect yourself, but I knew not what happened to you after."

"My only wish was to come home. I lost my way for a while in the woods. After finding my mother and sisters, I asked the elders for direction. They had a vague idea where these mountains were. They helped me find the way." Draping Bannon over a shoulder, I patted his back. "We should go. I worry we're still too close yet. We've walked slowly."

"The river will be challenging. Are you prepared to swim? I know how much you hate cold water." A smile emerged.

I remembered being a child in his arms, the two of us bathing in a river many, many seasons ago. I had clung to him, hating every moment of the experience, but I had been a smelly, dirty little girl, needing the cleaning.

"There's the smile I've missed," he murmured. "I'm glad to see it."

I got to my feet, working Bannon into the leather holster. "I loathe cold water, but it must be done. I doubt Bannon will like it either."

"We can continue down the river, if you like. We needn't cross it."

"I want to watch the cave this evening. I have to know if he comes. If we climb the mountain, we can see it at a safe distance." Glancing at where the sun sat, we needed to hurry. "We haven't time to debate it. We should go."

He nodded. "Very well. Lead the way, my love."

Emerging from the forest, we neared the rushing torrent, the water cutting a wide path through the trees. A rocky embankment graced either side, while thick reeds jutted between the rocks, some stalks reaching my shoulders. Alarmed by the prospect of having to cross, I glanced at Ronan.

"It's high here," he commented, a worried look on

his face. "We should go down further to a shallower part. We can't risk this, not with Bannon."

I nodded, feeling apprehensive. "And you've fished here?"

"Indeed. The fish are quite good." He patted his belly. "Tasty."

"I hope it's better ahead." Danger lurked in deep, swift-flowing water. If Bannon somehow came free of the carrier, I would never see him again, the current taking him. "We can only hope."

With Ronan in the lead, we ventured further, walking by the edge of the river, finding a shallower part, which relieved me greatly. Boulders had tumbled from the mountain here, creating a narrow bridge. The water gushed around it, the rocks appearing dark and slick.

"We go together," said Ronan, reaching out a hand. "It's not so bad."

I wore leather around my feet, wondering if I should remove it. "I'm going barefoot."

"Me too."

We took a moment to divest the footwear, tossing them into a satchel. "I'm ready." Bannon remained quiet, the boy awake. "Hold on, little one."

Ronan's fingers grasped my wrist firmly. "I won't let you fall. We go together."

Stepping into the water, I shivered at the cold, but, thankfully, it only came to my thighs. Some of the rocks shifted as I stepped on them, forcing me to fight for balance, but with Ronan's help, we crossed a moment later, standing on the other side.

He smiled. "That wasn't so bad."

"We need to hurry now. It's far later than it should be. I want to climb the mountain and find a place to camp."

"We've time before sunset. Are you tired?"

"No, but Bannon will need to be fed in a while. I

want us to be out of the valley by then." I sat on a rock to replace the leather on my feet.

He took a sip of water from a bladder. "Aye, it's a good walk then. I hadn't expected such exercise. I should be used to it, though. All I've been doing is running around the woods searching for you. Now, we're still in the woods."

I frowned, feeling guilty. "I'm sorry. It's my fault."

"No. You were taken. That's not your fault. Everything you've done was for your survival." He tied leather to his feet, eyeing me. "I should be grateful you're so resilient. You've done well for yourself and our son."

"I wish we could just live at the cave and be in peace."

"We will. The cave won't disappear."

"No, it'll remain. It's people who go away."

"And they return." He stood, inhaling deeply, a smile appearing. "We'll come back in a day or two, no longer. It isn't the end of our peace or anything terrible, Peta. It's a moment for us to be together." He reached for me. "Being with you brings back every good memory I've ever had. Some of the happiest times of my life have been with you, my love."

Melting into his arms, I inhaled his scent, musk mixed with hints of sun and evergreen. "I feel the same. My happiest times were by the river so long ago and then when I found you again at the cave."

"And more are to come." He kissed my forehead. "Nothing shall part us ever again." He took my hand. "Let's walk. It's all uphill, I'm afraid. I don't look forward to it. Shall I carry Bannon?"

I hadn't thought of that, pausing. "That would make it easier for me."

"Then give me the boy."

Slipping the leather from my shoulders, I grasped Bannon. "Your father wants to carry you."

Ronan slid his arms through the contraption. "All right. He doesn't look like he weighs much."

I helped Bannon in, his little legs sticking out on either side. "How's that?"

"It feels like nothing. Let's walk." He strode forward, so I had to run to catch up. "We should make good time now."

I smiled at that, finding his attitude pleasing. Bannon seemed to enjoy traveling on his back, Ronan holding a spear in one hand and a bow over a shoulder. I carted everything else and the bundled up bedroll. We cut a path through the forest, the land untouched here, the birds noisy. The incline began almost immediately, winding upwards. I glanced at the tops of trees soon enough. Not used to such an arduous hike, I stopped to catch my breath, staring at the surroundings with my hands on my hips.

"Are you all right?"

"I'm fine."

Ronan waited for me. "I'll slow for you. I'm sorry."

"We need not climb the entire mountain."

"No, of course not, but we should go a bit higher. I want to find a flat spot to camp for the night."

Not having recovered yet from days already spent walking, I steeled my resolve. "Onward then." I joined him a moment later. "Go. You needn't wait for me."

"I do. I don't wish to have distance between us. You first, my love."

I stepped before him. "I'm fine, Ronan."

"You are, but we needn't walk so fast. You've only just returned from a long journey. We really should've stayed at the cave and faced this man."

It had been my fear that led us to this place. "A few days is all we need. Once Greggor isn't a threat, we'll go back." My body protested each step, the mountain growing rockier and steeper. The sun dipped lower, the shadows expanding, nearly reaching us. It would not be long before sunset.

"A little ways more, then we rest for the night. I wish to be with you, Peta. I still can hardly believe you're here."

I smiled at that. "We've been separated too long in this life."

"Not again."

Each step brought us higher, the terrain rocky, although bushes and trees grew in patches of earth. I cast a glance over my shoulder, seeing the side of the mountain where we lived in the cave, although brambles helped to hide the opening, but I knew where to look. If Greggor came, we would note his approach. We ventured higher, finding a suitable place to rest for the night.

Ronan reached for Bannon, freeing him from the leather. "We shouldn't make a fire. It'll be seen."

"I know. It's going to be cold tonight." I hated sleeping in the elements, but it could not be helped. "I wish there was a cave." But even that would reveal us if we made a fire, because of the drifting smoke and the light shining from the opening.

"We'll sleep with Bannon between us."

I took my son, the boy fussing. "He needs to be fed."

Ronan tossed down the bedroll, which consisted of several thin pieces of hide, one for our backs, one for a blanket, and the other rolled up as a soft place to rest our heads. There wasn't anything else to do. No need to gather wood for a fire. I sat with Bannon, letting him feed.

"I miss my comfortable home," grumbled Ronan.

"I'm sorry." I blamed myself for his discomfort.

"No, you were right." He squatted next to me, touching my face. "We couldn't risk it. If this person comes, then we might've fought. Someone would've been injured, no doubt. I'm certain he travels with men. From what you've said, he's ruthless. He's a leader accustomed to getting his way in all things. He would've taken you and

Bannon. I can't lose you again, Peta."

I touched his hand, pressing it to my cheek. "You won't."

"This is worth the risk of losing you. I'd never forgive myself, but then again, I'd be dead." A hard gleam flickered in his eyes. "The only way he's going to take you from me is if I'm dead."

A chill ran through me that had nothing to do with the wind. "I don't know if he would kill you. I don't want to find out."

He stared at nothing in particular, a look of distaste passing over his features. "It's not much, but we're reasonably hidden here. We can see everything. The forest's that way and the prairie over there. It's a good position."

Bannon crawled from my lap, getting to his feet. "Da ... da ... da ... "

Ronan grinned. "There you are, lad. You'll soon speak." He reached for him, hugging him. "You're more beautiful than I could've imagined."

It brought me such joy to see them together like this. "He does look like you. He has the same eyes and nose."

"I wish I could've been there when you had him. It must've been terrifying giving birth alone."

"I had little choice. He was easy. The gods were kind to me that day. They watched over us." How would we fare later? I glanced at the valley, feeling the chilly advent of night, and there would be no fire to warm our bones. I felt a twinge of jealousy for the occupants of the cave, knowing the luxury in which they slept—a warm fire and plenty of soft fur beneath them.

But ... would they be so lucky when Greggor came? I prayed he behaved mercifully. If he hurt my friends, I would never forgive him.

Three

Not being able to make a fire, we sat with a pelt over our shoulders, Ronan holding Bannon in his lap. The shadows of evening surrounded us, while insects chirped in the bushes. Chewing on a piece of meat, I eyed the valley, seeing a swath of darkness where the river flowed. A small patch of light emerged from the cave in the hill, its occupants enjoying a warm fire and a hot meal.

"I don't see anything yet," murmured Ronan.

"No." Tired from the hike, my thighs and calves felt sore from having climbed half the day. I picked at a scab on my knee. "I wonder if he'll come."

"You were so certain he would."

"I am." I hated that I yearned for Greggor, wishing I did not feel this way. Time would hopefully alleviate the sentiment, weakening it. "I have to relieve myself."

"He's about to sleep." Bannon's head fell forward, the boy struggling to stay awake.

"Put him down. He can sleep in the middle." Without daylight, only the orb in the sky offered illumination, yet, despite that, Ronan and Bannon appeared entirely in shadow.

"Don't go too far. We killed two cats, but I assume there are more."

I felt reasonably safe, not having heard a growl or seen any fecal matter or paw prints. "I killed one myself. Maybe the rest left?"

"Just take care. I don't know if there's a den near here. I'd rather not risk it."

Taking a spear, I nodded, although I doubted he saw me clearly. "I won't go far." I ventured a few steps away, concerned where the drop might be. Not being able to see properly, I stepped on something sharp. "Ouch!" After squatting behind a rock, a light in the distance caught my eye. Staring at it, I noted others as well, a line of lights moving across the prairie, counting five of them.

"Peta?"

"Yes?"

"I see something."

"He comes." I felt a moment of panic, realizing that although we had crossed the river and climbed partway up a mountain, we were not far away from danger.

"I assume it's one torch for each man. I count five of them."

"Not many, but ... enough." I sat beside him.

Bannon slept now, the baby breathing softly, a pelt draped over him.

"You were right. We left just in time."

"I pray he doesn't harm anyone." Chewing on a nail, I could hardly guess at Greggor's mood, but it appeared he left as soon as he knew I had gone missing. "He'll find the cave. If we can see it from here, so will he."

"Or he'll pass directly beneath it and not look up."

The line of lights flickered, slowly moving over grassland, where they would soon smell the heated pool. "He's smart. Even in the dark, he'll know."

"I'm glad we didn't make a fire. With any luck, he'll just pass by and leave us in peace."

I somehow doubted it would be that easy. "I hope that's true."

We watched the advancing men, while the inhabitants of the cave went about their business, not realizing trouble came. The light from the torches suddenly disappeared, the trees of the valley hiding them.

"They're at the base of the hill. Let's hope they continue on."

A yellowish light illuminated the entranceway of the cave. Anyone near enough could smell the smoke easily, the aroma of meat grilling distinctive. Holding my breath, I saw a flicker again, my spirits sinking. The men climbed! They had seen the cave.

"Well, I suppose it was too much to ask they didn't look up," muttered Ronan. "The dog should've alerted Enwan to trouble by now."

No sooner had he said that then a man appeared before the cave, with another behind him. "I see Enwan and Bondo. They've come out." Their thin, black forms stood before the entrance, as the torchlight approached. I swallowed nervously, the palms of my hands suddenly sweaty. "Oh, please don't hurt them, Greggor. Please."

Ronan's arm went around my back. "I almost wish I were there to help them. There are only five men. We could've taken them."

"We can't risk it." Greggor and his men were built for fighting, with strength and muscle twice the size I had seen on other men.

The strangers reached the opening, the light from the torches flickering, exposing the forms of several people. I held my breath, praying violence did not ensue. From this distance, we could not hear a word spoken, although some sort of discussion occurred. A moment later, all the men disappeared into the cave.

"What's happened?" I whispered, afraid my words might carry across the valley, but that would be impossible.

"They've been invited in."

We watched for a long while, nothing happening at all, but a man suddenly appeared in the entranceway, his form a black outline. "Peta!" he yelled. "Peta!"

I gasped, shocked.

"I reckon that's Greggor?"

"It is." I felt the most ridiculous urge to run down the mountain to reach him. "That's … him."

"Peta!" he shouted, the sound carrying.

"So, he did come for you. As far as I can tell, he's not slaughtered anyone. I imagine Enwan invited them in for supper. He's told some lie about you not having come. Or perhaps he said you left already. I don't think we're in danger."

Had the ploy worked? "I pray he doesn't harm anyone. I could never forgive him if he did."

"He has no reason to."

"Men have killed for less."

"I should be jealous. There's a party of men searching for you. He seems very determined."

"He'll give up when it yields nothing." All sorts of thoughts drifted through my mind, worry, relief, loss … and confusion. "They'll sleep there tonight, I suppose."

"I'll watch for a while longer. I'd like to know when they leave. If they go back the way they came, then it's safe to return, because they'll go home. If they continue down the valley, I fear they'll end up turning around. They'll realize no one's been down that way. Then they'll come back."

"What do we do then?" I had not thought of that.

"We might have to take a trip around the mountain and see what's on the other side for a bit. A few days at most. Then we'll come back when it's safe."

"We can manage that."

He touched my face. "I've missed you."

The tenor in his voice skimmed down my back, the meaning clear. "You have?" He had brought back another woman to satisfy his needs. "But you've Leota."

"And you had Greggor."

"I was his captive."

"Yet, you let him bed you."

I pursed my lips, not having a response to that. "I had little choice," I lied, knowing Greggor would not have forced me.

For a murdering heathen, he did have some honor. This idea conflicted me endlessly. As far as I could tell, his men had behaved themselves, Enwan and Bondo inviting them in. I imagined him sitting by the fire, perhaps on the very pelt where I slept last night. It felt odd knowing he was so near, yet … I could not see him.

"Come here." Ronan drew me onto his lap. "You care for the man."

"No." Wrapping my arms around his neck, I shivered, feeling the chill in the air against my bare shoulders.

"You're cold."

"A little."

"Let me warm you."

His lips met mine, the feeling soft and languid. I kissed him in return with equal sweetness. He lifted one of the pelts over our heads, while lowering me to where Bannon slept. I threaded my fingers through his hair, finding knots.

"You've not been groomed properly," I murmured.

He chuckled, "Now that you're back, you can see to it. I miss your shells and braids. I shall fix your hair and adorn it as it should be."

Pleasant memories returned of a time when we were entirely devoted, so deeply ensnared in the rapture of love. We were the only two who existed, and that was enough. I wished fervently to feel that way again.

A hand cupped my breast. "You're still so soft."

I touched his back, my fingertips pressing into the firmness of muscle. Then I boldly grasped his buttocks, squeezing. A shiver of pleasure drifted through me. "I remember this."

"I've missed you." As our lips merged, a hand landed

on my belly, slowly moving to my womanhood, where he felt me. "So wet," he murmured against my mouth. His fingers probed—seeking, a thumb running circles over sensitive skin. He settled between my thighs a moment later, his manhood hard and urgent.

"Oh, Peta," he groaned.

I clung to him, my teeth nipping at the salty skin of his shoulder. I trembled in his arms, meeting his thrusts, as I lifted my hips to match him. The sounds of our mating drifted, the heat of our bodies warming the skin thoroughly, despite the breeze. He slid his hands beneath my buttocks, lifting them, while hoarse, ragged breath filled my ear.

"Peta!"

Shuddering, I flung my head back, gasping as sensation flooded, the release of pleasure strong and swift. "Oh, yes!" We clung together for a long moment, his weight substantial. Shifting, he fell to the side, but a hand remained upon me. I gazed at the stars overhead, a sparkling contrast to the dark of night.

Ronan touched my face, caressing my cheek. "Do you think you can forget him?"

Basking in the warmth of the encounter, I hadn't expected the question, feeling slightly irritated by it. "I've made my choice. I came back to you. This is where I belong."

"I love you, Peta. You'll always have my heart."

I hated the guilt I felt, kissing him, whispering, "I love you."

Four

Ronan slept with Bannon curled up next to him. I chewed a piece of meat, eyeing the valley and the cave on the hill. Smoke drifted from the opening. I sat with my thoughts, a variety of conflicting feelings distressing me. I waited for someone to emerge from the dwelling, eventually seeing a man, who came to stand on the ledge. Even from this distance, I knew who it was—Greggor.

It was so odd to think of him in my home, having slept where I sleep, sitting before *my* fire. If I stood and yelled, he would see me. Hidden behind rocks and shrubs, I watched him gazing at the valley, his eyes drifting slowly from one end to the other. Another man appeared behind him, a conversation ensuing.

A thinner, taller man appeared—Enwan. I breathed a sigh of relief, knowing Greggor had not harmed my friends. Enwan and Bondo invited them in for the evening, offering a warm fire and shelter. Bondo suddenly came out as well, holding a spear. I had to wonder what Greggor thought of him, being a half-breed. He strode down the hill, presumably to hunt, while several men stood in discussion before the cave.

What will you do? Where will you go?

A hand touched my shoulder, making me jump. "Oh!"

"Sorry," murmured Ronan, coming to sit behind me. "I didn't mean to scare you." He squinted in the light of morning, his eyes sleepy. He stared in the direction of the cave. "Now I see your interest."

"I must know where he'll go now. You do wish to return home, don't you?"

"Yes." He gently massaged my shoulder, his fingers kneading a tight muscle. Sleeping on a thin pelt offered little cushion to the hardness of rock. "If he goes the way he came, then we return. If he continues down the valley, he'll soon turn around. We can't go back then, not for a while."

"That's what worries me."

Ronan dug through a leather satchel, pulling out several strips of dried meat. "He didn't kill anyone, from what I can see."

"No. Bondo's just left to hunt. I saw Enwan."

"He's not entirely unreasonable, although he did steal my woman."

I shrugged, staring at the cave, where several people stood, all of them Greggor's men. "I wonder what they'll do." Enwan appeared then, being taller and thinner. He led the way, the other men following him. "Where are they going?" A moment later, they emerged at the base of the hill, having ventured down the path.

"A bath."

"Oh, yes, of course."

"He's leading them to the water."

"Why would he do that? Why not just send them on their way?"

"Maybe their stench is overwhelming," chuckled Ronan.

"I wish I could have a bath. I ... long for the cave."

Ronan nodded. "It wasn't all that comfortable, but I adore being alone with you." He kissed my shoulder.

"Yes, that was nice," I murmured.

His arms went around me. "Your boy sleeps well. He didn't wake once."

"He's better about that. He's your boy too." Silence filled the air after that statement, as we watched the men disappear around the bend, presumably arriving at the heated pool.

When Bannon woke, I fed him, draping a pelt over his head to shield his eyes from the sun. I watched the valley carefully, seeing the group of men return to the cave, but they did not stay long.

"It looks like they're leaving."

Ronan held out a bladder. "Have some water. You must be parched."

"Thank you."

"The moment of truth has arrived," he murmured, sitting and resting his arms over his knees. "Where will he go?"

We did not have to wait for more than a few moments, the men winding down the path to the base of the hill. They did not turn for the grassland, heading in the other direction, traveling further into the valley.

"I feared that," said Ronan, frowning. He sighed heavily. "We'll have to go elsewhere for a while. They'll be back when they realize no one's been that way."

"I … oh, why don't they go away?" This new development annoyed me.

"He's determined to keep looking for you."

Bannon crawled out of my lap. "I have to change you. You're stinky."

"We need to find water. Once they're further away, we'll go."

"And where is that?"

"Around the mountain. I've wondered what's on the other side for a while now. It's our time to explore. We'll be gone a few days. We can make a fire and hunt."

That did not sound unreasonable. "All right."

"Long enough for him to go away. When it's safe, we come home."

I pondered that, holding onto Bannon's hand, as he walked unsteadily. "Then we should tidy up. There's no reason to linger." The prospect of another day of walking dampened my spirits, but Ronan's plan remained sound. We could not risk returning to the cave—not yet.

***

Instead of climbing down the mountain, we went around it, although there wasn't a path and the hike proved challenging. When we reached the other side, the descent began, a green valley emerging, where the river continued and more mountains spanned the distance. Beyond the valley lay a border of trees, where the edge of the forest began. I had expected to see prairie, surprised by the thickness of the vegetation.

"That's going to hide us rather well," said Ronan, smiling.

We had stopped to eat, Bannon crying of hunger, and now we walked again. "The water looks refreshing."

"It's the same river."

"Yes, I know."

"We'll find a place to make a shelter. I'll hunt something tasty."

"Or I can."

"You look tired, Peta. You've done nothing but walk for days now. You should rest."

"I hope it's a good shelter. I want a fire."

"He can't see us here. We can make as big a fire as you like."

My legs protested the downward climb, rocks sliding loose beneath my feet, some tumbled down the mountain, making loud cracking noises. I cast a nervous glance over my shoulder, worried about predators and people, not knowing what we might find in these woods.

"Clans live here, somewhere."

"I can't say." He waited for me, holding out a hand. "You nearly fell there."

"I'm fine."

"Let me take Bannon."

"I've got him. You're carrying everything." He had my bow and spear, along with his weapons and the bags and bedding. "I want to find a nice spot soon."

"It's a good ways still."

"Well, down is easier than up." The gravel from the mountain left a layer of filth on my arms and legs. It covered Ronan from head to foot, even his face dirty. I surmised I looked the same. "We're so dusty."

"Indeed," he chuckled.

I frowned at that, preferring to sleep indoors and indulging in heated water for cleaning. I licked parched lips. "I plan to fling myself in the water. I don't care how cold it is."

"Me too. Go on."

He let me pass, keeping a lookout behind for trouble. The rocks continued to shift beneath my feet, some digging into the skin painfully, despite the leather barrier. I inhaled dust at times, smelling the earth in my lungs. Once we finally reached the bottom, I glanced up, stunned to have come so far. A swath of white graced the tip of the mountain, but that stood at an enormous height. I would never climb that high.

Ronan suddenly held up the bow, affixing an arrow. "What's the matter?" Alarmed, I wished I had my weapon, but it remained over his shoulder.

"Game." Letting the arrow fly, it landed out of sight, having torn through a thicket.

"How can you see anything?"

"I might've gotten it." He waited for me, taking my hand. "It was a stag. I hope it didn't escape." We came upon the animal a moment later, the arrow jutting from its head. "Ah, this will make a fine meal." He gutted the creature, the entrails sliding to the ground in a bloody heap.

I reached for the leather bags and spears, knowing he would have to carry it on his shoulders. "We should look for shelter."

"Onward then." He grunted, hoisting the stag upon his back. "This way."

Having walked the day away, we watched the sun disappear behind the mountain, the coolness of early evening approaching. Bannon babbled incessantly, the baby happy at the moment, but that would not last. We slowly approached the river, finding it not as deep here, the water glistening invitingly.

"You go first," said Ronan, dropping the carcass at his feet. "I'll hold Bannon."

Sliding the leather from my arm, I grasped my son, handing him to Ronan. "Go to your father for a moment. He'll need cleaning too."

Ronan grinned. "I've got it." He tossed the carrier to the ground. "Let your mother bathe, little one."

"Ba … ba … ma … "

"He's trying to talk."

I smiled at them, although Ronan held Bannon awkwardly, not used to handling babies. "I'll be back." Leaving the leather skirt at my feet, I ventured in, finding it chilly. Not desiring to spend too much time in these conditions, I sat, washing my face and arms, while my hair floated around me.

"I can bathe him quickly. He won't like it." Ronan approached with Bannon, the boy crying at once, stunned by the cold. "There, there. This won't take long." He kicked his legs, fighting the water, but Ronan held him securely, the two of them submerging.

My son's cries rang out, the noise carrying. I eyed the forest, worried someone might hear us. "I've got him." I reached for Bannon. "He's being too loud."

"I'm sorry. You're right. We should be more careful."

"Shush now. Shush. I trained him to be quiet before. I don't know what happened to that." Standing upon wet rocks, I untied one of the leather bundles, draping it over him. "There. That's better, right?" The portion around his buttocks hung wetly, needing to be wrung out. "You're going to be fine." Tears glistened in his blue eyes.

"Ma … ma … no!"

I stared at him. "Did you say no?"

He pointed to the water. "No! No! No!"

"Your first words." But those hadn't been his first. He had called Greggor papa before, but I had to forget about that.

Ronan approached. "I didn't mean to upset him."

"I was like that, you'll remember. I hated cold water. He just told me no."

"That's everyone's first word. I'm sure I said that too when I was small."

Bannon's lower lip protruded. "No! No!"

I rolled my eyes. "Oh, my. We'll never get him to say anything else."

"Give him to me, so you can ready yourself. We shouldn't dally. It's getting darker by the moment, and we need the light to find shelter. I pray the gods are kind to us. I want to find something comfortable."

"I'd like that too."

Five

The wooded area did not yield a cave, although we found a small, secluded copse, where the soil felt soft beneath my feet. Surrounded by trees and bushes, several species sported thorns, creating a natural protective barrier. Ronan worked to erect a simple structure, cutting branches and leaning them together, tying them with leather twine, although we brought only enough to secure the bedrolls.

I let Bannon play, the boy toddling around on grass, his happy shrieks filling the air. He hadn't been free to explore like this since I left Greggor's clan. He stayed within the enclosure, while I foraged for firewood.

Bannon leaned upon the stag's carcass, while drool dribbled to the fur of the animal. "What are you doing?" I held an armful of branches. "Why are you letting him play with our food?"

"I didn't know." Ronan tossed down a stone. "The shelter's mostly done. I can't do more now. It's getting dark. I'm looking for rocks, then we'll have supper." He ogled his handiwork, a satisfied gleam in his eye. "We can pack the roof with grass tomorrow. It'll help keep the rain out."

"I hope we don't have to stay too long."

"A day or so, maybe more."

I took Bannon's hand. "Stop touching that. He's our supper." The child grasped the antlers, babbling happily. "You'll hurt yourself."

Ronan strode away. "I'll be back."

When he returned, we settled in for the night, the forest dark and breezy, although the fire helped warm the small shelter. Ronan built it before the structure, grilling meat in the flames. The smell made my mouth water, the prospect of fresh meat a pleasure. Bannon and I sat on the bedroll, the ground feeling softer than the rocks on the mountain.

"Here you are." Ronan held out a stick, meat dangling from it. "It's done."

"Thank you." I ate, chewing. "In time, I'm going to mash meat for Bannon. He's bigger now. He should be able to eat it."

"He has a few teeth already." Ronan scooted nearer, his thigh brushing mine. He eyed me. "Your breasts are bigger."

"They're heavy."

"You've a babe to feed, that's why."

"They were even bigger before, when I wasn't able to feed Bannon for a few days. Now I don't make as much milk."

"I wonder what it tastes like?" He grinned.

"You may try it, if you want."

He nodded, holding out a branch with meat. "I just might."

"I like the cave better. There's more light to work after it's dark. We don't have to sleep as early or rise as early." I often sat around making baskets or sewing things or sharpening arrows.

"There are benefits, yes. We'll go home soon enough. Once this Greggor person realizes you're not here, he'll give up."

I felt the oddest sense of loss whenever Greggor's name was mentioned. "I hope so." Bannon crawled over to me, fussing. "What is it?" I held him to me, the boy suckling a nipple. "Sungir had a hollowed out rock. He would crush herbs and things in it. He had another rock that fit his hand perfectly. It was rounded on the end. He used to work nuts and dried leaves into tiny pieces. I could make meals for Bannon the same way. He eats berries now, but they have to be very ripe."

"You and Saffron and Leota can share ideas about such things. I know little of what food babies eat. If I ever had an ailment, I'd see the healer."

"I know some."

"You know more than that. I saw what you did at the cave. You made a stand out of branches and hung herbs. Enwan and I didn't touch it."

"I did that before Bannon came. I wanted to have everything ready, if I needed it. But, I didn't need it."

"You're very brave. I don't know how you managed alone. I was worried about you. I prayed you found someone to help you."

"I didn't. I had to do it myself." I hated being alone, memories returning with the impression of loneliness. "I'm glad you brought back women. I told you to make a trap for them, remember?"

"I do," he chuckled. "You said we should dig a hole to catch two-legged creatures."

"Yes, I said that. Sungir used traps for woodland animals and protection."

"We didn't have to resort to that. We found them on our travels."

I yawned, glancing at my son. "You go sleep now." Bannon crawled to the pelt, grasping at a thin leather cover. "That's a good boy."

Ronan leaned in, smelling of smoke and musk, the firelight flickering in his eyes. "For all your adventures, you're truly no worse for wear."

"I am unharmed." *Mostly.*

From the outside, I appeared as always, not having been marred by man or beast, but my innermost feelings had shifted. I hardly had time to dwell on this change, wishing it to go away. I wanted to be the old Peta I knew, the girl who cared for nothing other than her family and her man. I had Ronan with me now, his thigh pressed to mine, but I knew of another that lurked … searching for me. I had to push it from my mind.

"We should sleep," I murmured, wrapping my arms around his neck. "I wish nothing other than this quiet. We needn't rise early to watch if an enemy approaches. We're hidden and safe."

His lips brushed my cheek. "Might I love you again?"

"Yes, Ronan," I breathed. "I'd like that."

***

Despite having a roof made of branches, I still woke early, light filtering between the leaves. Bannon fussed once during the night, and I fed him, the boy sleeping between us for warmth. I sat up, brushing hair from my face. Needing to relieve myself, I crawled from the enclosure. The scent of pine filled the air, while a thick, greyish mist lingered.

Without leather on my feet, I did not go far before squatting. I listened to birdcalls, the sounds of the forest alive with all manner of insects and animals, the fluttering of wings over my head. On the way back, I stopped to pick up branches, finding an abundance of dried wood nearby. If anyone had been here, they had left no sign.

"There you are." Ronan appeared, a spear in his hand.

I smiled, remembering the gentleness of his caress the night before. "It's peaceful."

"Bannon's still sleeping. We can smoke meat, if you like. It must be done today, or it'll go bad."

That would require sturdy branches and a bigger fire. "We can."

"Will you forage?"

"Yes, I'll take Bannon. I'll teach him how to pick

berries. He might like that."

"Then we've much to do. I'd best prepare the meat."

I nodded. "I'll see to Bannon." I dropped the bundle before the shelter, eyeing the smoking fire. Noisy black insects buzzed around the dead stag, the animal only partially eaten. It was a shame to waste so much meat, but much could still be smoked.

Ronan worked to make the fire bigger, erecting sturdy branches to drape meat over. After feeding and changing Bannon, we ventured from the enclosure. I held a leather bag, which swung at my side.

"Let's look for berries, shall we?" Never wanting to be in the wilderness without some means of protection, I carried the bow and a satchel of arrows. From where we stood, I could smell smoke. "We shouldn't go too far." Bannon toddled along, wearing leather tied to his little feet. He fell over a branch then, crying. "Oh, no!" A cut on his knee began to bleed. "You'll be fine. It's just a scratch."

Ronan appeared, holding a spear. "Something wrong?"

"He fell. He's fine." I smiled, appreciating the sight of him, his easy smile and handsome face filling my vision. From beneath the leather skirt, his thighs broadened and then narrowed at the knee.

"You're beautiful, Peta."

"You look very well yourself."

He grinned crookedly. "I'm glad you think so."

Bannon, having recovered from the fall, wandered off, stopping to peel bark from a tree. "Don't go far."

"I should watch the fire. I might burn it all down, if I'm not careful."

"We'll walk around here. I'm hoping there's a bush with berries or something nice to eat. My feet hurt."

"Bannon's found something."

I glanced his way, seeing a rounded piece of wood in his hands. "What's that?"

Ronan frowned, pursing his lips. "Let's have a look." Bannon nearly stumbled again, catching on a root. "What have you there, boy?" He took the item from his hands, turning it around.

"No!" he protested, reaching his hands up. "No!"

I gasped, clearly recognizing what looked like a human skull. "Oh, no. It's … that's a person."

"Was." Ronan held it up, turning it from side to side. A gash appeared at the top of the head. "He or she met a bad end."

I shivered, glancing around, looking for any sign of trouble. "Where did you get that, Bannon?" But, I knew he would not answer me. Picking him up, I balanced him on my hip. "I'm going to have a look."

"I'm coming with you. I don't think we should let him play with it, Peta. It's not right. It should be buried."

I only half listened to him, focusing now carefully on the ground, seeing what looked like a bone. "There." I pointed at it.

Ronan picked it up. "A part of the dead person, no doubt. That doesn't look like any animal I've ever seen."

"And there." A small pile of bones appeared.

"That's … more than one person." Ronan frowned, holding a bone with a foot attached, the bones there tiny. "Many people. Someone tossed them in a heap."

"Or killed them in a heap." A sense of unease drifted through me. "I don't know. Is it safe here?"

"These don't look new. They've been whitened by the sun." He examined a leg bone, holding it up. "The birds chewed this rather well."

"Birds don't chew."

He brought it to me. "What do you make of that?"

I stared at what looked like small gouges notched into the bone. "I don't know." I took it from him, examining it. "The teeth of some animal, I suppose."

Ronan lifted the spear tip to it. He then fit it into one

of the indentations. "Or ... a tool made them."

I shook my head, finding this all far too disturbing. "We might make camp elsewhere." I ventured around, eyeing the ground, finding what looked like a circle of rocks. "An old campfire." I knelt, feeling the ashes. "Cold." A breeze moved a branch nearby, catching my notice. Seeing what hung from a tree beyond, I gasped. "Ronan!"

His expression had lost all humor, as he strode to the tree, looking up. "What madness is this?" A body hung from a limb, although it was nothing but bone now, swaying in the wind.

"Who would do that?"

"Someone was here." He used the spear to shove aside bushes, his eyes scanning the ground. "There are old spear tips and tools. Look. Another pile of bones."

"Some sort of graveyard?"

"No."

"What if there's a cat den? We're in danger, Ronan."

"Whatever it was is gone."

"What is it?"

"I surmise they were eaten."

"Well, yes. Animals have been through here."

"No, not animals. Other people ate them. They used tools to cut away at the flesh on the bones."

My mouth fell open, as a wave of queasiness had me holding my stomach. "Why?"

"I don't know. There's plenty of game." He scratched his neck. "Where did all these people come from?"

"Are the ... people who ate them still here?"

"No. We're the only ones."

"I don't want to stay longer, Ronan. I wish we could go home."

He sighed. "Another day, then we'll travel elsewhere. I like the copse. It's a shame about ... " he nudged a bone with his foot, "the dead people."

Six

Bannon sat on my lap, while I hummed to him softly. A robust fire hissed and crackled, Ronan cooking meat. He held out a sizzling piece for me.

"Thank you." I tore a chunk off with my teeth, the savory flavor filling my mouth. "It's good."

"We've plenty."

Bannon felt heavy, the boy tired from walking and playing all day. "He's nearly asleep." I found a flat stone and another that fit my hand, intending on crushing some meat for him to eat. The smell of smoke lingered, meat drying on several branches, a contraption Ronan made. "We're provided for."

"Indeed. The gods have been kind today."

"But what of those … bones?"

"It was something that happened long ago, Peta. I wouldn't worry over it."

"All those people died." We examined the pile of skeletons, finding most with crushed skulls or broken necks. "They met a violent end."

Ronan shrugged, chewing. "It's not uncommon."

"I don't want to encounter whoever did that."

"We won't. They're long gone. Perhaps it was a disagreement between clans. The losers … met their end."

"They killed little ones as well. What sort of clan has no regard for children?"

"Enwan and I came across some less than friendly clans in our travels. They would not let us pass through their land. I feared we might have to fight them, but luck led us to safety."

"We should be wary."

He smiled slightly. "Always, my love. One must always be careful."

I gently moved hair from Bannon's eyes. "He's asleep." Getting to my feet, I placed him on a thin pelt inside the shelter, kissing his forehead. "Dream well, my precious boy."

Ronan held a piece of meat over the flames using a stick. "He's a good baby. He hardly ever cries."

Eyeing the trees, I glimpsed the glowing orb of the moon through the branches, the night quiet, although the fire crackled. "I tried my best to train him not to cry. It doesn't always work, though."

"Come sit with me." He patted the ground beside him. "Have some more food. You need to eat."

Scooting in close, I felt the warmth of his thigh against mine. "I'm quite satisfied, Ronan."

His arm went around me. "I am too." His lips brushed my cheek. "You're all I've ever wanted. You and Bannon and whatever children we might have in the future, if the gods are agreeable."

"This is paradise. It's never too hot or too cold. The game's plentiful. I only wish for a hot bath tonight. My back aches."

His hand drifted down my spine. "I can help."

Wrapping my arms around his neck, I inhaled his musky scent. "You need a bath too."

"We're dusty. In another day we'll go home."

"I know."

"Where we'll sleep in comfort."

"With your other woman," I murmured dryly.

"I know you're sore about that. I'm not blind. I'm sorry."

"I never thought I'd have to compete for your

affections."

"You don't. I belong to you, Peta, first and foremost. You've returned with an unexpected surprise as well. He's the reason we're far from our comfortable shelter. He's the reason we're hiding in the woods."

"Yes, it's regrettable." I did not want to think about Greggor; just the mention of him left an empty pit in my belly. Had he left the valley yet or did he continue to search for me? It would be impossible to know. "We each have something to forgive the other for."

He squeezed me. "And we shall. I'm not angry. You had to survive. You needed to find that man to get our son. I brought Leota home to expand the clan. It won't be long before we've more children."

I thought about the possibility of another baby, realizing I had not bled yet this moon cycle. "Yes."

"We've eaten all we can tonight." He tossed a charred piece of meat into the fire. "Let's settle in to sleep. We must decide what to do tomorrow. I think it's too soon to return home."

"I agree." I glanced at the forest around us, glimpsing what looked like a set of eyes. Some animal lurked. "We should keep the weapons close at hand."

"Yes, of course."

"Something's in the bushes."

"A small creature, harmless."

"I haven't heard the growl of cats, which is good."

"No, nor wolves. It's … very quiet this eve."

I crawled over to the shelter, fingering the spear. "Are you coming to bed?"

"Yes, my love."

***

The screeching of a bird woke us far too early, the animal in a tree over our heads. I wanted to wring its neck to shut it up, but such a thing was impossible. Annoyed, I burrowed further into Ronan's side, his arm going around me. When Bannon fussed, I pressed the boy to my breast to feed him, hoping for a little more sleep.

"We needn't do a fire," murmured Ronan, a yawn escaping him. "The meat should be dried. I'll pack it away."

I listened to the birds, the noisy one still causing a ruckus. "It's too loud. Can you throw a rock at it?"

He laughed at that. "The cave provides a barrier, doesn't it?"

"To many things." I longed to be home, but it wasn't safe to return just yet. "I have to relieve myself." Bannon continued to feed, the boy hungry. "It's too early." My voice sounded tired, gruff.

"Rest, Peta. There's no need to charge into the forest. We aren't going anywhere. We're just waiting for your lover to leave the valley."

I frowned. "Don't call him that."

"It's what he is."

"Was, briefly. He's … he has people to manage. His clan is rather large. I'm certain they need him. He'll soon see the folly of his ways. Chasing after some woman … he hardly knows. He'll realize how stupid he is."

"Perhaps."

Finished with feeding, Bannon slept again, snuggling in soft leather. I slipped from the shelter, squinting in the bright light of morning. Venturing a little ways, I squatted to do my business, hearing the snapping of a twig behind me. Alarmed, I spied Ronan approaching, breathing a sigh of relief.

"Let's find some water," he said, urinating into a bush. "I could use a wash."

"Is Bannon asleep still?"

"Yes."

"Will he be safe alone?"

"We won't venture far." He held out a hand. "Come, Peta. You worry too much over everything."

Striding into the trees, I eyed the forest warily. "With good reason. My family disappeared on a peaceful day just like this one. We bathed in a creek, and I went home before them. When they did not return, I went back to find them, only someone had stolen them. I don't trust … the peace. I've learned to be wary of it."

"You disappeared while we hunted." He squeezed my hand. "We've suffered many a shock, haven't we?"

"Too many, too many unpleasant surprises. I'm tired of it all. I desire nothing more than to tend to my family from the safety of a clan."

"Which is exactly what Enwan and I plan to do."

The sound of trickling water reached my ears. "Let's not dally. I don't want to leave my son alone too long."

"Nor do I."

Approaching the brook, the water flowed clear straight to the bottom. I knelt on wet rocks, tossing it into my face. "It's cold."

Ronan discarded his skirt, stepping into the creek, which reached his knees. "Dreadfully cold!" He sat, making a face. "Gods' teeth." Then he washed his face and hands, tossing water over his shoulder. "Won't you join me?"

"I think not." I made quick work of bathing, shivering at the icy sensation, my skin tingling. "It looks good enough to drink."

"I've had some. It tastes fresh." Dunking his head beneath the surface, Ronan scrubbed his hair, emerging with sodden locks. "I'm finished with this. I can't stand it another moment." He jumped to his feet, hurrying for the embankment. "Let's go, Peta."

An inkling of trouble brought my attention to the woods again, my ears alert for the slightest sound. "I need to see Bannon." Terrified that something might have happened to my son in our short absence, I ran towards camp, my breath catching in my throat. I heard nothing other than birdcalls and insects, the world waking with the sun. "Bannon!"

Ronan came in directly behind me, his hand grasping a spear. "He's sleeping, Peta. Don't wake him."

"Bannon!" If anything happened to my son, I would never forgive myself. He had already been taken once from me. Memories of those feelings returned, the horror of not knowing where my child was far too real and unpleasant. I never wanted to relive such a thing again.

"He's fine."

I reached the shelter a moment later, seeing the lump beneath the pelt. Relief swept through me. "Thank goodness." I eyed Ronan. "I don't like to leave him. I won't again."

"Of course not." He knelt before me, a smile on his face. "You're an excellent mother. You should always trust your instincts on these matters."

"I haven't always, though. I've been wrong before. I paid a heavy price for being wrong, Ronan."

"I know, but it ended well. We're reunited. The gods brought us together. We're a family, my love."

I grasped his hand, while a wave of sweet emotion drifted through me. "We are." I hugged him. "I'm sorry. I'm sorry for it all. I do so love you."

He held me close, his mouth by my ear. "I love you."

Eager to show him how I felt, I kissed him. "We won't ever be parted again."

"Don't dream of it."

Seven

I ground up meat for Bannon, mixing it with water to make a soft paste. He sat on Ronan's lap, as I fed him using a short stick. Satisfied he could now take solid food, I happily changed his soiled garments and took him foraging, while Ronan followed, helping to pick edibles.

"These are good." He held a clump of green grass with roots dangling.

"Yes, but they're better boiled. We've nothing to boil anything with."

"I can dig a pit and line it with skin. We fill it with water and drop a few hot stones in." A crooked grin emerged. "We'll make do."

"It would be delicious. I'm looking for berries and mushrooms. I'm hoping for nuts."

"Then let's continue."

I eyed him askance. "You don't mind doing woman's work?" Men rarely foraged, finding the task annoying. I adored searching for things, wondering what I might find around the next bush, but men preferred to hunt, exerting themselves and killing things.

"I'd tan hide with you, if I had to. I can best admire you this way, anyhow. You move with an easy grace. Your limbs are long and enticing. I especially like it when you bend over to pick something up."

A tingle ran down my spine. "Ronan!" I carried Bannon on my back, the boy babbling happily.

"He'll be ready for a nap when we return. I'll be ready for mating." He strode past me. "Let's see about those berries now, shall we?"

I grinned at his broad shoulders, the skin tanned and muscled. "Yes, my Lord." Stunned I had uttered such words—words I had only ever spoken to Greggor, I prayed he had not heard me. Ronan continued, seemingly oblivious to being called a lord. I hadn't meant to do it, the phrase slipping easily from my lips. It brought back every memory I had of Greggor, the bittersweet torment of being in his arms. I pushed the thoughts aside, determined not to ruin the beautiful day—a day I should be enjoying with my family.

Before returning to camp, I gave Bannon to Ronan, the boy fussing, wanting a nap. "Watch over him, will you?"

"What are you doing?"

I glanced at the tree before me, the branches thick and inviting. "I plan to climb to have a look. Perhaps I can see something."

"More trees, is my guess." A smile lifted his lips.

"Just watch over him. Don't let him go far." I grasped at a branch, hoisting myself up. "I won't be long."

He stood gazing up at me. "Be safe, my love."

I climbed quickly, my lungs burning from the exertion. "I'm nearly there." The highest branches thrust far from the canopy, allowing for an unobstructed view, although Ronan had been correct. I glimpsed only forest all around with a mountain in the distance, the mountain that stood before our valley and our home.

"Anything?" he called.

I observed all directions, looking for smoke from a fire. "Nothing."

"That's good, I suppose. They've gone on."

Had Greggor given up so easily? Why did that thought displease me? "Possibly." Nothing seemed amiss in these woods. The land appeared peaceful, with ever-present birdcalls and buzzing insects. "I'm coming down." Grasping at a lower branch, I found my footing and descended, until I sat on the last one. "I'm hungry." Dropping to the ground, I snatched up a leather bag filled with nuts and berries. "I want to go back."

Ronan grinned. "It's sleep time." He held Bannon securely, the boy clinging to him.

He hadn't known his son for long, and yet they began to bond, which relieved me. "You keep him. I'll carry the spear."

"Yes, Wife."

I giggled at that. "From the smell of it, you need another bath."

"You'll have to take me as I am. I've no desire to get in cold water again."

"Nor I."

We ventured the way we came, although the shadows of the day broadened, darkening the forest floor, which smelled of damp earth. Bannon fussed now, his cries resonating. Once at the shelter, I fed him, the boy sleeping almost instantly. Placing him on a thin pelt, I covered his face with soft fur, admiring how sweet his features appeared, how pink his little mouth looked.

An arm went around my middle. "Come here, woman," growled Ronan. "You've teased me all day. I long to have you." He pulled me onto his lap. "This is where you belong."

"What about the food?" My belly growled. I suddenly missed having Shay and Wildre about, the women making Greggor's meals for him. I had grown used to being tended to, not having to cook or clean. I had only to care for Bannon and … see to my Lord's pleasure.

Blast it! Why must I still think of him?

I forced the thought aside, focusing on Ronan's enticing lips, which he held slightly open. Kissing him, I closed my eyes, as his fingers tangled in my hair.

"You taste as delicious as I remember," he murmured.

"You kissed me not that long ago."

"And it was just as good."

I laughed at that, shivering at the feel of his hands on my back, pressing into my skin with firm fingertips.

"How soft you feel."

"How hard you are." I squirmed on his lap.

"I know now why men don't forage."

"Why?"

"All that bending over. I see everything when you bend, my love. That skirt covers little."

"I understand."

"We wouldn't be foraging for long. I'd have you against a rock just as fast, mating you, and then no work would ever get done."

I smiled at that, caressing his cheek, feeling the coarseness of the hair that covered his face. "We've time now to mate."

"Oh, we shall," he laughed huskily, mirth shining in his eyes. "I intend to pleasure you."

"Is that so?"

"Yes, as you pleasure me."

"Then no more talk." I placed a finger to his lips. "I wish only to feel this moment."

***

I snuggled into Ronan's chest, the man beside me snoring softly. Safe within the confines of the shelter, I heard only the sounds of insects. Bannon slept at my back, the baby not having fussed yet. Ronan and I mated, the aftermath producing pleasing sensations, although I felt distinctly tired now. Closing my eyes, I drifted, my mind thoughtless, my body yearning for sleep, but a distinct rumble caught my notice.

Sitting up, I flung hair over a shoulder. "What was that?"

"Huh?" Ronan grumbled. "Go back to sleep, my love."

"Listen," I whispered. And then I heard it again: the low growl of a predator. "Cats."

"What?"

"They're near." The rumble echoed once more, although this time closer.

Ronan jumped to his feet, grasping the spear. "Arm yourself, Peta!"

All hope of sleep now forgotten, I picked Bannon up, placing him in the leather holder that I slung about my back. He continued to sleep, blissfully unaware of the danger. Ronan stood by the opening of our flimsy shelter, having tossed wood onto the dying fire to wake it. The cats did not like fire in the least, avoiding it whenever possible. A growl echoed, a warning of the approaching predator. I fixed an arrow in the bow, holding it before me with my feet apart, my eyes traveling from side to side, worried of what lurked in the darkness.

"Are they coming?"

"Shush!"

The flames in the fire burst to life, igniting around several branches and offering illumination. Something shook the branches of a nearby bush. I held my breath, praying a cat did not pounce on us, the possibility a real threat. I had killed one on my own once, the task necessary for my survival. Ronan and I stood just within the confines of the shelter, the structure made of sturdy branches and a grass roof. It provided a barrier to the rain and the sun, but little else.

A low rumble sounded alarmingly close. I continued to eye the trees, fearing, yet anticipating the glow of yellow eyes. I saw them a moment later. "They know we're here,"

I murmured.

"Prepare yourself." He held the spear, his stance wide, while a determined expression pinched his features. "Be strong."

Despite the blaze, the flames lifting into the air, a cat suddenly appeared across the way, having sauntered from the trees. A halo of hair framed his face, the animal fearsomely majestic. Two female cats emerged directly behind him, their fur far shorter. I did not wait another moment, aiming at the big cat, letting the arrow fly. It arched upward, returning just as fast, embedding in his side. The creature growled with displeasure.

"Well done, Peta."

The move startled the female cats, the animals darting into the forest, while the male howled in agony. I needed to finish him off before he pounced, preparing another arrow and drawing it back. It landed between the creature's eyes, which ended his suffering at once.

"It's finished," I whispered, breathing a sigh of relief.

"We can't stay here."

I shook my head. "No, it's clearly not safe."

Ronan sighed. "We'll leave at first light."

"I wish we could go home. I don't like being out in the open like this."

"We need a larger clan."

"Or the shelter of our cave." I had fortified it with thorny brambles to ward off the cats, which had worked so far. "Perhaps we can go home."

"Maybe."

"What if they return? We've just killed their leader. He looked to be the elder, didn't he?" Wolf packs had a certain order with leaders and subordinates. I assumed the same held true for a den of cats.

"I assume. I don't know. I'm tired, Peta. I hadn't expected this tonight. I shall be awake now."

"So will I."

"I've a cat to skin and meat to cook. We might as well make a late meal of it."

I patted my belly, which bulged slightly from supper still. "I'm hardly hungry."

"Let's gather wood and smoke the meat. The fire will keep them at bay."

"I hope so."

He smiled slightly. "You're as skilled as any man with that weapon. You hardly need me."

I found that stunning. "I do need you, Ronan. I've no wish to be alone. I hate it. I want you and our clan. One day, we shall have the home we dream of—a home of comfort and peace."

"The gods have been kind so far, my love."

"I don't know if I'd call it kind, but we're together now."

Eight

After feeding Bannon, we gathered our things and left the shelter. The newly acquired pelt from the cat the night before smelled of damp fur and blood. It needed to be dried in the sun, but that would have to wait until later.

Ronan stopped walking to peer behind a bush, moving aside the branches. "The cats have been here."

I sniffed the air, smelling the freshness of the day. "It's from last night."

"Perhaps. The fecal matter looks too dry to be fresh, though."

"I wish to return home now."

He glanced at me. "We know not if it's safe, Peta. I can't risk meeting this Greggor person and his men. They might still be in the valley."

The low growl of an animal resounded. "Where did that come from?"

Ronan pointed to the trees. "That way."

"Towards the valley."

"We can't go there. Let's give it a few days, just to be safe."

My shoulders slumped, but not from Bannon's weight. "I know, but I don't like it."

"We'll look for a rocky place or a cave to make camp tonight."

"It's all woods. I don't see a mountain anywhere. From the treetop yesterday, the mountains are a good distance."

He nodded pragmatically. "Then we'll look for another clan."

"There are no people anywhere near here, other than our cave."

"I've seen other clans on my travels."

"Bad people who mean ill."

"And good people. We shall be very careful today. If we find traces of others, we'll approach with caution."

"Or we'll be eaten before that happens." I heard another growl, the sound sending a shiver through me. "We're wasting precious daylight. We should walk." I grasped the bow, the weapon at the ready.

Ronan patted a bulging leather sack. "We've enough meat for days."

I hurried after him, his legs far longer than mine. "I'm not hungry in the least."

"I hate cats being about, but they are delicious."

Giggling, I stepped on a rock. "Ouch."

"The forest has provided well."

"How do you know where to find other people?"

"I don't. We'll walk away from the valley and the cats. Something must live in that direction."

"I'll climb a tree later. Maybe I can see something."

"If need be." We spoke little after that, my thoughts slipping from one worry to another, and, by the time we stopped to drink water, I questioned all of our decisions again. "I haven't heard a cat in a while."

"I haven't seen any scat." He tossed water in his face, his knees sinking into the mud at the edge of a creek.

"Bannon's hungry. I haven't time to crush meat for him. He'll have to be content with my breast." I released the boy from the leather carrier. "I know you hate all of this, but you've been very good. He's been quiet."

Having gotten to his feet, Ronan held out his hands. "I'll hold him. You wash yourself." He straddled him on his side. "He's a good, fine boy." The baby's golden hair blew in the breeze. "He's everything I could've asked for and more."

I adored seeing them together, their bond growing by the day. Bannon babbled happily, arms flailing and sturdy legs kicking. "He wants to walk a bit."

"I should make a harness for him with a lead. That way he can walk and not run off. I've this terrible fear of him going missing. A few steps and he'd disappear into the woods. It could happen in an instant."

That worried me. "Then we'd never find him."

"When we're with a clan, we'll have time to make such a thing. I've seen it done before. Children can be unruly. They have no fear. They don't understand the danger until it's too late."

When I was a child, I had seen a cat saunter into a clan and snatch a baby from its mother. It happened after all the men left to hunt. "Even a clan can't insure safety."

"But it helps." He touched my face. "I've made you frown. I've upset you with my talk. I'm sorry. I don't mean to bring up every horrible thing in life. I can't risk losing you or Bannon again."

"And you won't." I forced the ugly thoughts away. "You're right. We'll make a harness so he can walk with us. We'll manage him better that way. He won't be so heavy on my back." Speaking of my back, I felt an ache there, my hands drifting to my spine. "I'm sore. I wish we could sit in the hot water. It soothes away tiredness. I miss it."

"In good time. Let's walk a bit further."

I nodded. "Very well."

***

Before the nightly shadows overtook us, the sun drifting over a far off mountain, I climbed a tree, grasping one branch and then another, until I stood at the highest point, the orange glow of sunset warming my face.

"What do you see?"

"Trees."

"Any sign of a fire, smoke?"

I gazed in all directions, observing the mountain that stood before our valley in the distance. "No." But then a thin line of greyish smoke drifted, catching on the wind. "Wait!"

"What is it?"

"A fire." I pointed. "That way."

"The way we came." Ronan frowned. "Come down, Peta. This might not be good."

Climbing carefully, I lowered to another branch. "Why?"

"One small fire means it's a group of people, not a clan. If you'd seen a clan, it would've been many fires."

"True." I had nearly reached the ground.

"If it's the way we were, then it's someone following us."

I lowered to my feet, gritting my teeth. "And now what do we do?"

"We need to keep walking. If they're following, they'll know where we are from our footprints. We've broken branches along the way. We've eaten nuts and left the shells." His lips thinned. "That'll lead them straight to us."

"What if it's not Greggor? It could be people traveling."

"I doubt it. I trust nothing."

I remembered something Sungir had taught Ara and me many seasons ago. "Why don't we leave a false trail?"

"What do you mean?"

"We travel on for a way and make a few prints and some broken branches. Then we turn in a different direction, and trod carefully. We wear heavier fur on our feet."

"They'll see through it. Men aren't stupid."

"I don't know what to do then."

He stood with Bannon in his arms, the boy chewing on a dried bone. "Your fur idea is sound. If they come from there," he pointed behind him, "then we go there. We travel carefully. No eating. No heavy footprints. Don't touch the branches."

"I'll cut some fur."

"We need to hurry, Peta. It's growing darker by the moment, and we haven't made shelter. I fear we'll be out in the open tonight."

"Yes, that's the feeling I get." I sliced through the cat fur, although it had yet to dry completely. It smelled foul, although that could not be helped. "Here you are." I held Bannon, as he tied pelt to his feet.

"It's quite soft. I shall walk in comfort." A grin emerged.

"It does feel nice."

"There's enough for a pillow later."

"Although the smell isn't to my liking."

"No, it's rank, but it can't be helped."

We set out again a moment later, venturing deeper into the forest, walking on a bed of damp leaves. "The smoke wasn't near here. They've made camp for the night."

"Whoever they are. We need to look for shelter before it's dark, but we can walk a ways first."

"I pray so." I yawned, exhausted after spending a day on my feet.

"You're tired."

"Yes, my feet hurt, my back aches. I ... don't relish this in the least."

"It's not forever, my love. We'll find another clan soon enough."

"I don't know if I should pray for this or fear it."

"It's a risk, but ... we'd be safer with other people."

"Or not," I muttered, having doubts over the scheme.

Venturing longer than we should have, the forest grew eerily dark now, the sounds of night animals drifting around us. I felt the chill of the earth, the smell of wet dirt filling my lungs. Not finding a single boulder to hide behind or a crevice to make shelter in, we faced the possibility of sleeping beneath the stars. I glanced at the glowing orb in the sky through the branches, finding it to be rather round and large.

"It's so big tonight."

"Yes," murmured Ronan, holding the spear before him. "We've lost them, whoever they were."

"Perhaps." They could just as easily find our path at daybreak, if they desired to follow us. "I haven't heard a cat."

"It's been quiet."

"Where do you propose we sleep?"

"We should've stopped a while ago. We've almost no choice in the matter now. I wanted to put more distance in, and we've done that, but now we're without shelter."

"We can drape a pelt overhead from some branches and sit beneath. It might rain." The moisture in the air filled my lungs. "Rain comes."

"I was afraid of that, but you're right."

"Then we'll sit beneath a pelt and make a fire."

"I'll gather wood."

"It's good the moon's so big. I can see the ground."

He reached out to touch my shoulder. "You make the shelter. I'll gather the wood. We'll be settled before it's truly dark. Then we'll have a nice meal."

"All right," I said wearily, realizing I would agree to almost anything, if it meant not having to walk any further.

Nine

I had not closed my eyes for more than a moment when I felt a keen sense of danger. Fearing Greggor had found us, I braced myself for the confrontation, truly worried he might kill Ronan and I, or worse, but what could be worse than death?

Ronan, having sensed the same warning, stood before the shelter with a spear in hand, his eyes trained on the forest, where a collection of glowing lights appeared, as men approached with torches.

"This will be your lover," he intoned bitterly.

"I don't know." I held the bow with an arrow ready to fly, Bannon sleeping at my feet. I did not have time to put him in the carrier. "I pray they're just passing through." Our fire died down a while ago, only embers flaring in the coals. "We didn't make noise. They can't possibly see the fire."

"And, yet, they seem to know exactly where we are."

The low din of voices—many voices—carried in the forest. I could not make out what they said, although, as they drew near, I understood them to be of the white race. We braced ourselves for trouble, ready to protect Bannon with our lives. The first man stepped from the foliage, his hand wrapped around a thick branch that held a bundle of burning thatch. He did not look like Greggor, wearing nothing other than a fur skirt. Several beaded necklaces hung from around his neck, while inquisitive eyes roamed over us. Three other men came up behind him. None of them looked as if they belonged to Greggor's tribe.

I wanted to breathe a sigh of relief, but we could not know what they intended. I held the arrow up, aiming at the man's chest. He noted this, a sober gleam in his eye.

"Are there more of you?" he asked in a clear, understandable voice.

"No," said Ronan. "We're traveling through. This is my wife, Peta and my son, Bannon. I am Ronan."

"She means to kill me."

Ronan nodded. "Aye, and she can. She's a good shot, far better than I'll ever be."

"I'm Clayton, leader of my clan. We spotted your trail yesterday, and we've been following ever since."

"Why concern yourself with two people?" asked Ronan. "We're of little matter."

"Because you're walking directly towards our encampment. We prefer to know who comes before trouble is on us."

"We mean you no harm," I said.

Clayton pondered that, holding a spear in one hand and the torch in another. "Where do you travel from?"

"A great distance," said Ronan. "We're without a clan at the moment, but we desire one."

"There's a group of men searching for a woman of her looks," said a man behind Clayton. "We came upon them a day ago."

"This is my wife," said Ronan. "She's *my* woman, and no other."

Clayton nodded. "They're looking for her. The man said she's as fair as the daughter of a god." He took a step nearer, holding out the torch. "With light hair and blue eyes, just like this one."

"Which can be said of any woman," I muttered, swallowing a twinge of panic. By the sound of it, Greggor roamed nearby ... somewhere.

"They're looking for a woman traveling with a man

and a baby. I do believe we've found them."

"What shall we do?" asked the man behind him. "They're gone now. Does it matter? They're nothing to us."

Clayton shrugged. "I don't know. I haven't decided on anything just yet. It's the clan I worry about. We've had enough trouble with cats recently and hostiles."

Lowering the bow, I glanced at Ronan. "What now?" We had reached an impasse.

"This is my wife," he repeated. "I know nothing about a man searching for a woman. I care not," he lied easily enough. "My wife and I are looking for a clan to live with, if they'll have us. That's all. We don't wish anyone harm. We're beholden only to ourselves."

"And this Greggor person means nothing to you?" Clayton stared at me. "This man who's traveled a great distance to find his woman and son."

"Like I said, she's mine."

"I don't know of what you speak," I lied, praying he would not see through me. "I'm with my man and child."

"We should shelter for the night," said Clayton, nodding pragmatically. He seemed to have made up his mind. "Go gather some wood, Belland. We can decide what to do come first light. I weary of the day as it is."

"We've plenty of meat to share," offered Ronan. "We invite you to our fire, if you like."

"You invite us?" laughed Clayton, the sound gruff. "Ha! That's a fine jest. You're on clan land, stranger. You've trespassed far enough for one day." His gaze strayed to me. "You've a comely woman, though. I might ... be persuaded to invite you to our encampment."

"Persuaded?"

"We can discuss it further after we've a fire." He motioned to his men. "Make camp. We're here for the night."

***

The men brought their own pelts, sitting with us to share dried meat, while a robust fire warmed me to the bone. A light, congenial conversation rang out, easing whatever worry we had about their intentions, although I sensed the appraisal of each man, an interested glimmer in his eye. The third man's name was Egor, the man younger than the other two. Bannon woke shortly after, wanting to be fed. He fell asleep quickly enough, despite the noise of chatter.

I sat near Ronan, his arm about me. "They seem … safe enough," I whispered.

"Aye, safe enough, but there's something they want."

"I know what it is."

His arm tightened around me. "I don't mind sharing you with Enwan, but three strangers is another matter."

Clayton sat close enough to overhear our talk. "We won't harm your woman. We mean only to spend a pleasant evening by the fire."

To their credit, they appeared clean enough, their aroma slightly musky from travel, yet not noxious in the least. Light-skinned and fair-eyed, they sported long, tangled hair and messy beards, not having cut them in a while. Ronan preferred to be better groomed. Egor wasn't as muscled as Clayton and Belland, his lanky body slightly concave. He picked at his teeth with a stick, sitting with his legs crossed before him.

"Your woman's beautiful," murmured Belland. "Such a sweet-looking creature with soft eyes and a pink mouth."

I had never been flattered so, the feeling odd.

"What are the customs of your clan?" asked Ronan. "Do you share women?"

Clayton smiled slightly. "To a degree."

"Do you share your wife?"

"Sedat's of a fragile nature. She nearly died birthing

my daughter, Bea. Our healer warned she might not survive another pregnancy. I don't wish to see her so ill again, so I leave her be. The other women can mate with whom they wish, although their men oftentimes complain about it. There have been some ... disagreements. On the whole, we live in peace. I wish to keep it that way."

It heartened me that he seemed to care about his wife's welfare. I took a sip of water from a bladder, nodding into the flames.

"Your woman seems healthy enough," remarked Belland.

"She can take care of herself." Ronan pointed to the cat pelt. "She killed that animal yesterday."

Clayton's eyes widened. "Indeed?"

"She's a fine hunter. She's been alone often in her life, fending for herself."

"I need no man," I murmured, marveling at the truth of that statement. "Although I prefer them. I don't like to be alone."

"Lord Greggor said the woman he searched for was proficient with a bow. You have one just as he described."

"She's *my* wife," grated Ronan.

"Why argue the matter?" asked Egor. "She's with her man. She's unharmed, from the looks of it. I'd rather mate than argue."

Clayton's eyes drifted over me. "Let's come to the terms of the agreement."

"And that is?"

"Will you share your woman?"

Ronan glanced at me. "And if I don't?"

"Then you'll be escorted away from our lands."

"Perhaps we should just go. We can live elsewhere."

But how long would Greggor continue to search? I bit my lip, considering the predicament. "We do need a place to stay for a while."

Ronan leaned in, his lips by my ear. "I leave the

decision to you, my love. It wasn't that long ago you killed three men who desired to mate you."

"They stole me from my home. They gave me no choice in the matter. They were disgusting."

"And these men are not?"

"They don't look mean. When men are evil, I sense it. I feel sickened to my belly."

Ronan mulled that over, saying, "I'll share my wife, but you cannot harm her in any way. If she pleads for you to stop, then you shall stop. If she finds something disagreeable, then it shall cease. She has the final word."

"Then you may join our clan, if you wish." Clayton held out a hand. "Come here, woman."

The object of their singular attention, I felt more than a little overwhelmed in that moment, yet curious about what might occur. Being the only woman among four lusty men, I questioned whether or not I even possessed the stamina to please them all.

"They won't hurt you," murmured Ronan.

Taking a deep, fortifying breath, I got to my feet. Eyes followed my every move, the impression like fingertips grazing sensitive skin. Tossing hair over a shoulder, I licked suddenly dry lips. "What will you have me do?" I whispered.

Clayton's mouth fell open. "Gods' teeth, she's beautiful."

Untying the skirt at my hips, I let it fall to my feet. The heat of the fire warmed my skin, while the flames reflected in my eyes. In that moment, I felt an odd sense of strength, knowing I held more than a little power in this situation, despite being the only woman at camp.

Ten

Soft snores filled the air, where I lay between Ronan and Clayton, an arm from each man about me. I thought I heard Bannon fuss, but the boy drifted to sleep, not needing to be fed. Exhausted from mating half the night, images drifted through my mind of what I had just experienced. I had never been pleasured so completely before, mated in nearly every way imaginable.

"Are you all right?" whispered Ronan.

I hadn't known him to be awake. "I'm fine."

"Then you should sleep."

"I will."

He kissed my cheek. "You satisfied me greatly, Peta."

"I did that for everyone," I giggled.

"And you took pleasure as well."

"I remember everything, Ronan."

He yawned. "Sleep now. It's almost dawn. You'll be exhausted."

I scooted nearer to absorb his warmth, closing my eyes. I woke a while later to the sound of men speaking, my face hidden under a pelt.

"He's a strapping little lad," said Clayton. "You must be proud to have such a son."

"I am."

"He looks like you."

"He should. He's my son."

"It makes me doubt this Greggor person. He said the boy was his, but he's as fair as you and Peta."

"You should doubt it. I know nothing about Lord Greggor. I care not about the troubles of other men. It's hardly my concern, if he can't keep his woman. I wish only to live in peace with my family."

"You're a lucky man to have such a wife."

"She's the only woman I've ever wanted. I've known her since she was a child."

"Where do you come from?"

"A land where it's colder. We traveled a long way to find paradise. This place is warm and bountiful. We prefer it warmer."

"I see."

"We were nearer to the mountain a day ago, where we came upon piles of bones—human bones. People were murdered most violently. What do you know about it?"

"About piles of bones? Nothing. I've not seen that."

"It was done a long time ago."

"There are rumors of a half-breed clan, but we've not had any dealings with them."

"Here?"

"Yes. They're odd-looking. We've encountered the dark people here and there, but we leave them alone. No one wishes to mate them."

"Peta's an orphan. A dark woman by the name of Kia took her in when she was little. My wife can speak their language. She's lived with both tribes."

"I see. That's interesting."

"A white hunter, who was a hermit, taught her how to use the bow. She has some healing skills as well."

"Can she aid in childbirth?"

"Yes, of course. She had Bannon by herself."

"That's remarkable. Far too many women die giving birth."

I flung back the pelt, squinting into the sunlight. "It's impossible to sleep with all this chatter."

Ronan grinned. "You're awake."

"Where are the others?" I realized then that only Ronan and Clayton remained at camp.

"Washing up, I reckon," said Clayton.

"I need to do that."

Bannon came to me, holding out a hand. "Mamma, Mamma!"

"I fed you not that long ago." He settled in my lap, suckling at my breast. A yawn escaped me.

"You've exhausted my wife."

"We're all exhausted." Clayton held out a bladder of water. "Have a drink. You must be parched."

"Is there anything else other than dried meat?"

"If we're lucky, Egor and Belland will return with something tasty."

"Is your encampment comfortable?"

"It is." A smile appeared, crinkling the edges of his eyes. "Why do you ask?"

"Are you out in the open or is there a cave? Have you built dwellings?"

"We've many huts. Some are smaller, others are larger, like mine."

I liked that response. "Good. I prefer a real dwelling or a nice cave."

"Most people do."

"My least favorite is sleeping in the open."

"Only when we travel."

"When can we go?" I suddenly felt eager to settle down somewhere for a few days and rest. I desired a bed of soft pelts and a warm fire.

"Soon. After we eat, we go."

"Good."

***

Belland and Egor returned with several small woodland creatures, which we skinned and cooked over the flames. With bellies full of delicious meat, we followed Clayton and his men deeper into the forest where a swift running river flowed. After crossing, I shivered, soaked through to the bone. Bannon hated it, crying.

"I'm sorry. I know you didn't like that."

Ronan tossed a pelt over us. "This should help."

Clayton shrugged, water dripping into his face. "There was no way around it, I'm afraid. It's even wider down stream."

"We're close to home," said Egor. He wrung out a sodden skirt. "We'll reach our people before sundown."

"I'm glad," I murmured, shivering.

Ronan drew me to him, hugging me with Bannon between us. "There, there. Once we start walking, you'll be warm again."

"I fear having to come back this way," I whispered. "You know we must return the way we came."

"I've noted it. We can do it, when the time comes."

"How long do you propose we stay with these people?"

"A short while. Perhaps one moon cycle."

"That long?"

"It's not that long, Peta. Long enough for Greggor to give up and go home. That man's an irritation."

"He's gone elsewhere."

"We can only hope."

"Let's go," called Clayton. "Make haste. I wish to see my wife and child. I tire of the walk."

Egor and Belland strode ahead, leaving Ronan and I to follow, with Bannon in my arms. When we stopped a while later, Ronan carried him on his back. The sun stood at its highest then, the heat bearing down upon our heads, as we crossed a small prairie. Everyone held a spear at the ready, their eyes darting in all directions, looking for trouble. I never felt entirely safe out in the open like this, but it ended soon enough after we slipped into the cover of trees.

Resting for a moment beneath the shade of a heavy

branch, I watched as Bannon and Ronan shared a meal, Ronan having mashed dried meat between two stones. Weary from little sleep and too much walking, I yearned for a nap, my back aching.

"You look tired," commented Clayton. "I'm sorry we … were so demanding last night." He sat next to me, his feet encased in fur.

I eyed him through partially closed lashes. "I am tired. I shouldn't be this tired. I've traveled further on less sleep and done better."

"Perhaps you're with child." He eyed my belly, which protruded slightly.

I had been thinking along those lines as well. "I … don't know."

"You're not being entirely truthful with me, Peta."

I stared at him. "What do you mean?"

"There are things you haven't spoken of or you're both lying about it."

"What things?"

"About where you live, where you've been."

"Ronan told you about himself. I've nothing to hide."

"Except you're being hunted by some man from a clan far away. He wasn't happy in the least. He was quite angry to be searching for you. Men don't journey to find a woman."

I hated to speak about this, wishing to change the subject. "How much further must we walk?"

"Before it's dark. I shall be home." His hand stroked my thigh. "I desire to mate you again."

"You've had your fill."

"Hardly. That was but a small taste."

I sat up, alarmed by the direction of the conversation. "I've something to do before we go." Intent on finding water, I darted between the trees to a small brook, although I sensed I wasn't alone. Knowing Ronan had not followed, I turned to face Clayton, whose broad shoulders filled my vision. "I don't need a minder." From the eager look in his eye, I doubted that would dissuade him.

"This will be quick." He grabbed me, brushing aside the skirt.

"Chief Clayton!" I gasped, finding myself pressed to the rough bark of a tree. I could easily fight him, scratching and kicking, if I desired, but I let him have his way. I trembled as his fingers slipped between my thighs. "Oh!" He lifted my hips to mount me, his manhood begging entrance.

"Hold onto something," he directed gruffly.

I did as he asked, finding the encounter fiercely arousing, an image of Greggor appearing in my mind. Something about this reminded me of him, because he could be gentle, but also rough. I clung to the tree, experiencing various sensations, all of them centering on pleasure. I uttered something unintelligible, moaning. I felt him within me, his movements quickening, pushing me to the tree, where jagged bark scraped my cheek.

"You feel good," he murmured. "So soft."

He grasped my hips firmly, while I struggled to remain standing, my knees wanting to give out. When I thought I could take no more, I shattered, the force of the pleasure swift and stunning.

"Oh! … " I bit my lip to keep from crying out.

Clayton moaned throatily, finishing as well, leaving traces of his seed within me. An arm went about my belly to hold me up. "The tree wasn't the best idea." His mouth lingered by my ear. "I'd take you anywhere, though."

I needed his support, my thighs trembling. "I … don't know," I said stupidly, not having a response.

"We should wash up."

"Yes."

I cleared my throat, casting a wary glance over a shoulder, wondering if anyone had seen that. My mother often disappeared into the woods to mate with the men of whatever clan she lived with. I always questioned the appeal of such a thing, now I knew.

Clayton touched my cheek. "What a shame to mar such a pretty face."

"Am I scratched?" He towered over me, his presence one of strength and authority. It did not surprise me at all to know he was a leader.

"A little. A little blood."

"It's nothing then. I've had worse."

"Peta," called Ronan. "Come along. We go soon." He stared at me from a distance, holding Bannon in his arms.

"Yes, I'm coming." From the look upon his face, he knew what I had been up to, although he said nothing. "Just a moment."

Eleven

We arrived at the encampment before sunset, greeted by several inquisitive dogs that came to bark at us. A group of men approached with a few women, who lingered at a distance. I noted how dark they all appeared, with long, nearly black hair and brown eyes. The children ran about, while the aroma of cooking fires made my mouth water with the anticipation of a meal.

"Chief, you've returned," said a man holding a spear. "And who are these people?"

"An addition to our clan, Barcelo." Clayton turned to us. "This is our healer. Barcelo, this is Ronan and Peta and their child, Bannon."

His astute gaze raked over me. "The woman the dark-haired lord was looking for. Why would you bring her here?"

"She says she's not that woman."

"And you believe her?"

"Her child is fair-haired. It doesn't belong to the man. It hardly matters anyhow. I've invited them to live with us."

I felt distinctly uncomfortable being stared at by the healer. I could not fathom why, but he wasn't someone I could like, nor would I ever mate him.

His look remained dour. "I've seen trouble coming for a while."

"We're aware of all your visions. You've had them often enough, and nothing's happened."

"This one's trouble. I've seen her in a dream. She brings destruction. I fear we're doomed now. I knew it the moment that man arrived searching for her."

"And he's gone away," Clayton said, frowning. "We'll never meet with him again. I don't wish to discuss it now anyhow. I desire to see my wife and child. I need a warm meal and a soft bed." He glanced at those standing around. "Please make these people welcome." Then he whispered, "Enough talk of doom, Barcelo. I tire of it."

"My visions always come true, Chief."

"Not this time."

"Nothing good will come of inviting them here. If you seek to keep the peace of the land, you should send them on their way at once."

"Enough!" he bellowed. "Sedat! Where's my wife?"

"I'm here, Chief." A woman emerged, carrying a little girl. "Here I am."

"Find a hut for these people. Make them comfortable."

"Yes, Chief."

"Then make supper. I'm starving."

"A meal's been prepared." She glanced at Ronan and then me, her features pleasant enough, with dark hair braided down her back. "What a handsome boy."

"This is Ronan and Peta, and their son, Bannon."

"Thank you for being so kind," said Ronan. "We mean you and your clan no harm." He spoke to Barcelo. "We're hardly a threat to anyone, I can assure you. We've been traveling for a while. We seek shelter for a ... short time. We won't stay long."

This announcement seemed to appease the healer, who nodded. "Good. Then you go soon enough. I shall consult the rocks again and ask for guidance."

"Rocks and leaves," muttered Clayton. "I don't need to know what my future entails. It doesn't interest me. I live for each new day." He glanced at me. "I find nothing threatening with either of these two. You may stay as long as you wish. I pray it's longer than a moon cycle. I don't see why it can't be for the end of all of our days."

His wife glanced between us, her smile faltering. "Well then, I shall show you a hut, although it isn't very clean. Something can be done about it quickly enough, though."

"Thank you," I murmured, bowing my head slightly. I felt acutely aware of Clayton's interest, realizing I had some power over him, the man enamored of me. If I had declined to mate him, would Ronan and I still be wandering around the forest? One had to wonder.

***

The hut in question appeared well thatched with a spacious interior, the floor lined with soft pelts. Surprised by how big it was, I set Bannon down, the boy rolling onto a pelt with a grin on his face.

"You should be comfortable here," said Sedat, the woman wearing a short leather skirt with colorful beads sewn in a pretty pattern.

"It's big and nice," murmured Ronan. "Thank you." He glanced at me. "Better than expected, isn't it?"

"They live well here. All the huts are sturdy-looking." My belly rumbled. "I'd like some meat, if we have a few pieces left."

"A meal's being prepared now," said Sedat. "They'll make you a fire in a moment. You need do nothing other than rest. The chief said so." She bowed her head. "I bid you a good evening then. I've my husband and daughter to attend to."

"Thank you, Sedat." I glanced at Bannon, who got to his feet to run around. "He's rather happy."

"There are many children his age here. I'll introduce you when the sun rises. We can forage together, if you wish."

I delighted in her kindness. "I do. That would be lovely."

"Good. Your food comes soon." She slipped from the hut.

I glanced at Ronan. "What do you think?"

"We'll sleep well tonight."

"Let's wash up before dinner. I'm filthy. My skin itches with layers of dust."

He picked Bannon up. "He needs his garments changed. He stinks." The boy shrieked, giggling. "All that time in the carrier, and now he's far too lively."

I giggled, "I see that. We'll let him run around until he's tired. A good meal will help too."

"We can only hope."

"Let's go then."

We walked from the camp, standing at the edge of the river, the water quite cold. When we returned, someone had made a fire before the hut, the blaze burning warmly. An assortment of wooden platters held meat and greens, and a bowl filled with berries. I marveled at the fare, surprised by the generosity of the clan. Several members came to introduce themselves, their easy smiles and friendly manner putting us instantly at ease.

Ronan lay upon a pelt with a hand over his belly, a grin on his face. "I feel like a chief. I've never been so attended to. That meat was delicious. They seasoned it with something."

I chewed, staring absently into the fire. "Everything was wonderful."

"I've never met a more agreeable tribe."

"They'll expect us to help them. We can't lay about all day."

"This is your doing."

"What do you mean?"

"It's rather obvious the chief favors you."

"Then I shall use that to my advantage—to our advantage."

His smile fell. "Will he steal you away like Greggor?"

A twinge of guilt prickled me. "I came back to you, Ronan." I crawled over to him, sitting by his side. Bannon played with a carved piece of wood. "I feel nothing for him, if that's what you ask. I don't care either way what he wants, as long as we're together and happy. We should stay here until it's safe. I prefer a bigger clan. I feel safe here. They've men aplenty to keep the cats at bay and other predators."

He touched my face. "I agree."

"You know me like no other. The feelings I have for you run deep." I spoke the truth, although I knew I could love more than one man at a time. With Greggor, it had been wild, reckless passion, while the sweet affection I felt for Ronan brought a measure of contentment.

"Then I trust you."

"Everything I do is for our survival. I wish nothing more."

"It's my wish too." A hand wrapped around the back of my head. "Kiss me, Wife."

I smiled, as emotion brought moisture to my eyes. "Oh, Ronan." With a full belly and a comfortable abode, I marveled at our fortune, grateful for this moment.

Our lips met, as his tongue delved into my mouth, producing enjoyable sensations. I grasped his face, kissing him wherever I could, while his hand slid down my back and beneath the skirt. Tossing a pelt over us, we soon joined, the mating unhurried, the kisses far too numerous to count. I found myself beneath him, holding him closely between my thighs, while he drove deeply, rubbing against my heated flesh. In that moment of oblivion, I closed my eyes and shuddered, while clinging to him, helpless to think of anything else.

"Ronan!"

"My love," he breathed against my throat. "You're all I've ever wanted."

We lay tangled in each other's arms, the sound of Bannon playing filling the hut. When I did not hear him, I tossed back the cover, worried about the quiet. He ate berries from a wooden bowl, his lips purple.

"You better not choke. He's eating a fistful at a time." A hand stroked my shoulder.

"He's fine. Come back to me."

Laughing, I returned to the comfort of Ronan, sighing with happiness. "What shall we do now?"

"I'll kiss you all over again."

"So soon?" I felt his mouth at my throat, his kisses drifting to my chin.

"Aye, so soon. I don't want to share you with anyone else tonight."

"I don't wish to be anywhere else."

"Then kiss me."

Twelve

Someone cleared their throat, a man standing in the doorway of our hut. He said, "If you wish to hunt with us, we leave soon."

Groggy and hardly awake, Ronan slipped from the warm pelt, leaving me with Bannon.

"I'll come."

"We gather at the edge of the woods."

"Very well." He touched my hair. "I worry about leaving you. We know nothing about these people."

"I've my bow. I can manage, if need be."

"I do like a good hunt."

"I wonder what sort of creatures they kill in these parts?"

"The same as anywhere else."

"Bannon and I will be fine." I yawned, stretching my arms over my head. "I want to meet the women. I've longed for female companionship for some time. Bannon should play with the other children and know what it's like to share his toys."

"The few he has."

"Yes."

"Then I'll go. Stay safe, my love."

"And you." I closed my eyes, sleeping for a while longer, until necessity drove me from the hut to relieve myself in the woods where the clan made a latrine. They dug pits for this, the stench nearly overwhelming. When I returned, I found Sedat at the hut, holding a little girl.

"Hello."

She smiled. "I want you to meet my daughter, Bea. She's a little older than Bannon, but they might be friends."

"Ronan and I thank you for your kindness."

"You needn't."

"The shelter was perfect. I haven't had such a good sleep in a while." I ducked my head to enter, finding Bannon curled up with his eyes closed. "We've been traveling and sleeping in the open. I don't like that very much. I prefer a roof and soft furs."

"My husband instructed me to make you as comfortable as possible."

"Then I shall have to thank him."

"Are you hungry?"

"I've some nuts leftover from the last meal."

"We forage in the cool part of the day. Will you join us?"

"Yes, of course." I ate a nut, chewing. "How long have you been at this camp?"

"Many seasons."

"And all your family's here?"

She shook her head. "No, they're gone. I had brothers and sisters, but they perished."

"I'm sorry. Was it sickness?"

"Some fell ill, while others disappeared. A group left to hunt and never returned."

I thought about Ronan hunting, suddenly worried over him. "That frightens me."

"Our men are strong. They've killed all the cats in the area. They fought hostile clans and won. I'm not afraid. I fear little now, except my health."

"I'm sorry about your health, but news of the other brings me relief."

A woman appeared in the doorway, her face in shadow. "We're gathering to go, Sedat."

"This is Braya. She's as close to a sister as I have now."

I smiled at the young woman. "Hello. I'm Peta."

She waited by the doorway. "Welcome."

"Thank you."

Sedat got to her feet, picking up Bea, who gazed about in interest. "I shall prepare then. We won't go far today. We need some greens for the evening meal. We'll cook whatever the men bring back."

"I'll ready Bannon." I touched his forehead, hating to wake him, but it could not be helped.

She nodded. "I'll tell the women to prepare to go."

***

Foraging with others, their chatter filling the forest, brought back memories of when my mother and sisters were with me. I found the women easy to speak to, their kind eyes and open manner appreciated. We ventured a ways from camp, leaving a few women behind, along with two men, who stood guard. Searching for anything edible, we often stopped to pull things from the moist earth, the smell of moss and dirt filling my senses.

"He does well in that," commented a woman, pointing to Bannon's leather carrier.

"I've traveled great distances with him like this."

"Alone?"

"Yes, I'm often alone. Whenever I think my life is settled, something happens to ruin it. Then, I find myself alone." I frowned at those words, wondering why I had uttered them.

"I'd perish alone," said another woman. "I've tried to hunt the little creatures, but my traps always fail. I could live off nuts, but I'd be terribly weak in the end. It's just the same as dying, I suppose."

"Ladies," admonished Sedat. "We needn't worry

about this. Our men will always protect us."

When we stopped to eat, I held Bannon in my lap, although he was eager to play with the other children, most of them a bit older. He ran after a little boy, disappearing behind some bushes. Worried over losing him, I sprang to my feet, my heart pounding in my chest. I found him a moment later, engaged in play, which had me sighing with relief.

"The children watch over each other," said Sedat. She stood behind me. "He's fine."

"But they disappear in an instant. Something can snatch him away."

"Boys play all day, and they're always home by supper. When they get older, they'll hunt with their fathers and the elders of the clan."

"Yes, but he's too young, too … fragile."

"In time you'll not be so worried."

"I doubt it." Memories of past disasters loomed in my mind, from floods to cat attacks and kidnappings. I trusted nothing other than the aim of my bow and the sureness of an arrow. To appease her, I said, "Yes, perhaps."

"We're nearly done here. We've enough to support the evening meal."

I smiled at Bannon, who appeared to enjoy the other boys. "This is a fertile place. It's warm and green. Many things grow here."

"We've not seen a cold season. I prefer it mild like this."

"I've known the cold. I don't like it."

"Nor do I."

"We go!" called a woman. "Gather your things. Don't forget your children," she laughed. "Come along!"

After placing Bannon in the carrier, I fell into step with Sedat and Braya. Women walked ahead, while others came behind. Some brought spears and sticks. My mother always carried a sturdy stick when she foraged to ward off predators. I thought of her in these moments, missing her terribly and wondering where she and Ara and Maggi had gone. They had scattered after the raid on their clan. I prayed they were well and not mistreated, although I doubted I would ever see them again.

Returning to camp, I lay Bannon down for a nap, while busying myself with a pelt, scraping it in the sun and leaving it to dry over a rock. Few men remained in residence, although two stood watch on each side of the encampment, their eyes trained on the forest. Built within an open space, many huts littered the area, some not large in the least. Clayton gave us one of the bigger ones, the structure roomy enough for a large family.

Men returned later in the day, some carrying game over their shoulders. I waited for Ronan, having gathered firewood for the evening meal. He appeared shortly, a smile on his handsome face. Blonder than the other men, his hair hung past his shoulders, the breeze tossing tendrils into his face.

"How was your day?" I asked, getting to my feet.

He hugged me, smelling musky. "We ventured further than I would've liked. We killed a few stags. I'm tired."

"You should've stayed with me. We've walked enough as it is."

"I had to do my part, to show them I'm no weakling."

I gazed into his eyes, seeing their clear blue sparkle. "You can rest now. Come inside."

"I smell, Peta. Let me wash up first." He kissed my cheek. "Were the women nice to you?"

"Yes, very friendly. They let Bannon play with their children. I … I like this camp." I did feel entirely at ease here.

"I can't find any fault yet with it, but nothing's

perfect. I overheard Barcelo ranting about you. He believes you're ill luck. I tire of his complaints, but what can I do?"

Speaking of the healer, I glimpsed him at a distance standing with Clayton. The chief, feeling eyes upon him, turned to look at me. "We won't be here more than a moon cycle. We've our own clan to return to."

"I found evidence of a cooking fire not long abandoned. Someone's been through recently. I don't know if it's Greggor or not, but they're leery of strangers. They sent a few men to investigate. They'll follow their trail like they followed ours. If they leave clan land, then it won't matter."

Would Greggor return to this place? Was he still in the woods searching for me? "Go wash up. We mustn't worry over it. It's nothing more than people passing through."

"Perhaps." He kissed my cheek. "The fire looks good. We shall have a nice meal tonight. Clayton's invited us to his shelter, but I'm tired."

I spied the chief approaching. "Go wash up. We'll discuss it." As he strode away, I prepared myself to speak to the leader, wondering why he approached. "Good evening."

A hint of a smile softened his features. "How's the hut?"

"It's too big for us. It's ... very nice. Thank you."

"I've been told not to make you too comfortable."

"We won't stay long, you needn't worry."

He scratched his chin through the tangle of a dark beard. "I've invited your family to supper."

"Thank you for the offer, but my man's tired. We can cook our own food. We don't wish to be a burden to you or your family."

"You're not. I wish to see you later."

Now I understood the invitation, my instincts prickling with awareness. "I ... perhaps." He was chief, though, while we were guests. It was hardly wise to disregard a directive from the leader of a clan. "We shall come."

"Do you find me repulsive?"

Stunned by that question, I said honestly, "No." Being a younger man, he appeared handsome enough, his behavior kind. I had seen no evidence of cruelty in him, but I had hardly been in his company long. He was an attentive lover, giving as much pleasure as he received. "You and your people are very kind."

This seemed to satisfy him, a smile appearing. "You're safe here, Peta. I wish nothing other than your happiness. I ask only for a little bit of attention."

"I understand." I eyed him carefully. "If I refuse, what would you do?"

He crossed his arms over his chest. "I'd not like it. Women do not refuse me. However, I prefer them willing. You're not a prisoner, nor will you be. I've invited you out of good faith. It shall remain so. If you wish to leave, you may go, but I'll try to convince you otherwise."

Those words put me at ease. "Thank you."

Ronan approached. "Good evening, Chief."

"I've spoken to Peta about the meal. I offer our hospitality this eve."

I knew him to be tired, smiling sympathetically. "We can cook our meat over their fire." Bannon crawled from the hut, getting to his feet, where I picked him up. "Where are you going, little one?"

"We accept your invitation," said Ronan.

"Come as soon as you can." This seemed to please Clayton, who grinned, turning on a heel. "I'll be expecting you."

Ronan glanced at me. "It's unwise to deny the chief, I suppose."

"It's the least we can do."

Thirteen

With plans to leave before the next moon cycle, we soon found ourselves delaying because Bannon fell ill. He cried endlessly, feeling hot to the touch. I scoured the forest for herbs, drying them on a wooden stand and grinding them into medicines. The boy's illness lasted only a few days, his recovery swift. Noting my skill with herbs, Clayton's wife, Sedat, brought her daughter around for a cure, the girl suffering a reddish rash. When I mixed a healing poultice that worked, other women came for advice and medicine.

"You'll anger Barcelo," warned Ronan, speaking of the clan's healer.

"I'm no threat to him. I'm only making tea for people."

He shook his head. "He'll not see it that way. He already doesn't care for you."

"I'll be careful."

"You'll do just as you please, as usual."

I grinned at that. "You do know me rather well."

"I do. It's useless trying to tell you what to do."

"I'm often right about everything."

He shot me a look. "You annoying little baggage." A smile appeared. "If I wasn't so blindly in love with you, I'd take a switch to that perfectly formed behind."

I smiled coyly, enjoying teasing him. "You wouldn't dare."

"I would. It's time you learned some obedience."

"Ha!"

He grabbed me, kissing me. "You enjoy this, don't you?"

Wrapping my arms around his neck, I pressed myself to him. "Being together again is the only thing I've ever wanted, Ronan." My smile fell, as emotion washed over me. "All the time I spent alone, I thought about you. Whenever we part, I worry it's the end. Every moment is precious. I've learned enough about life to know that."

"You worry too much, but I understand. We won't ever be parted, Peta."

"It's been good for a while. I don't want anything to ruin it."

"Nothing will."

"I pray you're right. Finding this clan has been a blessing from the gods. Are they finally smiling upon us?"

He touched my cheek softly. "Yes, my love. You needn't fear their wrath. We've come through the fire. Now we're free to be who we are."

"I want to believe that."

"Do, because it's the truth."

***

The clan enjoyed celebrations, people often wearing colorful feathers and beads to dance around the fire, their customs odd, yet entertaining. They made instruments with wood and bone, blowing through them to create a pretty sound. This reminded me of evenings spent in Sungir's hut all those seasons ago, where my sister, Ara, and I played music and sang. It was the only way to pass the nights during the cold season when white blanketed the ground.

We lived in warmth now, the seasons mild, with plenty of edibles to pick and game to kill. I ate so much; my belly began to swell, although I suspected it to be because I carried another baby. I assumed it to be Ronan's, anticipating another blue-eyed, blonde infant once I grew even larger. Having given birth before, I did not fear it, although I preferred not to experience it alone.

Despite Clayton stealing me away on occasion to mate, I spent all of my time with Bannon, and when Ronan returned from the hunt, we sat around the fire and tended to our son, the boy growing by the day. Having killed big game, the men gone for most of the day to participate, we prepared for an unusually large feast. I grew tired easily now, not foraging as long to return to nap with Bannon. When I woke, I heard voices, the sound of someone laughing.

"Mamma!" My son pulled my hair. "Mamma!"

"I'm awake, you little scamp. You smell. I need to change you." A yawn escaped me. I longed to sleep more, our bed comfortable, with several layers of soft pelts and plenty of leather blankets. "Where's your Pappa?"

"Mamma!"

I sighed, tossing back a blanket. "I hear you."

Ronan appeared in the doorway. "We eat soon, Peta. I let you sleep longer. We're having a fine celebration tonight. More meat than any clan can possibly eat in one sitting. You should see it."

"I can smell it." A reddish gash appeared on his arm. "You're hurt. What happened?"

"A small scratch. It's nothing. The hunt was ... rather vigorous."

"I better tend that or it'll fester."

"Yes, my love." He grabbed Bannon. "He's smelly."

"I'm aware." I tossed hair over a shoulder, the strands thick and unruly. "Take him to the river to wash." I held out a folded piece of leather. "Here you are."

He gave me a look, which bespoke of his distaste for the job at hand. "It's hardly fitting for a great hunter to be minding the children, isn't it?"

My look remained impassive. I waited for him to do as I asked.

"If men laugh at me, and they will, they'll think me weak."

"You're more man than any of them, Ronan." I'd seen men lift their fists to their women and beat their children, finding such behavior abhorrent. Ronan had never done such a thing.

"Dadda!" intoned Bannon, squirming in his arms.

"Aye, you say that." He looked tired in that instant.

"I can do it, if you truly don't want to."

"I should wash anyway. You need your rest, Peta. You're growing another child." A smile escaped him. "We feed well tonight. We'll get a portion of meat to smoke. The women will work the hide. The beasts provide greatly. I want to tell you about the hunt, how magnificent it was. It reminded me of the clan by the river. I wish Enwan had been here to take part. He would've appreciated the skill it took to bring down the creature."

"From the look of that scratch on your arm, it must've been troublesome." The scratch was more of a gash—a deep one. "Once you've washed, I need to see to that. It might require sewing."

"Then we go." He held Bannon. "I shall return with a clean child."

I giggled, "Thank you, Ronan." I watched them walk away, smiling at the sight of them.

Later, by the fire, the chatter of happy voices resounded along with the cries of several babies, as we partook in the feast. I chewed on a large chunk of meat, the juice dripping to my belly. Wearing a leather skirt and several carved wood necklaces, I sat with Bannon and Ronan, sharing a pelt with another family. Their dog waited for a piece of meat, which I tore off with my teeth, handing it to him. Bannon ate too, but his portions had to be smaller, so he didn't choke.

"Here you are." I gave him meat.

"How are you?" asked a voice behind us.

I turned to see the chief, who wore colorful feathers in a necklace. "Well, and you?"

He patted his belly. "Full."

Ronan laughed, "I'm still eating. I can't remember this much meat. It's been many seasons."

"We've had a good hunt. Poor Jumba will recover from his broken leg. There's always someone with a serious injury to attend to." He eyed his bandaged arm. "I see you've a wound."

"Peta's taken care of it."

I longed to have a look at Jumba's leg, Sungir having taught me how to set broken bones when I was a child, but the healer would never allow it.

Clayton's eyes roamed over me. "She's adept at the healing arts. I'd like to give her permission to openly treat my people, but Barcelo would balk. I must defer to my healer. It's the way it's always been."

I nodded. "Of course." Although I felt it foolish, I kept these thoughts to myself.

"Please enjoy the evening." He petted the dog at my feet. "The merriments have only just begun."

As he walked away, someone blew through a bone instrument, the sound pretty and lilting. I sat back, leaning into Ronan's arms, while Bannon played with another boy, the two of them prattling happily. My husband's hand landed on my belly, his lips by my ear. "You look so beautiful like this, Peta."

"What do you mean?"

"With child. I prefer you like this."

"I see."

"So round and perfect. Your breasts are heavy. You prepare to have my baby. I wish to be with you when this happens."

I had been thinking the same thing. "Yes, this time,

we'll share it together."

"I can't imagine how difficult it was for you to give birth alone."

"The gods were kind that night. I wasn't truly alone. In my mind, I saw my mother and sister. They helped me."

"It's still remarkable."

"Not unheard of. Women do it. We've often little choice. The other day Lucita gave birth foraging. We helped her, but she should've been in her hut."

"She's had five children, Peta. She could've given birth standing on her head."

I laughed at that, feeling deeply content. "True, but you never know. Even someone who's had many children might have trouble."

"But you were near. You know what to do."

"I suppose." I stared into the distance, seeing men and women dancing around a large fire, while the healer tossed stones to the ground. "Oh, goodness," I muttered. "There he goes again."

"He thinks he's a seer of the future."

"Half of what he says doesn't happen. He's ... I think he's not right in his head."

"He predicted the hunt."

"Which is hardly seeing the future. The clan intended to kill a great beast. There were enough men. You knew where to find the animals. The hunt proved fruitful because of proper planning. I could've predicted such an outcome."

In the distance, Barcelo stood over the rocks, his hands held up before him. He prepared to foretell some prophesy, people quieting, even the babies ceasing to cry for the moment.

"He's about to enlighten us," I whispered, giggling.

"You shouldn't make fun of him."

"And yet, that won't stop me."

Ronan chuckled in my ear, "My disobedient wife."

He slapped my bottom.

"Ouf!" I grinned, kissing him.

"Listen, people!" shouted Clayton. "Barcelo's about to speak. What see you, healer? Shall more good-fortune come our way? How will the gods bless us this time?"

"Nay, it's not blessings that come," he said darkly, his face twisting. "It's ... something else." He knelt, throwing his head forward and moaning. "No!" he shouted. "No!"

Annoyed with the dramatics, I said, "Must he behave like this? He's scaring people out of their wits. He does this to strike fear in the hearts of the clan. It gives him more power."

"Shush, Peta," whispered Ronan. "Not so loud. It's disrespectful."

I bit my lip, keeping further thoughts to myself, but I found the display annoying.

"Hear me people!" Barcelo shouted. "I see a grave warning in the stones. We must prepare for trouble. It comes. I do not know in what manner it comes, whether by storm or disease or cats, but something comes. It wants to destroy us. There's nothing we can do, unless we prepare."

I glanced at Clayton to observe his reaction. He nodded pragmatically. "We shall, as always, remain vigilant."

Barcelo fell to his knees, moaning. A murmur drifted through the clan, the women appearing horrified. I rolled my eyes at the spectacle. The celebratory mood shifted, people huddling together to speak amongst themselves, while one woman wept openly. Why did he have to ruin a perfectly good evening?

"What are your thoughts?" Ronan stared at me.

"We shall discuss it later."

"Leaving?" he whispered.

He always knew what I had in mind. "Yes."

"I agree. It might be time."

Fourteen

Bathing Bannon in a stream, I let him play in the shallows, where the sun heated the water, although it still felt cool. He did not care in the least, splashing around happily, the clear water exposing smooth rocks at the bottom with tiny fish swimming.

"You're a good boy," I murmured, smiling, as sunlight lit my face. Having foraged for most of the day, I enjoyed this moment of relaxation, having nothing to do other than watch my son. "Did you find a rock?"

"Mamma!" Bannon held a stone, which looked purple.

"That's pretty." It reminded me of the one I wore around my neck, although I had forgotten it at the cave. Ronan had made the necklace for me as a child. "You should keep it. Your father can make a necklace for you." I wasn't sure if he understood me, but I spoke to him regardless, hoping he might learn more words. "Stone. It's called a stone."

He grinned, flashing new teeth. "Mamma."

"Yes, my love." I yawned, desiring a nap. "What is it?" He babbled happily, gathering several stones. He stumbled from the brook, naked. "Are you finished?" He peed into a bush. "Good boy. We should go back. I'm tired."

I held his hand, not having brought a weapon, even leaving the bow behind. Living amongst Clayton's people, I felt fairly safe for a change. Not once had I seen a cat or any other predator. When we foraged, we saw only woodland creatures and stags.

"Your father should return soon with game. Are you hungry?"

"Da … da … da … " he babbled.

"Me too." The sounds of children laughing echoed, while their mothers tended cooking fires. We passed Sedat's fire, the chief's wife sitting before it. "Hello."

She nodded. "Peta."

"How are you feeling?" She complained of a bellyache earlier.

"I'm fine. I've seen Barcelo. He's brewing a concoction."

No one spoke of his visions from the night of the great kill, the man not having raved about it since. I wondered if it had all been for our entertainment, although I hardly appreciated the negative tone. He garnered far more attention by speaking of bad things and disasters. Most healers seemed driven by their need for power and control over others. When they spoke of impending doom, people clung to them out of fear, believing every word. Sungir had taught me to question everything, to think for myself. Having been cast out of his clan, he had a dim view of people, especially healers. I missed the old man, worrying I might have forgotten some of his teachings.

Women came to me in secret for advice about certain ailments, especially when what Barcelo gave them failed to work. "If you want me to help you, you need only ask," I whispered to the leader's wife.

"I shall keep it in mind." She smiled tiredly. "How are you? That belly grows by the day."

"Because there's too much food," I laughed. The evening meal always consisted of something delicious, with women bringing over numerous edibles. Clayton spoiled us this way, but I knew it was because he felt a fondness towards me. I remained in his favor, allowing him to mate me whenever he wished. I worried now how he would react when we told him we planned to leave soon. "I eat too much."

"My dear, that belly's not big because of food."

"I know." Bannon ran off to play with a little boy. "I've time still before the babe comes."

Her gaze narrowed. "You don't plan to stay long, do you?"

"We've talked about … leaving."

"I know you're my husband's favorite. I admit to feeling angry about it, but I've tried not to. He's with other young women too. You're not the only one."

I had known that. "Yes."

"He might be unhappy with this. I don't know."

"But you'd be happy."

"I … would. I like you, Peta. You're a hard worker, and you mind your child, but … "

"But you'd rather I be gone."

She nodded.

"We've friends waiting for us—a small clan in a cave. They must think the worst happened. I want to return before this babe comes."

Getting to her feet, she stood before me, although she wasn't as tall. "I would be careful how you discuss it with my husband. Tell it to him in a gentle manner."

"He wouldn't force us to stay, would he?" Clayton had always been reasonable, having watched him deal with clan business in a fair way. He rarely punished any of the people, although a few had to be dealt with harshly for stealing or misbehaving.

"I would say not, but I don't know. I can only guess his feelings for you. I pray they aren't as deep as I fear."

On several occasions I had heard Clayton utter words of love, which worried me. "I'm … I'm certain it won't be hard to reason with him, Sedat. "I'll speak to Ronan about it." Men returned to camp, several carrying stags over their shoulders. "There's much to do for the evening meal."

"I'm glad we spoke. I wish you and Ronan the best of luck."

"I hope you feel better. Thank you." I ran after my son, the boy playing with two others, who held sticks. "Come along. Let's sleep a little before supper."

"Mamma!"

***

Flames from a robust blaze cut through the darkness of the night. Holding a stick in the fire, I burnt a piece of meat, the edges sizzling. I had already eaten several pieces.

"You're quiet this eve," commented Ronan, who sat beside me.

"I had a talk with Sedat. She already suspects we plan to leave."

"I wish to do so soon. They're smoking enough meat for everyone. That should keep us on the walk home."

I glanced at the other fires. People ate, while others laughed in conversation, the soft refrains of chatter falling all around us. "I've not hated living here. It's been pleasant. They spoil us."

He nodded, chewing meat. "I agree. If we didn't have the cave to return to, I'd say we stay. I can find little fault with the clan. The leader's a reasonable man. The healer's a bit odd, but then again, they always are, aren't they?"

"True," I giggled. "They think they know all. Barcelo claims to see what'll happen many moons from now, but he's ridiculous."

"The clan holds him in high esteem. He's their holy man. He's healed people."

"While others die when they shouldn't. I don't want a healer with our clan, Ronan. I don't like it."

He tossed a stick into the fire. "It's too late."

"What do you mean?"

"You're our healer, you silly woman. The cave's filled with your herbs."

"That doesn't make me a healer. I use what nature gives me. Sometimes the plants fail. There are many ways I don't know. Sungir died before teaching me everything. I've trouble remembering most of what he said anyhow. It's been too long." I stared absently into the flames. "Too many seasons have passed." A dog barked, the sound echoing. "I've been thinking more and more about Sungir. I consider him my father, you know. He was a good man—the best of men."

"I wish I'd met him."

"He had hair as light as some of the pale rocks in the creek. Very light. Far lighter than Bannon's hair."

Ronan eyed the camp. "That dog's loud."

I hadn't thought of it, hearing him still. "Someone should give him meat." I grinned, picking at a dried piece of grass tangled in my hair. "There are so many animals here. Braya's dog had babies. They're—"

"Be quiet." Ronan held up a hand. "Something's wrong."

Although the dog continued to bark, no one paid him any attention other than Ronan, the din of chatter continuing, with someone laughing at a nearby fire. I eyed my husband, now worried over his demeanor, his eyes trained on the forest, which surrounded the encampment. This evening was the same as any other, relaxing and warm, while the children played.

"It's just a noisy dog."

Ronan jumped to his feet. "Take the baby!" he shouted, darting into the hut to retrieve a spear.

No sooner had he commanded me to move than an odd sound occurred, a loud shout that did not originate from the clan, but somewhere else. Another cry rang out and another. Some unseen enemy surrounded us, and, from the sound of it, there were many. All talking ceased then, men brandishing spears, while a woman screamed. I hurried into the hut to pick Bannon up, the boy sleeping.

"What is it?"

"I don't know, but you must go, Peta. You can't stay here."

My mouth fell open. "What do you mean? What'll you do? What's happening?"

But he could not answer, because of the appearance of some wild, filthy creature standing in the doorway of our dwelling. Stunned, I gaped at the man, who looked to be a mixture of the white and dark races, the pronounced ridge on his forehead giving him away. He hissed, baring brownish teeth. Lifting a spear, he prepared to kill us, although Ronan fought him at once, driving the end of the spear tip through his belly.

"Take the baby and run, Peta!" shouted Ronan. He grabbed me, pushing me to the doorway, where I stepped over the injured man. "Go!"

A scene of carnage and mayhem greeted my eyes, women screaming, while men fought, the camp inundated by these odd-looking, half-breed men, who came upon us in the night to pillage and murder. Not having a moment to even take a weapon, leaving the bow and arrows behind, I held Bannon to my chest, terrified of being slaughtered like so many of the men, women, and children of Clayton's clan lying lifelessly on the ground.

"Go, Peta! Go! I'll find you!"

Terrified over Ronan's well-being, I had to protect my son, his cries rising above the din. Doing as I was told, I hurried for the forest, passing several women I knew who lay bloodied at my feet. I could fight too, if need be, but I fled instead, darting into the cover of foliage, the sound of screaming in my ears.

Fifteen

Taking nothing other than Bannon, my barefeet smarted running through brush and on loose gravel. Despite the darkness, the moonlight offered a measure of visibility. Not knowing how far to go, I found a small foraging path, following it away from the encampment and the screams of people. Running with all my might, Bannon jostled in my arms, the boy quiet at the moment. I eventually stopped to take a breath, my chest burning.

"Gods' teeth," I muttered. "What's happening?"

"Mamma!"

"Shush, little one. I need you to be quiet." I pressed a finger to his lips. "Be very, very quiet."

Who were those men? From what little I saw before fleeing, they all appeared to look like Bondo, but far uglier. Ronan had spoken about encountering unfriendly clans in his travels. I also knew how Greggor treated dark-skinned people, although he promised not to kill them anymore, unless they proved hostile. Other clans I had been with did not breed with them, because the babies frequently died in infancy or grew with deformities that prevented them from living useful lives.

Clayton's people kept to themselves. They hunted and took care of their families, keeping predators at bay, although they had not been vigilant enough tonight. I huddled within a bush by a rock, listening to the distant shouts of men, praying Ronan survived. The crunching of leaves caught my notice, a dark shape suddenly looming over me. Gasping, I smelled the man now, his stench overpowering.

"Ganda punto," he said in a gravely voice.

Although I knew the dark language, those words made no sense to me. They spoke in their own unique tongue.

"Harrow punto!"

The tip of an arrow suddenly thrust through the leaves, startling me. I fell on my behind, encountering the side of the rock, which hurt. "Leave me be," I whispered, knowing he would not. I had no weapon to protect myself. "Go away!" I spoke the dark language then, but I knew he wouldn't understand it.

"Punto!" A hand thrust through the bush, fingers tangling in my hair.

"Ouch!" I screamed.

Bannon fell from my arms, the boy landing on the ground. He said nothing, not crying, his eyes wide with fear. Even for someone so young, he sensed trouble, keeping silent. The brute pulled me from the bushes.

"Gamba punto!" His foul breath fanned over my face.

Wincing from the pain in my scalp, I lifted a knee, kicking him in the groin. He grunted, slapping me hard across the face. My skin stung for a moment, the blow forcing me to my knees. Several troubling thoughts drifted through my mind, knowing my time was at hand. I had no weapon. I could not fight this man. From the wild, feral look in his eye, he certainly meant to kill me. In one last bid to save myself, I screamed, the sound carrying. Then I screamed again, even louder.

"Canno!"

His fist connected with the side of my head, the impact staggering. I coughed, struggling to breathe, as something crashed through the foliage. I hated cats and feared the larger woodland creatures, but I welcomed what came then, praying whatever it was might eat this man. A whimper from Bannon concerned me, the boy hiding in the bushes.

The half-breed heard it too, his posture stiffening. One of Clayton's men appeared with a spear in his hand. I reached for Bannon, hearing the guttural groan of my attacker, as the weapon pierced his skull. I grasped my son, bursting out of the bushes to run, seeing the shadowy forms of men fighting.

I thanked him silently for rescuing me, but I knew more men to be about, both friend and foe. Fearing for Ronan, I climbed a tree, hoping to hide and observe. The safety of a high branch had saved my life more than once before. Bannon clung to me, his little body trembling. The sound of fighting gradually lessened, although a woman screamed and then another. I grasped at thick branches, hoisting myself upwards towards the top, where I stood with a view of what had been the encampment.

Fire consumed the huts, with lifeless bodies scattered all around. Several groups of men continued to fight, their spears clunking loudly from the contact. I did not see Ronan, praying he wasn't among the dead. Holding my breath, I watched the final assault play out, the dark ones having the upper hand. Shouts came from the forest as well, men fighting there too.

"We'll stay here tonight," I murmured. "We can't flee just yet. They'll find us." I sat on a branch, holding my son. "Your father's a strong man. He'll survive this." But, I wasn't so sure, fearing the worst. "Are you tired? You should sleep, my love." I steadied my voice, trying to sound as calm as possible, not wanting to upset Bannon further.

I rested my head against the trunk at my back, hearing voices below: the sound of women. I wanted to call to them, to tell them to hide, but my instincts prevented it. I could not give myself away. I thought of pleasant, peaceful things to calm my riotous mind, but the occasional scream brought everything back, knowing the danger we were in. Bannon slept in my arms, while I listened for anything, fearing being discovered.

The first streams of light broke through the branches at dawn. Shrieks of vultures cut through the silence, the animals feasting on the dead. I waited for Bannon to wake, feeding him a short while later. Getting to my feet, I eyed what remained of the encampment, seeing the burnt ruins of various huts and bodies littered in heaps here and there. Nothing moved, not even a dog.

"They killed the dogs too," I whispered, feeling tired and miserable. Being with child, I longed to rest; I was exhausted and thirsty. "We can't stay here. I wonder if they've gone? It's a shame about the huts. All our things are burned. There's no meat left." I stared at the encampment for a long time, seeing nothing move, other than big black birds that swooped down to pick away at the bodies. "Ronan, where are you?" Tears filled my eyes.

Waiting for as long as I could, the sun higher now, I climbed down, fearing another attack, but the half-breed people had fled. I ventured into the camp, the smoke from the charred huts burning my eyes. Nothing stirred, other than the scavengers eating human flesh. Recognizing several bodies, I cringed at the sight, weary of all the death.

I managed to find a few pieces of hide and a spear, which I took. I came across a bladder of water as well, having a long sip. I gave the rest to Bannon, the boy drinking greedily. Sitting back on my heels, I frowned at what I saw, tears in my eyes.

"We're alive still. We can't be the only ones."

"Mamma." He tugged on my hair.

"Ouch." My scalp smarted from last night. I felt my face, which hurt as well. Bruises covered my arms and legs, with a few scratches. "I pray your father escaped." How would I find him? "Let's look for your pappa, all right?" I took Bannon into my arms. "Let's find Ronan."

As luck would have it, I found a bundle of dried meat behind a hut, pulling it open to eat a strip. Grateful for the meal, Bannon and I slipped into the forest, where I nearly stepped on a dead man, although he appeared to be one of the half-breed people. Several died in the skirmish, their appearances hideous. I had never seen these sorts of people before, their skin not as dark as my mother and sisters. The shapes of their faces were similar with a thick bridge above the eyes. I found another spear. Walking in a large circle, I saw nothing other than the bodies of Clayton's clan and a few half-breeds. Dismayed, I sat to rest, Bannon sleeping at my side.

Tired from stress and a lack of sleep, I cried then, feeling miserable and hopeless, worried even more now about Ronan. I had not seen him yet. I hadn't found anyone alive.

"Where are you?"

Holding my face in my hands, I wept deeply, my shoulders shaking. I hadn't felt such despair in a long time, memories of the past emerging. We had grown lazy at this clan, feeling safe and cared for.

"No place is ever safe," I whispered. "We let our guard down."

A few tears led to many more, my grief profound. I would feel better after a good cry, needing this time to process what had happened. I could not wallow for too long, though, needing to find shelter for Bannon. I cried to exhaustion, so weary I rested my forehead on my knees, with my arms around my legs.

"Hello."

The shock of hearing a voice brought me up short, a girl standing before me. She appeared tired and dirty, with dried tears running down her cheeks. I had seen her before at camp.

"Hello," I said, stunned. "How are you?"

"I can't find my mother."

I swallowed the lump in my throat. "Oh, you … poor thing." I held out a hand. "Come here." She took it, hers trembling. I drew her near, hugging her. "Where have you been?"

"They told me to run. I ran with my brother. I can't find him either."

"You're a brave little thing." I moved hair from her face. "I can't find my man."

"Nobody's alive," she said in a soft, shaky voice. "No one, but you and your baby."

"If we're here, then others are too. They're just scared. They're hiding."

"Do you think so?"

I smiled, feeling a jumble of emotions, knowing I had to take care of this little creature. "Yes. I've been looking around for a while now. I'll search again after my son wakes."

"I looked all day. There's a body that looks like my mamma, but … it can't be her."

"No, of course not. She's somewhere safe." I felt awful for this child, knowing her family had perished, but I had to ease her mind. "We'll look more in a while. Are you hungry?"

She nodded.

"I found some meat." I pulled out a piece. "Have some."

"Thank you." She ripped off a chunk with her teeth.

"What's your name?"

"Silla."

"That's a pretty name. I'm Peta, and this is Bannon."

"I've seen you."

"Yes, I was with your clan."

"What will happen now?"

"We eat and rest for a bit, then we look for … our

people."

"I'm glad I heard you crying. I hope you're better now."

"I'll be fine when I find my man." I sucked in a long, uncomfortable breath. "I haven't found his … body among the dead. I know he's alive—somewhere."

Sixteen

When Bannon woke, we walked off together, foraging here and there, finding bodies scattered in the woods. It looked as if the half-breeds found them and killed them as they fled. An ill, awful feeling lodged itself in my belly. How much longer would I search for Ronan? I could return to the cave, which seemed to be my only choice now.

Poor Silla found her brother's body and her father, the girl's shoulders drooping. I tried to comfort her, but she knew now that no one in her family survived.

"It was my mother then," she said sadly. "The body I saw earlier. I don't want to believe it."

"No, I wouldn't either." I watched her carefully, as she fought back tears. "You can be sad. You can cry. I'm going to cry myself to sleep later." I forced a smile, feeling wretched. "I don't know where my man is. He's not among the dead."

"What if they took him?"

I hadn't thought of that. "Why would they? They killed everyone." The squawking of vultures filled the air, the creatures swooping in to eat human flesh. An idea struck me. "Perhaps I ... should look for tracks." Among our dead, there had been a few half-breeds, the men appearing shorter in stature, with stocky, thick legs. Their feet weren't as long and thin as ours. "Can you watch over Bannon for a bit?"

She nodded.

The boy played with rocks, oblivious to our predicament. This was a blessing.

"I'm going to look at footprints. Maybe our people ran far away. If I see prints and I don't find a body, then those people might've escaped."

A light danced in her eye. "Yes. That's a good idea."

"You stay right here. I'll be back." I gave her a spear. "You can use this." The weapon was twice the size of the girl. "We must protect ourselves now. There are animals who'll eat us. You have to be careful."

"I don't know how to use a spear."

"Hold it like so, and point it at your enemy, man or beast. I'll teach you how to use it, although I'm not very good with it. I prefer a bow, but mine burned in the fire."

She grasped the weapon, a look of determination on her face. "I'll keep Bannon safe. You find our people."

"I'll try," I answered honestly, the faintest bit of hope stirring in my breast. "If I can't find anyone, we'll have to leave."

"Where will we go?"

"There's a cave two days away. The people there are kind. They'll take care of us."

"Will you be my mother now?"

Something twisted in my belly, the sensation bittersweet. "Yes, of course. I won't abandon you, Silla. I'm trusting you with my son. I love him more than life—more than myself—more than the gods. I just ... need to find my man now."

"I can do it."

"I'll look for footprints. I shouldn't be too long. There's water in the pouch. You can give it to Bannon, if he fusses. I'll try to find something for us to eat too."

She nodded. "Good luck, Peta."

I stared darkly into the forest. "Luck's not been on my side often."

***

Moving in a large circle, I spotted various tracks, following them until I stumbled upon a body, the sight disturbing. The half-breeds did not care in the least about babies or children, killing everything in their path. I thought Greggor to be a heartless murderer, and he was, but these people spared no one. Greggor had let women and children live, killing only the men. He promised me he would never target the dark-skinned people again. We'd had many a discussion on this issue.

I found another half-breed body, the man lying on his side. As I passed, moving silently by, I thought I heard a moan, stopping to look at him. His skin appeared lighter than those of the others, with a pronounced bridge upon his forehead. He smelled dreadful, not having washed in a long time. Greasy, tangled hair lay about his shoulders, while a large gash in his belly revealed greyish entrails. Buzzing insects feasted on him, the sound loud in my ears.

I frowned, having thought him to still be alive. Hadn't I heard a moan? "Hello?" Ignoring the insects, I detected a faint sound, a man's voice perhaps? "Hello?" Grasping the spear, I held it before me, venturing towards where I thought I heard something. The moist earth revealed footprints, although these appeared thinner and longer than that of the half-breeds. "Is someone there?" A rustling branch made me jump, my chest pounding with anxiety and fear. I hadn't gone far when I saw a man's foot, the skin as pale as my own. "You there," I murmured, nearing. "Oh, my … " I nearly choked on my own tongue. "Is that you?" A man with lightly colored hair lay on his back, his face hidden by dried blood. I recognized him at once. His fingers clutched his belly, where a trickle of blood poured forth. "Ronan!"

"P-peta?" he murmured.

"You're alive!" I fell to my knees beside him, tears

streaming down my cheeks. "Ronan!"

He smiled slightly, although the movement pained him. "I'm not alive long, my love."

"No!" I shook my head, determined to see to his wound. "You're going to live." I lifted his hand, which revealed a puncture, but it wasn't centered directly in the middle. "I'll tend this. You're going to recover." Nothing would diminish the joy I felt at seeing him again—nothing. I assumed the wound to be the result of a spear tip. "Can you move at all?"

"I … don't know," he managed. "I thought you dead. They killed everything. I've never seen such violence. Not even the babies were spared. Who would do that?"

"I can't think on it now. I've you to care for."

"Bannon."

"He's fine. He's with Silla."

"Silla?"

"A girl I found."

"I'll … try to move, if I must. I fear you waste your precious energy, though, Peta. This wound … isn't survivable."

"Shush. I won't have talk like that."

He took my hand, his fingers feeling cold. "I'm happy to see you one last time. I worried I might die without saying goodbye."

"You will *not* die," I said sternly. "I need to move you. I don't wish to make camp near one of … those horrible men."

"I'll do as you ask, my love." His voice broke. "Whatever … you need me to do."

"I must bind the wound first." Removing the leather skirt from around my hips, I used the spear tip to tear strips apart, tying them together again for a long bandage, which I worked around his midsection. He groaned in pain, his face twisting. "I'm sorry." I brushed away the tears, hating how my emotions bubbled to the surface. I would not weep for him now, not when he still lived. "That should keep, long enough to move you." I grasped his arm. "Can you try to stand?"

"Yes."

I helped him to his feet. "That's good." I marveled at how easy that had been. One arm about his back, I held him as tightly as I could, slowly walking away. The ground where he lay appeared soaked with blood, which was troubling. "It's not far."

"I should've saved more people. I killed him and a few others, but it wasn't enough."

"You're not to blame for this. We were set upon."

"Barcelo foresaw the tragedy. His prophecy came true."

"I don't wish to discuss it."

"This didn't have to happen. We should've been more vigilant."

"It's too late now. I'm going to heal you, and then we're going home."

He struggled to lift one foot, then another, the progress slow. "You and Bannon should go now. There's no reason to ... wait for me."

"There's every reason. You're my man. You're my son's father. I'm not leaving without you." I lifted my chin, holding him tightly about the back. "We're nearly there. I'm going to make a fire and tend your wound. You'll be on the mend soon enough."

He said nothing to that, groaning with each step, as blood stained the leather around his middle. We reached Bannon and Silla a moment later, the girl holding my son in her lap.

"You found someone!" A smile lit her face.

"I did, but he's hurt."

Ronan grunted, falling to his knees. "My son," he murmured.

"Is this your man?"

"Yes, this is Ronan."

"You're fortunate to find him."

"That remains to be seen," I said with a hint of bitterness. The gods seemed to enjoy this game of theirs, giving me my dreams, only to snatch them away later. "Are you in pain?"

He nodded, grimacing. "Don't worry over me." His attention drifted to Bannon. "I can die in peace now. I've you and my son. I need nothing else."

"You're not dying, Ronan." I helped him to lie back, using a small pelt for a pillow behind his head. "I need to find some herbs."

"I'll gather wood for a fire."

"Thank you, Silla."

"Bannon can help me."

"He likes to run off, so be careful." I worried over that. "Perhaps I'll take him with me."

"I can watch him," said Ronan. "You get what you need. The boy will stay with me."

"I'll get wood here," said Silla. "I'll stay close."

"Thank you. There are plants for pain and others for healing. I'm going to gather everything I possibly can before it's dark. Then I'm making a strong brew for you. You'll be on your feet again in a few days."

"I admire you, Peta." He smiled sadly, a watery, dull look in his eye. "You'll exhaust yourself for nothing. I've seen enough wounds like this to know what it means. The spear went too deeply. It cut through my insides in a way that can't be mended."

I did not want to hear that. "You rest, my love. I'll be back." I nearly tripped over my feet, because tears distorted my view.

He has to live. I have to heal him.
Sungir! I need your wisdom. I need your guidance.
The gods … I curse you!

Seventeen

I found an inner strength, motivated by the fact that three people depended on me for their survival. I first made a sturdy shelter of thick branches and bundled grass for a roof. While hunting for herbs, I found discarded patches of hide, which I used for our comfort, lining the floor.

Cleaning and tending Ronan's wound, I brewed various teas to help his pain and keep him from feeling hot, but once the tea wore off, he felt worse immediately. Silla helped to watch Bannon, often foraging with me. We found green edibles and berries and nuts, but hunting with a spear proved impossible. I failed to hit anything, even stags unaware of my approach.

Discouraged by the situation, I remained determined to help my husband, sitting with him by the fire, watching the flames curling around a thick piece of wood.

"You do too much," he said softly.

"What?" Lost in thought, I glanced at him, hating how pale he appeared, with dark circles under his eyes. "What do you need?"

"You've prolonged my life a little, but we both know—"

I jumped to my feet. "Did you hear that?" I stared into the forest, seeing nothing other than the shadows of trees. "What was that?"

"It's nothing, Peta. Come sit. Listen to me."

I did not want this conversation. "I should check

your poultice."

"I know you're trained in the healing arts, but your skill cannot bring a man back from the dead."

"Stop it! Don't talk like that." Bannon slept with Silla, the pair cuddled up together on a pelt. I did not want to wake them, whispering, "Let's speak of this tomorrow." A cold-feeling hand closed around mine.

"Listen to me," he said softly, his tone even. "You've tried everything."

"No, not everything. There's one plant that's hard to find. When I find it, I'll make you a new brew, something that'll take the fever away for good."

"I fester on the inside. It won't stop bleeding, no matter what you do. You've closed the wound, but I'm bulging now, my belly filled with blood. Listen to me."

Tears filled my eyes.

"You must let me go, Peta. I'm not long now. I can feel it. I've tried to will myself back to health, but I can't. I've drunk everything you've given me, but it does no good. This wound is more than any healer can mend. I knew it the moment the spear went in. I felt it in my back. You must listen to me." He squeezed my hand. "You know the way home. When I'm gone, you should return to the cave, where Enwan and Bondo will take care of you."

I sighed, feeling miserable. "We were supposed to be together for the rest of our days. All those seasons without you. I thought they were punishment enough. When I found you again, I prayed the gods might show some mercy, some kindness."

"They have. We've been granted this time. I've my son, my beautiful son. You'll have another babe soon enough. Whenever you look at them, you'll think of me."

Swallowing painfully, I saw him through a veil of tears. "I want to keep trying to heal you."

"You're exhausting yourself running around the forest. You should go back to the cave."

"We will, once you're better."

He sighed. "Oh, Peta."

"No!" I said too loudly, determined to never give up. "I'm going to find that plant. If that doesn't work, then I'll open you up again and clean the wound. I should do that anyhow. I found something that might heal your insides."

"If you feel you must."

I drew closer, settling in next to him, my arm over his chest. "Yes, at least let me try. If I don't try everything, I'll blame myself forever for not doing my best."

He patted my arm. "You've done more than enough."

"And you're still with us."

"For now."

"For many, many more seasons, Ronan."

"I've always loved you, Peta."

Tears filled my eyes. "I love you."

"I've never been happier than when you came back to me. I still remember how filthy you were when Enwan and I spotted you."

"You made me bathe in the heated spring."

"Indeed. Then I saw what a beautiful young woman you were. I recognized the necklace I made for you. I knew who you were then."

"The gods brought us back together."

"They have a plan. We can't know it, but they do want what's best for us."

"I disagree."

"They've given us this time, this very precious time. These past few moons with the clan have been some of the happiest of my life. I don't regret a thing."

"And when we return to the cave, we can continue to live just as happily as we are now."

Another sigh escaped him. "Yes, I'm certain."

"You should rest. No more of this sad talk. When I find the plant I need, I'll heal you. You'll be good as new.

You might have a scar, but that'll soon fade."

"It will."

"Sleep, my love."

"Aye," he murmured. "I shall sleep. My dreams are only of you."

***

A noisy squawking woke me, something cold pressed to my side, while I hid beneath a thin pelt. In the dimness before dawn, I tossed the hide aside, sitting up.

"Shut up, you annoying bird." I heard the creature again. It sat directly above us, its form mostly in silhouette. The light had not risen high enough to penetrate through the branches. "Shush." Leaning over Ronan, I rested a hand on his chest, needing to reassure myself that he breathed. I felt the coolness of his skin, the sensation a shock. "Ronan?" My fingers curled around his neck, everything stiff and cold here. "No!"

No wonder that bird sat overhead … waiting …

Getting to my feet, I tossed the pelt over him, as tears flooded. I had to get away, away from the children so I did not wake them. Stumbling into the gloom of the trees, I ventured a short way, leaning against a tree for support. I wept then, the grief nearly too much. He tried to warn me last eve. He knew he did not have long. Now I wished we had spoken about every topic imaginable, until his last breath. Why hadn't I kissed him one last time? Anguish and regret mingled within me, feeling like the pricks of a thousand thorns. This was far worse than when my mother and sisters had gone missing.

"Why?" I glanced upward. "You cursed gods! You did this! How could you take him?" The bark of the tree scratched my cheek.

"Peta?"

I heard Silla. "Yes?"

"He's gone, isn't he?"

"Y-yes."

"I'm sorry. He told me yesterday his time might come soon. I ... am sorry."

This poor girl had lost her entire family in the raid. "You'll have to tell me what you spoke of while I foraged."

"Many things. He wanted me to know everything about you. He told me how he knew you when you were my age. He told me all about the great flood and how you were separated for many seasons. How you found one another again. How strong you are. He said you can kill cats."

I held a hand to my mouth, staring at her. "He said that?"

"He spoke all day, Peta. He said I must help care for Bannon. I won't be a burden."

"No, you're not a burden."

"I feel as you do. I miss my mamma and pappa. I miss my brother."

"I know," I breathed.

"We're all that's left of the clan."

"Yes."

"Don't be sad."

"I am now. I can't help it."

She stood there with only a thin skirt around her hips, her dark hair a riot of tangles around her. I had to take care of her and Bannon. This wasn't like the time at Sungir's hut, after my family vanished. I could not endlessly wallow in the misery of loss. Bannon and Silla needed a safe place to live—they needed food. I wanted nothing more than to collapse in a heap and weep for a season or two, but I could not. Not now.

"We'll have a burial," I said.

The other day I helped Silla find the bodies of her parents and brother. We dug shallow pits and placed them inside, with rocks on top. This seemed to help her mourn, as we prayed over their graves. It eased them into the eternal life, where the gods lived. I needed to bury Ronan now. I had to find the strength to do so.

"I can help you."

"That's kind ... Silla."

"Ronan spoke of your home in a cave. I'm to make sure you go there."

I hardly knew what to say to that.

"He said it's towards a mountain. I can't see a mountain. Can you?"

"I'll find it again."

She nodded, staring into the forest. "I'm hungry."

Without a supply of meat, the berries and nuts hardly satisfied us. We had to find bigger game. This task now rested upon my shoulders. "Let's bury my ... my husband. Then we'll ... we'll see about food."

"Yes, Mamma. I do like to eat. It would make my belly happy." She smiled slightly. Her hand touched my arm. "Are you all right?"

"I ... am ... will be fine." Bannon's cries echoed. "He's hungry too, no doubt."

Eighteen

It had been a long time since I felt the weight of melancholy, the emotion unwelcome, yet all too familiar. Traveling with a girl and a baby proved challenging, the pace slower than I would have liked. The carrier I made for Bannon fell apart after the first day, the leather not strong enough. I thought to make another of the hide we had, but the children slept on it. They would not be comfortable or warm in the night without it.

I failed to kill anything significant to eat, my belly always rumbling. We ate mushrooms and onions with whatever nuts and berries I found. We drank water from the leaves of trees after a rain. Time spent foraging slowed the pace further, but we needed food to survive. The evenings proved the worst, after I put Silla and Bannon to sleep and sat alone by the fire to stare into the flames ... thinking of what I had lost.

In these times, I allowed myself to grieve, crying as silently as I could, my shoulders shaking with emotion. I longed for the cave and a friendly face, knowing we headed in that direction, as I remembered where the mountain was compared to the position of the sun. At least I prayed I had the correct direction. I had been wrong in the past.

Feeling tired and weary, I stewed in my thoughts, most of them sad. "Alone again," I whispered. "But not alone. I've little ones to manage and another on the way. I can't live like this with three children. I need a clan. But even a clan can't protect me. Will I ever find peace? Why must people be so terrible to one another? I don't understand it. We did nothing to the half-breeds, yet they attacked us. They were ... scary and horrible. I hope I never see them again."

I had another thought.

"Where's their camp? Surely it's not anywhere near, or is it?"

I had seen no evidence of another clan or anyone traveling through. I once marked trees that led to the valley where the cave was, but those lay in another direction entirely. We were on the other side of the mountain, an area I did not know.

I wiped my cheek, drying the tears. "I miss you terribly, Ronan. How good you were to me. How sweet you were. I can't believe you're gone. I should've helped you. I could've killed men with my bow." Guilt tore through me. "I'm trained that way; yet, all I did was run." My shoulders hunched. "I'm a coward."

He told me to run. But, I still felt wretched over everything, imagining different scenarios, where Ronan and I saved the clan by killing the intruders. This was a fantasy. What if everyone had not perished? The bodies that littered the ground were of our clan and the half-breeds, but ... if everyone perished, there should have been more bodies.

"Many escaped," I whispered, having just realized that. "Yes, many ran like I did. We can't be the only ones alive." Clayton's clan might be in these woods now ... somewhere. I could find them in the coming days. "I hope they have food."

I clung to that thought, crawling over to Bannon and Silla and sleeping on the edge of the pelt. There wasn't enough of it to cover me fully, so I shivered most of the night, sleeping fitfully, until noisy birds woke me. After I fed the children some berries and gathered our things, we set out again, stopping a short while later to pick nuts.

"When will we be at your cave?" Silla eyed me expectantly.

Shrugging, I gazed at the canopy of green overhead. "We're going slower than I like. I need to climb a tree. We should be able to see the mountain now."

"Can I climb with you? I like to climb. I'm good at it."

I smiled, finding her enthusiasm endearing. "I need you to watch Bannon. You can climb after I come down."

"Yes, let's do that."

Gazing at my distended belly, I worried about how cumbersome it might be. "I'll have to be careful."

"You're getting big."

"Yes, but it's still far too soon to have this baby."

"My mother wanted another baby, but it didn't happen."

"I'm sorry." I hated to think about her family or Ronan, pushing those thoughts aside. "I'm going up now. With any luck, I'll know where we are. We can't be far."

"Yes, please. Then I can go."

Bannon played with rocks, sitting on a pelt. "Watch him." I reached for a branch, pulling myself up, which proved no easy feat. "Oh, my. I'm so heavy." Holding onto a branch, I stepped on another and then another. Midway up the tree, I noted what looked like smoke in the distance. "I see something!" Going higher, I reached nearly the top, the branches sturdy enough to stand on.

"What do you see?"

Looking down, I experienced a moment of dizziness, my breath catching. Grasping a branch with both hands, I feared falling. The children would be without help, if anything happened to me. I took a deep breath, struggling to right my senses.

"Let me see … just wait." I felt a little better. "I'm looking." Smoke drifted over the treetops in the distance, revealing what looked like a large camp, as there were several plumes over a wide area. "I see much smoke."

"That's something."

"Over there." I tried to point, but then felt unsteady. Gazing in all directions, I experienced a moment of confusion, not seeing a mountain. "Oh, what have I done?" I had been using the position of the sun as a guide, vaguely recalling where it sat in the sky in relation to the mountain, but now I had to wonder if I had erred. "I … can't be wrong again."

"Are you coming down?"

"Yes," I grumbled, grasping a lower branch. "I'll be there." Stepping onto it, I lowered to another and another, until I dropped to the ground.

"May I go up?" She appeared quite eager.

"Yes." I stood with my hands on my hips. "Please be careful."

"I'm a very good climber."

"All right."

She pulled herself up, while I sat with Bannon, watching him move rocks around. A camp resided not far from where we were, but I could not say who lived there.

It might be the half-breeds, Peta. It could be dangerous.

"I see smoke!" called Silla. "Over there!"

"I know," I said dully, worried over who they were.

"Do you think it's our clan?"

"I don't know. We'll approach carefully. They might be hostile." I knew then what I would do. "Come down. We go soon."

"Yes, Mamma." She descended lithely, hanging and dropping from branch to branch, reminding me of how I had been as a child.

"You go so fast. Please don't slip."

"I'm very good at this. I can do it."

I smiled at her bravado. "Yes, you're a good climber."

***

Knowing the direction of the clan, I planned to approach with caution and climb another tree to have a look at them, before they saw us. Being late in the day, most of the inhabitants would have settled in to cook dinner, the hunters returning as well. Most clans functioned this way, even the dark ones. As we neared, I spied small trails here and there, the paths worn down from many seasons of use.

"People indeed live here," I murmured, eyeing the forest warily. "If they have dogs, they'll bark. They can sense things like that."

"What will we do?"

"Take Bannon." I gave her the boy. "I'm climbing again to get a look at them. If they're the horrible men that attacked us, we must leave quickly. Do you understand?"

She nodded. "Yes."

"I'll be right back."

I grabbed a branch, stepping onto another and another, lifting high above the ground, where a clearing appeared. The inhabitants of the clan built simple huts, the structures scattered from one end to the other, with a thick forest as a border all around. I glimpsed cooking fires and people, their appearance similar to my own. Breathing a sigh of relief, I felt better now about them, hoping they would treat us kindly.

"I'm coming down." When I reached the bottom, Silla eyed me expectantly. "They're not the dark-skinned ones or the half-breeds. They look like us."

"They're our clan?"

"I don't think so. They've been living here a good while."

"Maybe our clan found them?"

"We'll go see. We should go before it's dark." I picked Bannon up. "They've fires and food. I'm starving."

"Me too."

I glanced at the sky. "Please gods; please don't forsake me. You've taken so much lately. Show some mercy." Silla waited for me. "Let's go."

Heading in the direction of the encampment, it wasn't long before an animal barked, the aroma of meat grilling filling my senses. On a path now, we approached the edge of the forest, but a man suddenly stood before us, having stepped from the bushes. He pointed a spear at me, his expression tense.

"Mamma!" cried Silla.

"We come alone," I said, my chest pounding. Another man appeared, and then another. Something warned them of our arrival, the dogs, no doubt. "I'm Peta. This is my daughter, Silla, and my son, Bannon." Surrounded, I waited for what they might say. "We're without a clan. We were attacked a few days ago. Please." I must have looked as haggard and tired as I felt, my shoulders slumping. "We seek shelter."

"Move aside," said a man's deep voice. "Aside!" The spear in my face lowered, as he came into view. "It's a woman and children. I doubt they've come to murder us," he chuckled. "Go back to your meals."

"But … she might be the distraction. Then they'll attack."

"I doubt it, Gart. She looks a mess." His eyes drifted over me. "Where's your man? Where's your clan?"

"My clan was attacked. My man's dead." Tears formed in my eyes. "I've nothing other than my children."

An authoritative air lingered about the man, his anatomy hidden beneath a long leather skirt. Muscled and scarred, he appeared to be Ronan's age, his hair dark, with a long, dark beard.

"I'm leader here. My name's Rourke."

"I'm Peta. This is Silla and Bannon."

"The boy's yours, but not the girl," he commented, intelligence flaring in his eyes.

"Yes, she's mine, but ... not mine. She's an orphan."

This word caught his notice. "We find many orphans."

"We were attacked most brutally by a group of half-breeds."

He tilted his head, frowning. "Half-breeds?"

"A clan of mixed race. Half dark and half white."

"They can't be bred like that."

"Yes, they can. I know of a man of mixed race. He's good and kind, but these people were ... " tears ran down my cheeks, "terrible. Silla's family was slaughtered. They killed my man."

He stared at me soberly, a hint of sympathy emerging. "You may stay with us, Peta. We've men who need a woman. I'm sure you'll be welcome at any number of fires." He held out a hand, gesturing. "Come."

I smiled through the tears. "Thank you ... chief."

"Rourke. I prefer Rourke."

"Thank you, Rourke."

Nineteen

Rourke led us into the encampment, people turning to look, whereby I noted how many here appeared quite pale, with long, golden locks, even the men. I had never seen a clan like this one, its inhabitants so similar to how I looked. Many sets of eyes settled on me, while I held Bannon at a hip, with Silla by my side. We moved to the center of the settlement, having passed various cooking fires, where something delicious roasted. My mouth began to water.

"Good people," said Rourke. "It's but a woman and her children. She says her clan was attacked by a mixed-breed race." He nodded at another man. "This isn't the first I've heard of such a thing, but now we've proof of it."

"We must be watchful," said the man.

"Yes, Shannon. We must." Rourke glanced at me. "Someone please give this woman and her children food and shelter. There are a few of you without women. You know who you are. You may present yourself to her directly. I wish to get this settled, so I can eat. We've outdone ourselves with the hunt. It smells delicious."

Several men hurried over, their expressions eager, curious. I eyed the first few, not finding any of them appealing, preferring to find shelter with a family. The taller, more handsome men had been spoken for, by the looks of it.

"Sabine?" A woman's voice rang out. "Sabine?"

Others approached, an older man standing before me. I wondered if he was the healer for the group?

"Sabine? Doesn't she look like Sabine?" The woman

pushed her way through, where she stood at nearly my height, with long, golden hair. Her blue eyes drifted over me. "No. No, this can't be. Look at her! Look! She looks like Sabine. Tell me she doesn't. Look at her."

I held Bannon closer, confused by what occurred. "I'm ... Peta."

She shook her head. "You look just like my daughter, child."

Of advanced age, fine lines appeared around her eyes and mouth, her skin spotted with freckles. Perhaps she wasn't of sound mind, the woman ranting and raving. A younger woman drew near, her appearance like mine. I had never encountered a female taller before. I found myself rising to my toes to stare directly into her clear blue eyes.

"Gods' mercy," she murmured. "She does look like mother, doesn't she?" A host of emotions passed over her face. "The same eyes, same nose. The same mouth."

"I'll take her," said a man. "I like her just fine. I don't mind all the brats. I did say I wanted a family, didn't I?"

Laughter drifted, someone saying, "You wouldn't know what to do with a woman, Blemmy."

The man's face reddened. "Shut up, you maggot! I've mated plenty. Your wife's taught me everything I know."

A fight erupted at those words, the men throwing punches, although laughter drifted around us, everyone finding it amusing.

"Enough!" bellowed Rourke. "I tire of this. Someone please offer the woman a fire and a meal. I wish to settle it now."

"What say you, Gerda?" asked the younger woman.

"We'll take her to ours. I wish to speak to her."

Several men grunted their displeasure, one saying, "I'll have her."

"So will I."

"Go away," waved the younger woman, her features stern. "Away! She's our guest now."

"I eat," said Rourke, striding away. "This matter's settled. Go back to your meals!"

"Come," said Gerda, a smile on her weathered face. "Let's have a meal. You look tired, my child."

"Thank you." I exhaled the tension I had been holding, happy to be with a family, although I questioned if Gerda was of sound mind.

An older man frowned. "I would've taken her to my fire."

"Perhaps another time, Horris."

"I'm not too old to care for a woman, you know. I can still mate."

I had never seen so many people of advanced age, marveling at the two that stood before me. "I—I'm quite happy to sit at your fire, Gerda."

When he failed to budge, she waved. "Move aside. Out! There's nothing to see here now. She's my kin. She's with me."

Her words struck me as odd, confirming my fears about her mental health. She led me to a hut, where a man sat by the fire watching over grilling meat. He had been one of the people in the woods with a spear, which he had pointed at my face.

The younger woman nodded. "This is my husband, Gart. My name's Mimi." She pointed to an empty pelt. "Please sit."

"So she's to be our guest?" Gart's attention lingered on me.

"She is."

"Come, let's sit." I lowered to the pelt with Silla and Bannon, eyeing the meat dangling in the fire. My belly rumbled with hunger.

"I suppose you'll expect me to feed her then."

"Yes, husband." Mimi sat next to me, with her knees drawn up. "Food for everyone, please."

Gart stared at us, his mouth partially open.

"Food." Mimi snorted. "Why do you look so stupid?"

He frowned. "I don't look stupid."

"You stare, husband. We wait for food."

"You look nearly the same. It's … odd."

A basket came my way, Gerda holding it. "Here you are. Berries and nuts and things. You may have whatever you want."

"Thank you." I shared the fare with Silla and Bannon, the boy crushing the berries into his mouth, leaving a stain around his lips. "We're very grateful."

"Here you are." Gart offered freshly cooked meat.

"Thank you," I murmured.

A baby cried, the sound emerging from the hut, which brought Mimi to her feet. "My girl wakes." She left to tend the infant, whereby Gerda sat next to me, her knee touching mine.

"Tell me about yourself, child."

I chewed on meat, my belly grumbling with hunger. "What do you wish to know?"

"Where do you come from?"

"I … don't know."

"You don't know?"

"I'm an orphan. Dark-skinned people found me and raised me, but we lived mostly among white clans. I can speak the dark language."

"An orphan."

"Yes."

Mimi returned holding a baby at her breast. "You took my place."

"Sit on the other side."

"She's so fussy. I wonder if her teeth are coming in."

"Look at us, Gart," said Gerda.

He tossed a stick into the fire. "What?"

"Look at us, at the three of us. Tell me what you see."

"Women sitting."

"That much is obvious. Is there anything about us

that strikes you as ... similar?"

He stared at Gerda and Mimi and then me. "I saw if before, yes."

"What about it? What do you see of our eyes and noses and mouths? Look at the shape of everything. Does anything look ... familiar?"

"I reckon so, Gerda."

"She looks like Sabine. She looks like my daughter. So many seasons ago, when we lived where the air is cold. We hunted that day, only to be attacked by a family of cats. My husband died from his wounds. When we fled, our little Crayben went missing. We searched high and low for her, but we never did find her."

That name sounded so odd to my ears, although ... a memory stirred, something in the woman's words ...

I had few memories of my early seasons, although I did recall a small white animal I used to play with, some sort of pet. It had been a type of dog, the animal unusually small, with black eyes. What had his name been? It lingered around the edges of my mind.

"She looks like us," said Mimi. "But that doesn't mean she's Crayben."

"You were so young, my dear. You wouldn't remember her anyhow. She was a season older than you."

"The only thing I remember is fighting over Beany. My sister wouldn't share him. I'd have to steal him away to play with him."

"Beany?" I mulled that name over, realizing it belonged to the pet I remembered. "A white dog." Gerda stared at me, as did Mimi. "It's one of the few things I recall. I had a white dog as a pet. I loved that animal more than anything. I don't know what happened to it. I don't remember anything else."

"By the gods." Mimi got to her feet. "Hold her, will you?" She gave the baby to Gart.

"Blast it, woman. Can't a man eat his meal in peace?"

"Hold your daughter." She thrust the child at him.

"No one mentioned it was a dog," said Gerda.

Mimi knelt before me, her pretty face filling my vision. "You're my sister."

"There are other white dogs," said Gart, the baby now in his lap. "You're all making a great deal over nothing."

"No, there aren't," said Gerda. "It was a special breed, brought over from a far off place. A man came through to trade. I remember it well. He had several puppies, which he offered in return for pelts and things. We took one. It was a present for Crayben. I confess to spoiling my grandchild."

As tired as I was, I could not possibly process having just found my long-lost family. This could not be happening. I offered Mimi a weak smile. "Let's think on it. Things will look clearer at daybreak."

"You're Crayben. I know it."

"Even if I am, I prefer to be called Peta. It's the name given to me by my mother, the only woman I've ever known as my mother."

"We can call you whatever you like," said Gerda. She grinned. "What a happy coincidence, eh? I'm astonished by the turn of things, but one never knows what'll come walking out of the forest."

I pondered that, horrible memories returning, even in a moment of such happiness. "It could be destruction. There are terrible clans about. I hope the men of the tribe are watchful."

"We're always alert," said Gart. "We take turns being awake part of the night, then someone else watches until morning. We're perfectly safe here."

Something unpleasant settled in my belly. "No. No place is ever safe. It doesn't matter how watchful people are. If the gods wish it, they can destroy all. I've seen it. Too many times."

Twenty

I slept in my own hut that night with Silla and Bannon; the woman who claimed to be my grandmother slept with us. Although a stranger, she felt comfortable and right, her presence not intrusive in the least. I woke to feed Bannon before dawn, although my milk had begun to dwindle. Thinking of Ronan, I felt sad, although being with family helped to soften the edges a little.

Not able to sleep any longer, I crawled from the shelter and tossed a thick branch into the fire, which eventually caught flame. Staring into the distance, I pondered the direction my life had taken, knowing the gods had led me here for a reason. I had to sacrifice the man I loved, but I had found my family.

I miss you so dreadfully, Ronan.

"Something troubles you," said a soft voice.

I turned to see Gerda, who sat beside me. "I can't sleep."

"You've had more than your share of misfortune, child. I'd like to know about your life."

A sigh escaped me. "I hate to relive it, but you should know, I suppose."

"We truly thought you dead. No child could survive without someone to look after it. You disappeared into the darkness after the cat attack, never to be seen again."

"I don't remember much. I … really don't." Not one memory returned of what happened then, a black void filling my mind. "I'm sorry."

"Trauma has a way of stealing our memory. I'm sure you must've been terrified."

"It's not the last time I've faced cats, Gerda. I've killed two in my life."

She eyed me askance. "You've killed cats?"

"Yes. I know how to use a bow. I lost mine the other night in the raid. I need to make another one." I vowed to find the right tree for the wood needed, feeling far too vulnerable without my weapon.

"Men have such devices here."

"I can make my own. I prefer it. It's smaller and easier to handle."

"You're skilled as a hunter."

"I am, but only with the bow. I can't throw a spear far."

"No. Only strong men can. Even the boys struggle with that." Silence filled the air for a moment, the conversation stalling. She said at last, "You're quite heavy growing another baby."

"I ate a great deal at the other clan. We had more than enough food—too much food." I smiled at the memory. "I've some time yet before I give birth."

"And you had a man?"

"I did. His name was Ronan. I've known him since I was little. He was a good friend. He took care of me. We lived with a clan by a river many seasons ago. They took us in, but only because I looked like them. They never really wanted my mother or sister."

"Because they were dark."

"Yes."

"Were you mistreated?"

"No, but we were never really accepted. They tolerated us. Then Ronan and Enwan arrived. They came from some other place. I liked Ronan from the start. He was always so kind to me, but he teased me. He was like a brother."

"I see."

"Then a great flood came. We were foraging at the time. My sister and mother and I climbed a tree. We managed to survive. So many of our clan drowned."

She listened politely, nodding.

I told her about the dark clan we found and how Greggor attacked. "I'll never understand why men kill for no reason."

"I've heard of that."

"Does this clan kill the dark ones?"

"We do not attack unprovoked. We've moved a bit over the seasons, sometimes meeting unpleasant people, but we only fight if we're threatened."

"That's how it should be."

"I've not seen many dark people, Peta. Those clans don't mix well with whites. I've heard of odd things happening when a man breeds with a dark woman. The babes are … often deformed."

"Some, I suppose. I've seen mixed-race people. I know of one who is kind. He's living with us—or he was."

"Your home in the cave."

I spoke to her about that. "Yes."

"Where you want to go back to."

"Yes."

"I hope we can persuade you to stay with us. This is where you belong, Peta. We're your true family."

By birth they were my family, but I knew nothing about them, other than they seemed kind. I thought of my mother and Ara and Maggi, missing them terribly. I thought about Ronan, a twinge of pain flaring.

"What are your thoughts? They aren't pleasant."

"I've a family already."

"And I'm grateful they took such good care of you, my child. I only wish your mother had lived. She never once stopped wondering what happened to you. She grieved her whole life."

"When did she die?"

"Many seasons ago, birthing a babe, who also died."

"I'm sorry."

"Your father died of injury after a hunt. The animal gored him."

"What was he like?"

"A tall, strong man. Everyone respected him. It happened two seasons after Sabine passed. He was never the same. They'd been together since they were children."

"And your man's gone too."

"Your grandfather died in the cat attack. He bravely fought it, but lost. Then you went missing."

I stared into the flames. "Our time together is so short. It can end—in an instant."

"You're grieving now. I see the pain in your eyes. I'm sorry. You've had much tragedy."

I hadn't told her of Sungir and what happened after. "I'll stay with you for a while, but then I must be on my way."

She didn't like that, a frown appearing. "No need to hurry off, Peta. You and your children are welcome to stay as long as you like. You're growing a babe. You should rest yourself. You shouldn't be out in the wilderness alone—ever, especially in your condition." Her arm went around my shoulders. "Let us take care of you. You're finally where you belong."

***

I filled half a basket with nuts, pleased with my efforts. Silla and Bannon picked mushrooms, although I had to be careful they weren't the type to make a person sick. Having been with Gerda's clan for several days, we fell into a familiar routine, the chores divided by gender, as they always were. The men hunted, bringing back tasty stags and woodland creatures, while we provided the rest.

At camp, I carried out a few pelts to be beaten, Silla helping me. She wore her long, dark hair in a messy braid, which I had done for her this morning.

"I can do it, Mamma. You don't have to work so hard."

A sigh escaped me. "I'm fine."

"Go rest."

She assisted me with everything, including watching Bannon. "You're a sweet little thing."

"I always helped my mother."

"I can see you did. She must've been proud."

"I don't know." Her smile fell.

I shouldn't have brought up bad memories, struggling myself with several that plagued me every day. "This one's clean enough." I pulled the pelt from a branch, holding it. "Bannon should nap soon." I spied him playing with a little boy. "He doesn't look tired, though."

"I can watch him."

The men had not returned yet from hunting. Women and children littered the camp, although a few men remained to watch over us. When the wind blew from a certain direction, the stench of the latrine drifted through the encampment. It smelled as if they needed to dig another.

"All right. I'll have a nap."

Crawling into the hut, I tossed the pelt to the dirt floor, settling in on the soft bed. I reached for a thin blanket of leather, pulling it over my face. I heard Bannon outside, his laughter drifting to me. Time alone always brought back memories—feelings of deep loneliness. If only I had been able to save Ronan. If only I could have cured his injured belly. I had tried every plant concoction I could think of, but none of them worked. The wound had been far too deep.

Despite being with family—my long-lost family—I

still felt alone. I carried on the best I could each day, waking with the sun and being helpful in camp, but a part of me felt oddly numb. I yearned to find Ronan's burial site, to weep upon the stones there. With each passing day, I remembered things I wished to tell him. He died without knowing how deeply I loved him—how much he truly meant to me.

Before sleep finally came, I allowed my thoughts to settle on another, a man I doubted to ever see again—Greggor. I had run from him, although I hadn't planned on it, Shay and Wildre arranging it. What would have happened if I had stayed? I had feelings for the man, the person I had sworn as an enemy so long ago. I forced the memories aside after returning to Ronan, but now I was alone again, and they grew with each passing day. I hardly had the strength to ward them off. Perhaps, if I weren't so grieved and lonely, they would not bother me as badly. Burying my head in the leather blanket, I wept, although I wasn't certain for what I cried.

Twenty-One

Every clan spent the evenings eating around fires, but not all sang, danced or played music. With some clans, mating occurred at all times of the day, especially those of my mother's race. White clans did this as well, although they weren't as open about it. When my sister's man wanted her, he motioned for her to follow him, leading her to their hut.

I spent the nights with my children, learning more about Silla and watching Bannon play with other little boys his age. He did not seem to miss his father in the least, not once asking about him. He was too young to truly know what happened. Perhaps, this was a blessing. I often worked the knots out of Silla's hair, braiding it or tying it with strips of leather. These simple tasks took my mind off my troubles, the melancholy I held at bay, but it never went away. If we were traveling and fending for ourselves in the wilderness, I would have survival to think about, but the clan provided ample food and shelter.

Guilt and grief circled, like the ravens or vultures that fed off corpses. I yearned for the safety and comfort of a clan—which I now had, but I could not shake this feeling of restlessness. I found my real family, Gerda and Mimi being more than kind, inviting me into their home. Why was their love not enough? What was the matter with me?

"I'll be back." I got to my feet. "Please watch over Bannon."

"I will, Mamma." Silla felt the new braid I made.

"Thank you. I love it."

"I enjoy playing with your hair."

"I want to learn to do it. I can do yours."

The thought of grooming myself struck me as odd. I had not cared to bathe lately or pick at my teeth or even untangle my hair. Why should I bother? "I suppose."

"You'd look pretty with braids."

Offering a faint smile, I nodded. "Perhaps. I'll be back." I had to relieve myself.

I passed several cooking fires, families laughing and eating. Someone played a pretty bit of music, blowing through what looked like a bone. The clinking sounds of stone scraping against stone rang out as well, men sharpening spear tips for the morning hunt. After finding the latrine, I came back through a line of trees, seeing the fires of camp between the branches.

A dog found me, making me jump. "Oh!" The animal sniffed my leg. I petted it. "Hello." The creature acted as escort, trotting up ahead, where several men glanced my way.

I heard one of them say, "She'd be handsome, if she did something with herself."

"Indeed," a man laughed. "That hair's been pecked away by birds."

Annoyed and embarrassed, I stomped back to the fire, sitting with my legs crossed before me.

Mimi approached, holding her baby. "There you are."

"I went to the latrine."

"I thought so." She smiled. "How are you feeling?"

"Perfectly well." I lifted my chin, glaring in the direction of the men that spoke so rudely, although they did not know I heard them. "I've got to find the wood I need to make a bow." Every day we foraged, I looked, but the tree in question remained elusive. "Or I'll make one with another type of wood, but it won't be as good."

"Why do you need a bow? The men provide. It's not

necessary to hunt."

"When I'm alone again I've got to kill game. We can't live off just nuts and berries."

"What are you talking about?"

"I've a clan waiting for me. I've spoken of them before. I plan to return soon."

"Please don't." She frowned. "Gerda will be terribly upset."

Although these people were my real family, I knew little about them, having no emotional connection to any of them. Such an admission sounded harsh, but I missed Enwan and Bondo, not to mention my mother and sisters. I would not give up hope of seeing them again. The gods had taken so much from me—the heartless bastards—they owed me my family at least.

"I don't mean to cause anyone pain," I said, watching men dance around a fire, stomping feet and chanting, kicking up dust. "I'm grateful to you all. You've been kind."

"You needn't go so soon. You can stay longer. I hope you don't leave."

"It'll take a while to make the bow and a few arrows. I'll be with you for another moon cycle, if not two."

She smiled at that. "You'll have the babe then."

"I plan to give birth at the cave." I had a thought. "You and Gerda are welcome to join me. Why don't you come with me?"

"To the cave?"

"Yes. We're a small tribe, but it's growing."

"I'll speak to mother about it, but I don't think she'd want to go. We know everyone here. We've been with these people all our lives."

"I understand," I murmured, picking at a jagged nail.

Silla came and sat, her little legs drawn up before her. "Am I going with you?"

She had overheard the conversation. "Yes, of course,

unless you'd rather stay with these people."

"I want to be with you, Mamma."

Her devotion touched me. "I'm honored to be your mother, little pet. You'd make a fine addition to our small clan." I had used my mother's term of endearment, which sounded just right.

Mimi's features remained downcast. "I wish you'd reconsider. You could stay with us forever. You shouldn't be wandering around on your own. Your man's dead. You can find another mate here. There's no reason for you to go. We're your real family anyhow."

Every word she said rang true, but I could not shake this unsettling feeling. It reminded me of when Kia and Ara and Maggi went missing in the woods after Sungir died. Something told me I should not stay here. I did not belong with this clan, despite the fact that I had found my birth family.

***

Several days of foraging proved fruitless in finding the wood I needed for the bow. I searched high and low for the specific tree, feeling frustrated. I noted how some of the men carried bows, their weapons appearing heavier, not as delicate as the ones I made. How I wished I had been able to take mine before fire consumed everything, but we did not have time during the attack. While picking at my teeth with a stick, I pondered the dilemma, Gerda approaching with Bannon in her arms.

"We're going to bathe, Peta. I do hope you come."

I cared little for such a thing, but I knew I needed to. Bannon and Silla could use a bath. "They hate cold water."

She nodded. "Most children do. Many women come. It's a bit of a walk to the pool, but it'll be worth it."

Getting to my feet, I grunted, suddenly tired, my back aching. "Yes, Grandmamma."

A smile lit her face, deepening the lines around her mouth. "I do like hearing that. I'm quite proud to know you, my dear. I prayed to see you again."

"The gods listen at times," I murmured.

"You're still so sad. It shows in your eyes. I wish nothing but to see you happy. A good swim will help. It'll wash away all that burdens you. It shall lighten your spirit."

"It might take more than water for that." I ran fingers through my hair, bits of ash from the fire the night before falling free. Beneath the leather skirt, my legs appeared greyish, my feet nearly black.

She motioned with her hand. "Come along. Let's not delay."

I fell into step beside her, muttering, "I've never been this dirty."

Silla approached with Mimi and her baby, while other women joined us, all of them bringing their children. We made a noisy group, everyone chatting, while one baby cried out its displeasure. The walk proved surprisingly brisk, the trail meandering down to a small waterfall, where the stream pooled into what looked like a glistening pond. Surrounded by vegetation, the place offered shade and privacy, women discarding their leather skirts and beaded necklaces.

A chorus of happy voices rang out, someone diving into the water. I worried they might strike their head on a rock, but the pool proved quite deep. The younger ones waded in and remained near the shallow end, while several women swam to the center, keeping themselves afloat.

Although cold, I gritted my teeth and brought Bannon with me, the boy kicking his legs.

"No, no, no!" he shouted, his eyes filling with tears.

"I'm sorry." He struggled in my arms, kicking and crying. "Oh, do hush. It's only for a moment. You'll get used to it." Other babies cried too, although that lessened after a while, the mothers washing them quickly.

Gerda waded to me, holding out her arms. "I'll take him. You go swim."

"All right."

Women passed around a lump of something round, using it to lather their hair, some sort of soapy concoction. Sungir taught Ara and I how to make such things, using wood ashes and oils. I took one, lathering my face and hair, scrubbing vigorously. Bits of dirt and debris floated around me, my hair having been filthy.

"Look!" exclaimed Silla. "I can swim, Mamma." She reached the center of the pool.

"Be careful." I waved to her. "Come here, so I can wash your hair."

A few women finished bathing already, standing by the edge of the water to dress, some leaving with their children. Gerda held Bannon, the boy happy not to be in the cold any longer. I had gotten used to it, feeling clean and invigorated. I missed the heated pool at the cave, yearning for the smelly, yet soothing water, but this would have to do for now. I emerged a short while later, approaching Silla, who shivered.

"We should've brought some leather." I smiled sympathetically. "I'm sorry."

"I-it's a-ll r-ight, Mama," she spoke through clenched teeth. "I'm f-fine."

"You're very cold."

Gerda tossed a pelt over her shoulders. "Not to worry. I've the cure for that."

"Thank you, Gerda." It gladdened me that someone had remembered such a thing. "I'm fine. I'll dry in the air."

"We'll go back in a moment." She produced a three-pronged, wooden comb. "Now, let's do something about that hair."

"Don't bother. I care less. You may tend to Silla, if you wish."

Her look grew stern. "Nonsense. You're in need

more so than anyone, Peta. It's best to work the tangles now, before it dries and looks like a rat's nest."

I sighed. "If you want to waste your time on such an errand, then so be it."

She chuckled, "It's not a chore, my dear. You're my precious granddaughter. If your mother were alive still, she'd be the one doing this. She loved you, dreadfully." The comb tangled in my hair. "Oh, my. This is a mess."

I sat on a rock, waiting for her to finish. "Tell me something more about my mother." She separated a portion of hair, working it with the comb.

"She was a good and kind woman, the best woman. She loved you and your sister. She spoiled you both. She made pretty skirts with beads and shells for you. You were a sweet, dutiful child. If it were not for the cat attack, we would've seen you grow. You would've mated with someone of our clan and had your children with us. Your mother never stopped wondering what happened to you."

"That makes me sad."

"She was never the same after you disappeared. They feared the cats took you away. Your father and his brothers searched for a long time. There was never any trace."

"I'm sorry." I glanced into the forest, knowing that danger lurked there, despite feeling safe and secure at the moment. "One day … you're with your family … the next … they're gone. I've lost people too."

She patted my shoulder. "I know you have. You're very brave, my dear. You were so little, yet you managed to survive."

"I'm always fighting death."

"Then you should stay with us. We can keep you safe."

I doubted any place was safe … no matter how many men a clan had to protect themselves … it did not guarantee peace.

Twenty-Two

My hair dried on the walk back to the encampment, the strands feeling lighter than before and softer. Being clean felt wonderful. My skin glowed, revealing a golden tan. My feet were no longer black. Silla smiled happily, skipping ahead, while Gerda held Bannon, the boy tiredly leaning into her.

"He's going to need a nap," she said, patting him gently.

"Truly. All the playing wore him out." I yawned. "I might sleep too."

She eyed my belly. "A woman in your condition should rest, my dear. No one would fault you for it either."

"I don't want to be lazy, Gerda. I've a good walk ahead of me soon." With that thought in mind, I vowed to try harder to find the right wood for the bow.

"Bah, no." She shook her head. "We must convince you to stay. You're with your blood family now. We care for you like no other." A misty, faraway look softened her features. "What a blessing it is to have you here. I adore you, Peta. You're so much like your mother. I see Sabine in how you walk and talk, how you smile. She was a beautiful woman—the most beautiful in the clan. Men stared at her wherever she went. They vied for her attention, but your father won her heart."

Toying with a silken strand of hair, I pondered that, missing Ronan in that instant. "My man was handsome. I wish you could've met him. If only I'd been able to save him."

"I'll know more about that when Bannon grows."

I did not wish to upset her, but we would not be here

then. Despite the warm reception and finding my family, my home was not with these people. Whenever I thought about the cave, I felt an odd sinking in the pit of my stomach—the impression that I needed to be elsewhere.

"Yes," I murmured. Silla dashed through the trees, where we followed, passing a cooking fire. "A little nap would be nice."

"I'll put him down. Please don't trouble yourself."

My sister approached. "You look much improved, Peta." She offered a smile. "You smell better too."

I laughed, finding that amusing. "Water can work wonders." A man sitting before his hut gaped at me. Several others turned to stare as well.

"You won't have trouble finding a mate now."

"I desire no one."

Gerda disappeared into the shelter with Bannon, emerging a moment later. A prickle went down my spine, the feeling unsettling. Several men stared my way, including Mimi's husband. I wanted to disappear into the hut to escape their notice, but I needed to eat something first. Chewing on dried meat, I sat next to Gerda, while Mimi tossed several branches into the fire.

"How was your bath?" asked Gart.

"Cold," said Mimi, crossing her arms over her chest. "My sister's clean now."

"So I see."

Gerda grinned. "Bannon didn't like it. When the season's warmer, the children enjoy splashing around in the water." She glanced at me. "We've a few men without mates. They could protect you rather well. They'll help raise your children."

It would be easy to stay here with these kind people. I could find no fault with them, except … I needed to be elsewhere. "Perhaps." But I would not take a mate here. I had to return to the cave.

"There's one right there." Mimi pointed. "Look at

him. His name's Gono. He had a wife, but she died in childbirth. She left behind three strapping sons who hunt with him. They say he can kill a great beast alone."

"That's rubbish!" Gart spat, a look of disgust on his face. "No one can kill a great beast alone. It takes all the clan. You're making things up."

I eyed the man in question, finding him to be muscled and tall, his legs slightly bowed. "I don't want another husband."

"She'll see things differently," said Gerda. "Give her time. They'll romance her one-by-one. She'll find someone to mate with—someone to love." A knowing gleam entered her eye. "Then she'll stay with us."

I've loved before ... but now it's all ruined.

"Please don't." I chewed the meat, worried now, because a man approached. "I ... I'm mourning anyhow. I can't run off with some stranger."

This did not discourage Gerda, the smile remaining on her face. "Here comes the first one. Look at him. He'd do well enough."

I groaned inwardly. "Oh, no."

The man approached, flashing yellowed teeth. "Good day," he said. "I've been meaning to welcome the newcomer. I apologize for not doing so before."

"You waste your time, Lendle," murmured Gart. "She doesn't want you."

He ignored that, staring at me. "I'd like to share supper with you. Would you agree to eat with me?"

"Thank you, but ... no." I offered a weak smile. "It's very kind of you. I'm eating with my family."

A hint of pink appeared on his cheeks. "I do hope you change your mind. I don't have a wife. I don't have children. I'd be happy to raise yours. My hut's rainproof."

Laughter rang out, Gart grinning. "My hut's rainproof?"

Lendle glared at him. "What will you have me do?"

"You'll need more than a rainproof hut, my friend."

"Shall I show her the size of my manhood? Perhaps, she'd like to see it. Many women have enjoyed it."

"Ouf!" Gerda waved him away. "Please, no. We're eating." A giggle escaped her.

Mimi snorted, but refrained from saying anything, although Silla asked, "What's a manhood? Can we see it?"

I gasped. "Certainly not. It's nothing to worry about."

"My thoughts exactly," chortled Gart. "It's too small to be of concern to anyone."

"Why you, arse!" Lendle flung himself at him, the men tumbling upon the grass, where a skirmish occurred, someone grunting in pain.

"Stop that!" Mimi shouted. "Get up this instant, you idiots!"

Several men laughed at a distance, someone shouting, "Knock some sense into him!"

I worried someone might be injured, although they stopped fighting then, Gart stumbling to his feet, where he spat blood onto the dried grass. Lendle grimaced, glaring at him.

"Go back to your fire," said Gerda. "If Peta wants to mate you, she'll say so. You've made your intentions clear."

He offered a weak smile. "I do hope you'll say yes."

"Go away!" shouted Gart, giving him a push. "I tire of this." As Lendle departed, he glanced at me. "Might I expect another soon?"

"What do you mean?"

"Men sniffing around every day."

I shrugged. "How would I know?"

Mimi touched her husband's face. "You're injured."

"Hardly." He shrugged, reaching for a piece of meat. "That was nothing."

***

Grasping a spear, I set out to find the wood I needed, leaving Bannon with Gerda. Women foraged, their voices drifting in the distance. I determined to go in another direction entirely, knowing I had not seen the right tree in any of the places we frequented while foraging. Mindful of being followed, I waited behind a tree, worried someone might be on my trail. When the path remained empty, I continued on.

The men hunted on the plains, having left at daybreak. Stepping from the path, I waded through what quickly became a wet, messy bog, with brownish water reaching my knees. Because of this, no one foraged here, the plants thick and green. All manner of birdcalls resounded, including the low hoot of an owl. Slithering things made ripples on the surface of the water, while buzzing insects bit at the skin on my arms and back. I waded in a large arc, slowly emerging, finding the edges of an embankment.

Gazing upon the filthy, sodden skirt, I shrugged. "I need another bath."

A moss-strewn ravine revealed itself a moment later, the rocks far bigger than any man or beast. I ventured around them, finding bushes bursting with berries, purple and ripe. I ate as many as I could, filling my belly with the delicious fruit.

"Blast it," I muttered, unhappily. "Where are you, you stupid tree? I only need *one* tree." Stomping my foot, I vented my aggravation, lifting my chin and cursing the sky. "Do you not want me to return to the cave? Is that why you're making this impossible?"

The gods wouldn't answer me; I knew this.

"Fine! I'll let it rest for now." Falling to my knees, I picked at the berries, tossing more into my mouth. "I might as well eat. I can't take them with me. I should've brought a basket." But, I had wanted to find the tree, knowing I needed to carry wood after chopping it down. "Um … these are good."

A twig snapping brought me up short, a prickle of warning skimming down my back. Holding my breath, I listened. The rustling of a bush revealed a man, Gart suddenly appearing. I released a deep breath, getting to my feet.

"What is this about?"

"You shouldn't be alone, Peta."

"I'm fine." His legs appeared filthy. "Why are you following me?"

"You seek something. What is it?"

"A certain tree."

Grasping a spear, he nodded pragmatically. "And you won't stop until you find it?"

"I need the tree."

"To make a bow."

"Yes."

"We've trees aplenty for bow making. Why not use them instead?"

"I'm looking for a lighter wood. I can't explain it. You have to see it. It makes a better weapon."

"And what would a woman know about that?"

I thought he followed to mate, but now I had to wonder. "I learned it from an old, wise man. His name was Sungir."

"Sungir?" His brows drew together. "Why does that name sound familiar?"

"He lived far away from here, where the air is cold. He was very old."

"It doesn't matter. Let me escort you, Peta. Mimi would be upset, if anything happened to you."

"You … you didn't follow me to … mate?" I watched him carefully, wondering at his reaction.

"That would be … a pleasurable idea, but I sense you've no interest in it." He lowered his gaze to my belly.

"You're ... quite large. I've no wish for it ... I suppose."

I giggled, feeling relieved. "I don't want to mate, no."

"But you have, clearly."

"Yes."

"To this Ronan person."

And another ... but I shouldn't think of him. "Yes."

He waved dismissively. "Let's find the tree, shall we? You made me walk through the muck. Mimi will insist I wash after this."

I grasped the spear, passing him. "I had to search in a new place."

"Tell me what the tree looks like. I've lived here many seasons. I might be able to help."

I felt a great deal more at ease now, not minding his company. "All right. It's tall and white and smooth." I glanced at him over a shoulder.

He nodded. "I might know where that is. This way."

Twenty-Three

After finding the right type of wood, it needed to be cut and debarked, the drying process lasting nearly a full moon cycle. Once completely dry, I sanded down the edges and filed grooves in the correct places. Sitting by the fire each night, I worked the bow, men often stopping by to have a look.

"Is that finished yet?" asked Mimi. She held her baby girl, Soland, to her chest.

"Nearly." I smiled, finding my sister's company pleasant. I had gotten to know her better, discovering we had many things in common. "This'll be a fine weapon."

"And you plan to leave us still?" She frowned slightly.

"I must."

"But, why?"

We argued the point repeatedly, my resolve as firm today as the day I walked into camp. "Because I … live elsewhere. The cave of the wind's my home."

"You say there are only a few people. That's hardly a clan."

"It'll grow. I'm hoping you and Gerda will come with me."

"Gart would never allow it. His family's here. This is my clan."

"And my clan's in the cave."

She sighed. "You're stubborn."

"People are waiting for me."

"What if they're not there?"

"Then I gather wood and wait for them. I've done it before. I had Bannon alone in the cave."

"I could never venture off by myself. I'd be ... too terrified."

"I'm always alone," I murmured, holding up the bow. It felt good in my hand. I had missed having a weapon. "I'm nearly ready to try this."

"Women don't hunt."

"So you've said, but I'll need to hunt food. Berries and nuts alone won't keep me strong."

"Then choose a man. There are several who'd take you, even in your condition." She eyed my belly.

"I'm aware of that." Not a day went by when someone didn't try to mate me. I could hardly go to the latrine without being followed. "Speaking of men." I eyed the approaching hunters, some carrying stags over their shoulders. "Supper arrives."

A warm smile lit her eyes. "My handsome man."

"I do like your husband. He's ... respectful."

"He says he's never mated you."

"No."

"I wouldn't be angry if he did. It's the way of it. I fully expected it."

"I don't want a man." That statement held a measure of truth, although I missed Ronan dreadfully.

"You do." She placed the baby on a pelt, the infant crawling to the other end. "You told me of the dark one, the man who left his people to find you."

I had confessed to her about Greggor, having a moment of weakness. "Yes, but he's gone. He's gone back to his clan by the lake."

"Perhaps."

That answer perplexed me. "Have the men seen anything?"

"They encounter travelers often enough, but no one how you've described."

Was Greggor still searching for me? He could not possibly be roaming the forests, could he? "That's all done with." The baby kicked in my belly. "Goodness, someone's growing strong."

"You shouldn't travel in your condition."

"I've done so before. It doesn't slow me."

"Please stay with us until after the babe's born. Don't go, Peta. I've only begun to know you. From what Gerda says, we played together often as children. We were inseparable."

"I've no memory of it. I'm sorry. I wish I could remember my own mother, but … I can't."

"I hardly remember her too. That's why I want you to stay. Is our clan not good enough? We're your people. We belong together."

I smiled sadly. "Everything you say is true, but … I've a mother and two sisters out there. They've gone missing."

"But they're … of the dark kind."

"Yes, but they're my family. I don't expect you to understand. My sister, Ara, is a remarkable woman. She's strong and kind. She may not look like me, but she's my sister in every way. Maggi's younger and so sweet. I miss them."

"I've seen the dark ones before. They're scary. They're different."

"They're just like you and me. They tend to their families the same way. They love the same. They fear what we fear. They only wish to live in peace. Some clans hunt them and kill them." I remembered the attack far too vividly. "There's a clan of mixed-breeds hunting and killing white clans. That's how Ronan died."

"Yes, I've heard stories."

"I hope they're far away."

"Gart said they came through, killing everything in their way."

"They did."

"You're lucky to be alive."

"I've never seen such brutality. I thought I had with Greggor's clan, but these people are worse. Greggor promised not to kill the darks anymore. He said he wouldn't."

"Do you think he'll honor that?"

"I ... don't know." All this talk bothered me, memories of horrible things returning. "This is mostly finished. It needs some leather twine, but it should be good. I'm going to try it tomorrow."

She eyed the bow. "I hope it breaks."

My mouth fell open. "What?"

"Then you'll have to stay."

"I could leave tomorrow, if I wanted. I can use a spear."

She frowned. "You're mean."

I touched her shoulder. "I know where you and Gerda live. I can come back to see you. I'll bring my new babe then. Would that make you happy?"

"We've been here too long. Rourke will move us to a fresher hunting ground soon enough. Then I'll never see you again."

I pondered that, knowing it to be a possibility. "Let's pray then that you stay a long time."

"Please don't go."

"I'm sorry, Mimi. There are things I must do. I feel it in my bones. I'm not meant to stay longer. I can't explain it, but ... something's pulling me home. I must leave."

***

I sensed I had a shadow, someone following me. Standing on the other side of a tree, I waited, wondering who it might be. Gart suddenly appeared, knowing I hid.

"You don't have to wait for me." He grinned.

"I prefer to do this alone." Annoyed, I scowled at

him. "I've things to do."

He eyed the bow. "I can see that. I'm dying of curiosity. Does that thing work?"

"It will, if I have the chance to try it."

"I want to see this."

"I didn't invite you."

"Weapons are for men, Peta. You're more likely to injure yourself with that thing. It looks far too frail anyhow. The wood's too thin."

"It's perfect, the best I've ever made." I lifted my chin defiantly. I learned from a master. With the right wood, it needn't be thick or cumbersome. "This is strong, stronger than you think. It doesn't require a man to use it." I stepped before him, daring him to challenge me. "All that's needed is skill, which I have."

His nostrils flared. "I should've mated you. I don't know why I denied myself. I feel foolish now."

"I don't wish it." Having the bow and several arrows, I could ward off man and beast, although I hadn't tried it yet. "You may watch me kill a stag, if you wish. Please be quiet."

"You're going to kill a stag?"

"Yes, I am."

He chortled, "I'd like to see this."

"Then follow quietly," I muttered, irritated he had invaded this moment. I desired privacy to acquaint myself with the new weapon, tweaking it here and there if needed. Now I would have to do so under his watchful eye. "Come along."

He stepped behind me, his presence annoying. Eyeing the forest, I spied blue between the branches of nearby trees, seeing open space. With leather tied around my feet, my footfalls remained silent. A skilled hunter, Gart trod just as softly. We emerged onto grassland, a family of stags grazing in the distance. I set an arrow at once, not wanting the animals to know of our approach. Aiming for a younger one, I pulled back on it, the leather creaking slightly. Then I let it fly, the arrow arching gracefully, the tip finding its mark a moment later.

I glanced at Gart. "It might be good you're here after all. I'll need someone to carry the thing."

He held a hand over his eyes, squinting. Then he looked at me. "You got it?"

"I believe so." The other animals disappeared, darting into the woods. "I can't be sure until I've seen it." I smiled triumphantly, more than pleased with the performance of the bow on the first try. But, then again, I'd made many of these over the seasons, each time producing a better weapon. Not waiting for him, I strode onto the prairie to retrieve my prize.

I gazed at the animal, the arrow embedded in its flank. It was still alive, so I cut its throat quickly to end the suffering. Gart neared, standing with his hands on his hips.

"Will you carry her?"

"Yes." He scratched his head, an odd look on his face.

"Is something the matter?"

"I wasn't expecting this."

"It's a stag, Gart," I teased. "I'm certain you've seen one before."

"I've never known a woman to hunt."

"Anyone can hunt, even children." I pulled the arrow free, wiping the blood off on dried grass. "Shall we?"

Hoisting the stag upon his shoulders, he grabbed the feet. "I should've mated you."

I snorted, turning for the forest. "So you've said."

Twenty-Four

I held my son's hand. "Can you say goodbye, Bannon?"

He smiled, exposing several tiny teeth. "Ba … bye."

"That'll have to do." I ruffled his hair. Facing Gerda, I swallowed a feeling of regret. Tears glimmered in her eyes. "We must be on our way."

"Please reconsider, child. Please."

Mimi stood next to her. "Can't you wait another day?"

"I've spent too many as it is." I should have left at the last full moon, waiting longer for another to come and go. With the size of my belly, the journey would not be easy. "I need to make haste."

"You're foolish," muttered Gerda. "Foolish woman. What if you find your cave, and no one's there?"

"I've given birth alone before." I shrugged. "I pray to the gods every day. I hope they show me some mercy. I found you all, which is a blessing."

Mimi hugged me. "I shall miss you, sister. If we never meet again, I hope you live a long and happy life. I wish you nothing but the best."

I held her close, breathing in her sweet scent. "I'll miss you. If you ever need a new home, come to me. I've told you how to get there. It's not too far. You and Gerda and Gart are welcome to live at the cave."

"If we find ourselves without a clan, we shall consider it," said Gerda.

I hugged her next. "Thank you. Thank you for being so kind to me. I needed a place to … grieve for a while. I'm so happy I found you. I'll never have to wonder about where I come from. I know my birth family now."

"Please come back to us, Peta. If you need a home,

we have one for you."

I stepped out of her embrace, wiping a tear from my cheek. "I will."

"You've enough dried meat?" Mimi glanced at my leather bundles. "How will you carry all of that?"

"Silla will help me. Bannon can walk a little. We'll share carrying him." I pressed a hand to my lower back, feeling the weight of the pregnancy. "We'll manage."

Gerda's astute gaze missed nothing. "You shouldn't be doing this, Peta, not now. You're too far along for such a walk. You'll be forced to sleep in the cold. You're easy prey for some animal. Please don't go."

"My home's not far. Two days at the most. I can manage." I glanced at Silla, the girl wearing a soft skirt with leather on her feet. We prepared for this, having gathered our things the day before. "Are you ready?"

"Yes, Mamma. I'm ready." She grinned.

"Give me a hug." Gerda held her. "You're my grandchild too. You're more than welcome to come back, if you wish."

Silla nodded, her eyes watering. "Thank you. You people have been very nice." She patted her belly. "I didn't starve here, not once. It sure was good being with you."

"And you'll like the cave too. It'll be your new home soon enough. Once this babe comes, I don't plan to leave it again. I long to raise my children there forever. My days of wandering around are over."

"I'd like to see your cave," said Mimi. "If the hunting isn't good, we'll have to leave. I don't like such changes, but we must go where the food is."

"You're welcome to join me."

"We belong here, child." Gerda smiled sadly.

With a bag of arrows and the bow across a shoulder, I reached for Bannon's hand. "We shall go then. Please tell Gart I said goodbye." The men had left to hunt, already. "Thank you for everything."

"Let us walk you out," said Gerda.

"All right."

Crossing the camp, we stepped into the woods, following a path for a while, until I bid my family farewell, hugging them again. They disappeared behind me, the branches hiding them from view. I felt a profound sense of loss, knowing I would never see them again.

"Are you sad, Mamma?"

"Yes."

"Should we go back?"

"No. I can't go back." The path dwindled to nothing a while later, the ground covered in leaves.

"Where will we sleep tonight?"

"It's too early to worry about it now." I gazed at the sun through the leaves of a tree. "We've a long walk before seeking shelter."

"Two moons, and then we're there?"

"I hope so." Glancing at my belly, I would not be able to climb a tree to see where we were. "I'm going to need your help. In another day, you'll climb a tree, and tell me what you see." I felt certain we traveled in the right direction, knowing the cave stood beyond the mountain, in the opposite direction of the setting sun. Or at least I hoped that was how I remembered it.

"I can do it." She grinned. "I'm good at climbing."

"I know you are."

With a cumbersome belly, I did not walk as fast as before, but we still put in a good bit of distance, the clan settlement far behind us. I remained alert for trouble, stopping to listen every once in a while, hearing nothing other than the sounds of the forest, the birdcalls and insects. After pausing to rest and eat, I pondered the journey so far.

Bannon found a bush with berries, picking and eating them until his fingers and lips turned blue. "You've eaten them all?" I smiled, pleased he traveled so well.

"Mamma, yes! Good."

"I'm glad."

"Can we go?" asked Silla. "I want to go further."

I eyed her. "Is everything all right?"

"I'm not tired. I can walk more."

Getting to my feet, I brushed grass from my skirt. "I know."

"Are you tired?"

My back ached and my feet hurt. "No. I'm fine. We shall go on." I reached for Bannon's hand. "Come along."

The waning sun brought in cool air, the night fast-approaching. After washing in a creek, we continued to walk, the trees blending into one after a while. I searched for the best place to shelter for the night when Bannon began to fuss in earnest, crying loudly. We settled on a camp near three trees, intending on sleeping between them. Tossing down a thin pelt, I set my son on it, the boy rolling back and forth while rubbing his eyes. The day had exhausted him.

"I'm sorry. I know you're tired." I gazed at the deepening shadows, listening to the humming of insects. "There's just enough light left to find firewood."

"I can help you."

"No, you need to stay and watch over Bannon."

"He's grumpy."

"I know. He's tired." Having walked all day, I yearned for a nice soak in a heated pool, wishing the trek home wasn't longer than a day. "Let me find wood." After lighting a fire, I sat with my legs crossed before me, chewing on a dried piece of meat.

Silla curled up with Bannon, the boy asleep. With any luck, he might sleep through the night. Used to the sounds of camp, I found the quiet eerie, concerned over the slightest noise. Whenever a twig broke, I worried someone might appear. One never knew if strangers were friend or foe, but my bow remained by my side nonetheless. When I could not keep my eyes open any longer, I lay by Bannon, pulling a worn leather blanket over my face.

In the morning, I sat up, inhaling the smell of the defunct fire, a greyish mist swirling through the branches of the trees. After tidying my hair and tying it with leather, I woke the children.

"Time to get up."

Silla muttered, "It's so early."

I had every hope of reaching the cave by nightfall. "We've a good long walk ahead of us."

"But I want to sleep."

"You may sleep as long as you like once we're home." I tugged on the leather blanket. "I need to roll this up."

"Ugh."

"Wake up, Bannon." He stirred, gazing at me with bleary eyes. "Good morning."

Despite being tired and cranky, I managed to get the children on their feet a short while later, the three of us trudging through the forest before the sun had fully risen. I yearned to rest, my back aching, but I knew I could not stop now. Silla found a sturdy stick, scraping away at it to smooth it out. She walked with it by her side. When we stopped to eat, I made her climb a tree.

"Go see what you can see."

"All right." Happy not to be walking, she grasped at the lowest branch, hoisting herself up. "I can do it."

I waited below, praying she did not slip and fall. "What do you see?"

"More trees."

"Go higher."

"All right."

I waited, eyeing her every move. "And now?"

She balanced on a high branch, her hand wrapped around another. "What do you want me to look for?"

"Do you see a mountain?" Pivoting precariously, I thought she might plummet to her death. "Be careful!"

"I see it!"

I hadn't realized I held my breath until that moment, gasping. "Where?"

She pointed in a direction. "There."

"What does the mountain look like?"

"Very big with white on top."

"Oh, thank the gods."

"It's so far away, Mamma."

"Yes," I said tiredly. "Another day of walking, no doubt. Do come down. Thank you."

She made quick work of climbing, jumping to the ground a moment later. "Is that where we're going?"

I nodded. "Yes. Let's see how far we get today."

"Another night in the forest?"

"Yes, I'm sorry."

"At least we're going the right way."

I ruffled her hair. "We are. Thank you for climbing, Silla. You've been a great help."

"Were we going the right way?"

"We were a little off."

"Then I'm glad I helped you. I don't want to get lost." She eyed the forest. "I … I like being with people more than out here alone."

"I don't like it either, but at least we have each other."

"You'd be lonely with only Bannon?"

"He'd keep me company, but he doesn't speak very well," I giggled, feeling relieved to be so close to home. "I'm grateful it's almost over. I've been gone too long."

"Tomorrow then?"

"In the evening, more than likely. It's a great distance away."

"I'm a good walker." She nodded enthusiastically. "I can do it."

"Let's keep going then. We've all day still." I felt a ping of pain in my belly, the sensation worrying. "Yes … we should keep walking."

Twenty-Five

We spent the night huddled together between two mossy boulders, while a steady rain fell. I found several branches, placing them upon the rocks and draping one of the leather blankets over to ward off the wet. I doubted we had enough dried wood to burn through the night, the prospect of being miserable and not sleeping at all very real.

"I don't like this," muttered Silla, her arms around her knees. "I'm cold."

Bannon snuggled into the only other remaining pelt, the boy sleeping. "It's not good, but we'll survive."

"Why does he get to be warm?"

"You and your brother will both be warm. After we eat, I'll make him share it."

"I'm tired of dried meat."

"It's only for a little while longer. Tomorrow eve we'll be in a comfortable cave. You'll have plenty of other things to eat then." Long, dark hair hung down her back, her thin shoulders shaking. I put an arm around her. "You poor thing. I remember what it was like to be so thin and young. I'm sorry."

"I'll be fine. I just don't like the cold."

"I don't either." I gazed at the small fire, the edges smoking from the rain. "We'll be lucky to have this for much longer." The leather above our heads grew damper by the moment. I feared it might leak completely later. "It's the last night." Whatever discomfort I'd felt in my belly earlier went away. I could not worry about that now. I had to trust the babe within me was fine.

"Is there more meat?"

I reached for the bag. "Yes, here."

"Thank you." She chewed, appearing thoughtful. "I do like—"

A low growl resonated, making the hair on the back of my neck stand up.

"What was that?" Silla whispered.

Knowing it to be a cat, I tried to sound calm. "A … an animal of prey."

"A cat?" Her brows rose.

"I believe so." Eyeing the spear, I experienced a moment of terror, holding my breath. Where was the animal? It sounded far too close. Perhaps, we had made camp near a den. During the walk, I remained forever watchful of danger and signs of paw prints and fecal matter. I hadn't seen anything to warn me of this. "It might be passing through."

We waited what felt like an eternity, not hearing another growl.

"Is it gone?"

"I don't know." I drew her nearer. "We should stay where we are. If anything comes, I've the bow. I'll take care of it." I shivered, my teeth clinking together. "It's going to be a long night."

***

After daybreak, with little sleep, I emerged from the shelter, placing my hands to my lower back and stretching. "I feel dreadful," I muttered to myself, eyeing the misty gloom of morning, the sun on the verge of appearing.

Not having heard another cat sound, we settled in to sleep, huddling together on the ground with only a pelt for comfort. I gave most of the bedding to the children, sleeping in the cold. I smelled of wet earth, with dirt and twigs trapped in my hair. Miserable and tired, I made my way about the shelter, keeping an eye on the bushes. Holding the spear, I stood still and listened, hearing nothing other than the noisy squawking of birds.

It's the last day. We should be home by nightfall.

Finding a swollen creek, the water gushing deafeningly over slick rocks, I knelt to wash, shivering at the feel of the water. I did not linger long, worried about the children. Upon my return, they continued to sleep, while the first streams of sunlight broke through the branches. I set about bundling our things and removing the sodden leather over the shelter. This woke Silla, the girl sitting up.

"What's the matter?"

"We should go soon. There's no need to linger."

"All right." She sounded tired—weary. "I slept badly."

"At least you slept," I murmured, tying the leather securely. "I'll wake Bannon. He can eat and walk." My son protested the disturbance, crying soundly, which I feared might alert any cats in the area. Placing a hand over his mouth, I shushed him. "Quiet," I whispered. "It's dangerous to be so loud."

Silla held a walking stick, her eyes on the forest. "I don't hear anything."

"You never know." I would not rest easy until I arrived at the cave. "Let's get things together." I took the pelt from Bannon, the boy's lower lip protruding. I could tell he wanted to cry, tears filling his eyes. "I'm sorry. Things will be better soon."

Angered suddenly by the situation, I bundled the pelt and tied it off. I could tolerate travel like this, the drudgery and discomfort manageable, but children shouldn't have to suffer in this way. They deserved to live in comfort within a watertight shelter with enough food and water. I vowed this to be the last journey I took, especially alone.

Taking Bannon into my arms, I held him close. "It's all right, little one. You're a good boy. It's going to be better later. The sun will warm you." He sniffed, trying his best not to cry out loud. I glanced at Silla. "Take my bow and the arrows, please. We should go."

"Yes, Mamma."

The rain from the night before made every step wet and filthy; my legs coated in dirt. Determined not to spend another night in the cold, I walked faster today, my stamina having improved. I carried Bannon for as long as I could, the boy eventually too heavy. He walked then, the exercise warming his little body. By midday, I spied a trail, realizing I neared the encampment where Ronan and I had been attacked. We spotted the first corpse a distance out, but all that remained were the bones.

Silla frowned. "It's a dead person."

"Yes," I murmured, trying not to stare at it. "Something bad happened here. We should keep going."

"Is that what we look like on the inside?"

"Yes."

"Oh."

Walking in a large half circle, I managed to avoid the center of the camp, seeing nothing other than the trees. I glimpsed another pile of bones a while later, but Silla did not see them. I thought to find Ronan's grave, but it would take too much time. Leaving the area brought a measure of relief. Nothing remained here but horrible memories. It dawned on me that I had underestimated the time it took to arrive at this camp. We might have to spend another night in the wilderness.

"Are you angry, Mamma?"

"What? No."

"You look upset."

"I … might've misjudged the distance. There's a chance we have to sleep outside again."

She took the news stoically. "It's all right. It should be nice, if it doesn't rain. Don't worry."

I sighed, feeling weary and sore, my back aching. "Perhaps we'll look for a nice spot in a little while. It's too early still."

"Yes, I know." She followed Bannon, the boy tripping over a protruding root. He caught himself before falling.

"That's a good boy."

Bannon tired eventually, where I had to pick him up. He had grown too big to carry on my back. I held him for as long as I could, setting him down a while later. Tired, I found a shady spot to sit under, reaching in the leather bag to find only two pieces of dried meat left. While Silla and Bannon picked nuts off the ground, I felt a moment of abject misery, cursing the world and all the gods. Gerda and Mimi had been right. I should not be walking all day long for days on end in my condition.

"Are you unwell?" Concern flared in Silla's eyes.

"I'm sorry. I'm just tired."

"Me too."

"I'll be fine. Give me a moment." Running fingers through my hair, I found tangles. Frustrated, I forced myself to stand, feeling suddenly dizzy. Sitting again, I waited for the feeling to pass. "I … we need more water." The bladder we carried was nearly empty. "We didn't take enough provisions for this journey."

"We have nuts." She held out a hand. "See."

"You eat them."

"You should have some too."

"Thank you." I appreciated the gesture, but I knew I needed more than a few nuts to feel better, my body aching.

After finding water, I searched for a place to rest for the night, although the sun still sat high in the sky. Exhausted, I needed a longer rest, having gotten the children up far too early. We found a dry spot near a group of trees, and had a warm fire blazing a short while later. Giving the last two pieces of dried meat to Bannon and Silla, I contemplated finding game to hunt. Perhaps a small woodland creature or a stag, but that meant I had to venture out and search for it.

Silla stared at me. "You're not feeling well, are you?"

"Not so much," I admitted.

"Let me find you something to eat, Mamma."

"You needn't do that. This is all my fault. I should've stayed with Gerda's clan until after the babe came." But, then I would have traveled with two children and an infant, the task impossible. I sighed, feeling deeply unhappy.

"You rest. I'll manage it."

"Please be careful. Take the spear."

She grasped it securely, a determined look in her eye. In that instant, she reminded me of when I was a child. I felt a twinge of pride looking at her, the girl disappearing into the trees. Worried now, I waited nervously for her to return, Silla carrying something in her arms.

As she approached, I smiled. "What have you found?"

She held a woodland creature, an animal that wore a hard shell for protection. "Supper."

I wasn't fond of the taste, the meat mushy and chewy, but it would fill our bellies sufficiently enough. "Let's cut it in pieces and cook it. Thank you, Silla. You've done very well."

"I nearly stepped on it. The gods always provide, don't they?"

"Um … mostly." I wasn't happy with the gods at the moment, but I had to admit they were kind to provide supper for the evening. "It's not the most tasty food, but we can eat it."

She grinned. "It'll give us strength to walk

tomorrow."

"I've every hope of being home then." I eyed a patch of sky through the branches. "No rain tonight. We should sleep well."

Bannon toddled over, kneeling to look at the animal in its greyish shell. He reached out to touch it, the creature snapping at him.

"Be careful," I giggled. "If he bites you, it'll hurt."

"Bad, no," he admonished. "Bad."

Silla lifted a spear. "Shall I kill it?"

I nodded, grateful for the fresh meat for dinner and the prospect of sleeping in dryer conditions.

Twenty-Six

We spent a pleasant night without rain, the three of us on a pelt with the leather blanket over our heads. I woke having to itch my leg, seeing a reddish bump. Sleeping in the open had its disadvantages, all of us suffering various insect bites. I tossed the blanket aside, moving awkwardly, my huge belly cumbersome. Leaving the shelter, I ventured towards the sound of water, dropping to a knee to wash my face and hands, glimpsing myself in the reflection. Flaxen, tangled hair framed my shoulders.

"I'm a sight," I mumbled.

Grooming had been the least of my concerns, the welfare of my children paramount. I did groom Bannon and Silla, though, picking twigs and leaves from their hair, combing the locks with my fingers. I remembered the days in the cave when Ronan and I would do the same. I used a sharpened spear tip to cut his beard. These memories brought back warm and wistful feelings. By all rights, he should be with me now. I would never see his friendly blue eyes again; his handsome smile, or have the chance to run my fingers through his hair.

"You are missed," I whispered. "You'll never be forgotten."

Although feeling tired still, I roused the children; grumpy as they were, and we began what I hoped was the final part of the journey. A little while later, Silla climbed a tree, the girl quick and agile.

"What do you see?" I held a hand to my forehead, the sun blinding.

"A mountain. We're nearly there, Mamma!"

"Which way?"

She pointed. "There."

"Good. We're going on the right path. Come down, so we can go." I picked Bannon up. "We've a bit of a climb coming. This is going to be tiresome. How I yearn for a good sleep on a comfortable bed, but it won't happen until we reach the cave."

Silla jumped to the ground, grinning. "Are we close?"

"Yes. Take the spear and that bundle. Let's be on our way."

She skipped ahead, her dark hair flying out behind her. "It's a good day, isn't it?"

"I suppose," I murmured, feeling a shooting ache in my back. "Just lovely."

Knowing how close the mountain stood, we did not tarry, walking at a brisk pace. Stopping to rest a while later, my legs protested, the calves quite sore. The path we took rose gradually, the trees thinning. We slowly ascended the side of the mountain, our feet crunching over rocks and leaves. After sitting to eat some nuts and take a sip of water, we continued on, rising now above the trees, where I craned my neck to glimpse a green valley. The view familiar, I gasped at the sight, seeing the tiny dark spot in the mountain across the way that revealed our cave.

Oh, the glory of the gods. I'm nearly home!

"There it is."

"What, Mamma?" Silla let Bannon down, the boy having tired feet.

I suddenly remembered the river. We would have to cross it. "Oh, the gods will have to help us. We're going to need it."

"What's the matter?"

"Can you swim?"

She nodded. "Yes."

"That's good." I had yet to teach Bannon, but I would soon. "I don't want to spend another night in the open. We've that valley to cross. There's a river at the bottom of it. Let's hope it's not too full." I placed a hand on my belly. "I'm … hardly fit to swim."

"I'll help you."

I eyed the girl, admiring her spirit. "It's almost over. Tonight we'll be with the people of my clan and comfortable."

"I'd like that very much."

"Let's go."

***

We reached the river later than I would have liked, the sun descending rapidly over the mountain. As luck would have it, the water wasn't as deep, although the current proved deceptive. Holding Bannon in my arms, I waded in with Silla behind me, the little girl holding up the rolled pelt.

"It's cold." She gasped. "Ugh."

Bannon kicked in my arms, trying to keep his legs out of the water. "I'm sorry. Let's hurry. It's not too deep." The river reached my waist and no further, which was a great relief. "Are you all right?"

"I'm fine."

Taking her hand, we waded to the other side, emerging with sodden skirts. "That wasn't too bad. It was very high before."

"I'm clean now." Silla grinned, flashing crooked teeth. "Nice and clean."

"It won't be long until the cave. I want to hurry, but we should be watchful." I eyed the trees, worried about what lurked there, what animals might be waiting.

"It's pretty here."

I had to agree, the forest in the valley especially lush, with an abundance of birds and insects, a few buzzing annoyingly. "Yes, but I've seen cats too, so we must be watchful."

She nodded. "I've got the spear."

Letting Bannon walk, we continued on, passing through the trees easily enough, where I spied a small path. During the time we had inhabited the cave, evidence of our occupation revealed itself in various trails that meandered in all directions. It would not be long now before we reached the base of the smaller mountain, the climb to the cave the last obstacle.

"What's that smell?"

"Our heated pool."

"And you bathe in that?" She made a face.

"It's the smoke that smells. I don't know why. Something in the ground heats the water. It doesn't leave your skin smelly. You'll have to try it to see. It's the most wonderful thing." I longed to have a bath, but that would have to wait. "Up we go."

Silla eyed the rocky path. "Oh, Mamma. Do we have to? I'm tired."

I ruffled her hair, grinning. "It's the only way you're going to reach the cave, my sweet girl." I heard the faint sound of a baby crying. "Oh, do you hear that?"

"A baby."

"Blessed are the gods." Tears formed in my eyes. "They're home. My clan's home."

"It's going to be all right." She touched my arm. "You don't have to cry."

"I'm crying because I'm happy and tired. Let's not waste another moment." I held her hand. "Come along, Bannon. Up we go." The path rose steeply, the ground rocky, although, as we climbed, the smell of something delicious teased our senses. Before we reached the entrance, a dog barked, the sound carrying. I grinned, remembering his name. "Putty." The animal appeared at the head of the pathway, barking noisily. "Hello, Putty. Good dog. You're a good dog." He ambled over, his tail wagging, and sniffed me. I petted him, Bannon doing the same, the boy enthralled. "His name's Putty."

"I like dogs very much." Silla reached out to touch the animal. "He's soft."

"Peta?" Enwan appeared, a spear in his hand. "Is that you?"

I nodded, swallowing a lump of emotion. "Yes."

"I thought never to see you again. Where have you been? Where's Ronan?" His attention strayed to my belly. "You're in a fine condition."

"We've been traveling, and I'm tired. I'll tell you all soon enough."

Bondo came up behind him, carrying a spear. Silla gaped at the man, his appearance so odd. A cross between the white and dark races, he sported long, blond hair and blue eyes, with a pronounced ridge over his forehead.

She grabbed my hand. "Mamma!" Fear shone in her eyes.

"He's not going to hurt you, my sweet. He's a friend."

"You've returned," said Bondo, grinning, which made him look less fearsome.

"Yes." We walked towards one another.

"And I remember this one," said Enwan, reaching for Bannon. "Hello there." My son eyed him with interest. "You were only a babe when you left. Someone's been feeding you well. You're heavy." He held him at his hip. "You look just like Ronan."

I passed him, gesturing for Silla. "Come along. I need to rest my bones." Bondo stepped behind me, the man's feet crunching over the rocks. "I'm glad you're all here. Is everyone well?"

"Leota had her baby," said Enwan.

"That's who I hear crying."

"Where's Ronan?"

I sighed. "I've some stories to tell."

"That doesn't sound good at all."

"No."

The opening of the cave stood before me, a thick bunch of thorny bramble blocking most of the entrance. Leota and Saffron sat inside, with their children. Their eyes lit when they spied me, Leota getting to her feet.

"Where's Ronan?"

I noted the baby in her arms, the infant's hair as pale as Ronan's. "Hello." I smiled tiredly, eyeing the space, happy to see it clean and as perfect as I remembered. "How are you?" Saffron's child crawled upon a pelt. "Hello, there."

Putty happily sniffed everyone, his tail wagging vigorously back and forth. He eventually settled on an old pelt, licking his paw. Enwan offered me a bladder of water, which I took.

"Thank you."

"Sit down, Peta. You look a mess. You smell … not so well."

"I know. It can't be helped."

"You all need a bath."

"Which we'll have after supper." I eyed the cooking meat, the aroma making my belly rumble. "I'm hungry."

Leota and Enwan exchanged a glance, their look questioning. She asked again, "Where's Ronan?"

Lowering to a pelt, I sighed deeply, hating to have to tell them what happened. "He's gone," I said simply. "We were attacked by a band of half-breeds. They … killed everyone, men, women, and children. They spared no one. We were lucky enough to escape, but Ronan was injured. It was a wound that would not mend. I tried my best. I did what I could." Tears formed in my eyes. "I fell short. I'm sorry."

"Half-breed men?" asked Bondo. "Where?"

"Over the mountain and beyond, but I think they were just passing through. We were with a white clan when it happened. We meant only to stay away a short while to avoid Greggor. We saw him come." My shoulders sagged. "Is there any meat?"

"Let her eat," said Enwan, his mouth flattening. "I'm saddened to hear this." He handed over a small basket. "Here. We just cooked it."

I motioned for Silla. "Come eat, my girl. Have some food."

Saffron gave us a basket partially filled with berries. "Here you are. What an ordeal you've had. We worried about you. We feared you'd never return."

Tears streamed down Leota's cheeks. "He's dead?"

Bondo embraced her, holding her tenderly. "It's not what you wanted to hear, but I'm sorry."

"I'd feared this. I had a … bad feeling. I knew something would happen. My boy will never know his father."

Enwan sat next to me, his legs impossibly long. "I've known that man most of my life. I remember the time we met on the plains, how we helped one another survive. I can't imagine being here without him. His loss is … so great."

I swallowed the meat, which seemed to stick in my throat. "I tried to save him." Bundles of herbs hung from a stand made of branches in the corner of the cavern. "I didn't have the right plants to cure him." The herbs I amassed here might have been useful. Would it have changed the outcome?

"What sort of wound was it?"

"A deep cut in the belly."

He nodded. "There was no hope then."

"I'm sorry. It's not how I wanted to return. I feel responsible for … all the ill that's happened. It's my fault."

"Don't blame yourself, Peta. You only did what you

thought was best. If you stayed, you would've encountered Greggor. He did come here."

"I know. We sat on the mountain and watched."

"He was … very angry to have missed you. I know he scoured the basin looking for you. He's come through here … several times."

That bit of news alarmed me. "More than once?" Would he return again?

"He's determined to find you. He knows this is your home—where you live—where you desire to be. He thinks you're his woman. He's mad with love. I've never seen anything like it."

The baby in my belly kicked. I placed a hand there, feeling the firmness of the skin. "I see. I … can't run any longer, Enwan. I'm tired."

"You're having a babe soon enough, from the looks of it."

I touched his face, relieved and gladdened to see him. "I've missed you. I've missed all of you."

Twenty-Seven

Saffron's daughter, Poppy, and Silla slept together that night, Silla taking the toddler under her wing. The cave provided warmth and comfort, the bedding thickly layered from seasons worth of pelts. I slept beautifully, waking refreshed and keen to bathe, taking Bannon with me.

I heard the crunching of rocks on the path, turning to see Leota. "Good day," I said, smiling.

She failed to return the favor, her features sober. "I wish to speak to you."

Ronan brought her back to be his woman when he thought I had perished. She hadn't taken the news of his death well. I nodded. "Can we talk in the pool? I need a good soak."

"Yes." She strode past me, her arms swinging at her sides.

The trail wound around rocks and boulders, ending at the base of the mountain. Another path led to the heated pool, the smell like something rotten. Reeds and grass surrounded the water, where I waded in, my feet sinking in the wet, slimy-feeling earth. The heat caressed my skin at once, the feeling exquisite. Bannon splashed on contact, a happy peal of laughter escaping him.

"I knew you'd like it."

Leota picked up a basket left on a rock. "You can clean with this."

Lumps of soap from wood ashes and oils sat on the

bottom, several partially used. Ara and I made soap similar to this. "Thank you." I took one. "I know I smell. I was too tired to bathe last night."

She sat on a rock, her feet dangling in the water. "I'm greatly saddened about Ronan's death."

"I am too." I let Bannon splash around in the shallower part, the boy chatting happily to himself. "It wasn't my plan."

"You say you were attacked by a band of half-breeds?"

"Yes. It was … the worst night of my life. It came on so quickly; no one knew what to do. The clan scattered. Ronan told me to take Bannon and run. I wasn't able to bring my bow. I regret not helping the men."

"That's not your duty. Women mind the children. They don't fight battles."

"I should've. I could have helped. Afterwards, I couldn't find Ronan. I thought he was dead. They killed all the men. I never saw anyone else after except for Silla. She managed to survive. Then I came upon Ronan in the woods. He lived for a while, and I thought I might cure him."

"And you failed?"

"I did."

"I wish you … I wish he never left. He'd still be alive." She gazed into the distance. "I love him. He brought me here to be his wife. You've robbed me of … all I've ever wanted. I don't want to hate you, but I do."

Her honesty cut me to the bone, the words like spear tips. "I'm sorry. I'm truly sorry. If those men hadn't taken me, none of this would've happened. Ronan wouldn't have left to find me. He wouldn't have met you and offered to care for you. You'd be happy with someone else right now."

"I wouldn't have met him then. He was … such a sweet, kind soul."

"You have his son to remember him by. When he grows, he'll look just like Ronan. He and Bannon are brothers." I scrubbed my face, feeling cleaner, but a weight settled upon me. "I hope we can live together, Leota. I don't want you to hate me."

"I've considered things. I've thought of leaving, but nothing has ever been this nice for a home. Enwan and Bondo provide. I'm fed and protected. I don't have the will to travel alone. I … can't do it."

"Perhaps more men will join us? It was always Ronan's wish to grow the clan. We've more than enough room in the cave." Soapy bubbles lathered my hair. "I hope you stay."

She frowned. "After you left, this Greggor person came with several men. We were terrified they'd kill us. I've never seen people so large. He demanded to know where you'd gone. Enwan told him you left with Ronan to live elsewhere. This news enraged him. He said you betrayed him, deceived him."

"Our history is … difficult."

"Angering such a man is unwise."

"It wasn't entirely my doing."

"But he blames you. Enwan spoke to him; he calmed him, although he was still very angry. They sat by the fire most of the night talking. I listened to some of it. That man's desperately in love with you."

I did not desire this conversation—especially so early in the day. Rinsing my hair, I waded towards her, water pouring from my shoulders. "I was with him for a while."

"Why did you come back?"

Shay and Wildre orchestrated my return, plotting it out carefully, because I had lost the will to leave Greggor myself. "I came back for Ronan. This is where I belong."

"But you have another who wants you."

I muttered, "If you need to blame someone, it's the gods. They meddle endlessly in our lives. I was perfectly happy with Ronan and Enwan. I never wanted to leave. I found them again after seasons of being apart. Then, one day, three men took me. They snatched me from my home. From that moment on, nothing's been the same. All I've done is fight to survive. My child was taken. I went to get him, finding Greggor." I refused to speak further on this.

"The gods?" Bitterness laced her tone. "The way I see it, you were never meant for Ronan. He was a means for this other man—this brute of a man with an angry face. He's the one you're supposed to be with."

I shook my head. "No."

"I question why I'm here. I lost my love and my son lost his father."

"I can't know what the gods want. I've given up trying to fight. I'll let them have their way now. I … I've my children to worry over. I'm sorry about Ronan. I miss him dreadfully. He was my love. He was all I ever wanted—"

"Until Greggor," she snapped. "You're better suited for him."

She hardly knew me, my blood beginning to boil. "What do you know about it? You don't have a clue about who I am."

"I've seen plenty."

"Then resent me forever, but it changes nothing." I flung my hands into the air. "Look at us! We live in paradise. We've plenty of everything. We can't ask for more. Men come and go. People die. Our lives are the blink of an eye." She sat unmoved, her features drawn. "You may not see it now, but you're here for a reason. You won't be long without a mate."

"I don't want another man!" she cried. "I want Ronan!"

"So do I!" I shouted, my anger surfacing.

"For the love of the gods," muttered Enwan,

appearing from the path. "Why are you yelling so early in the day? They can hear you across the valley, women." He dropped his skirt, wading into the water. Reaching for Bannon, he drew him into his arms. "Hello there, little man." His gaze strayed to me. "You look much improved, Peta. Did you sleep well?"

"I did."

"Good." He turned to Leota. "I know you're sore about what's happened."

"Sore?"

"Very sore. I'm sorry."

"Everyone's sorry."

"I lost my dear friend. I've hardly wrapped my head around it. When it sinks in, I'll howl from the mountaintop. There's little I can do now."

She shook her head, her eyes watering. "I hoped he'd come back. He promised me a life here, a good life."

"Which you shall have." He lifted Bannon, the boy giggling. "You'll mate another. We shall endeavor to make the clan bigger."

I glanced at my fingers, seeing the cleanness of the nails. "I do so love this water."

"So does this little one." Bannon kicked and laughed, his face a vision of youthful delight. He hardly noticed the fight that occurred, the child oblivious to anything but pleasure.

"Don't be angry with Peta. It's not her fault Ronan's dead."

"But it is. If they hadn't left—"

"Then Greggor would've killed him."

Those words bothered me greatly. I had feared he might do such a thing, but I never wanted to believe it.

"So, because of *this* woman, my man would've died either way. Is that what you're saying?"

The smile vanished from Enwan's face. "I'll not have this argument. Ronan's dead. There's little to be done about it. We must go on. Grieve for him, but blaming Peta won't make the pain any easier. I don't like to hear shouting this early in the day. Our house is one of peace. Everyone should be made to feel welcome."

"Are you leader now?"

"There aren't any leaders, but I'm oldest, I assume. I don't want the fighting. I've waited my entire life for this. I want a clan where everyone has a say." He glanced at me. "Why can't people get along? Why must there always be strife?"

"I haven't the slightest idea, Enwan. People can't agree on anything." I offered a faint smile. "It sounds like a dream. I pray you get your wish."

"Why do I get the feeling you're going to spoil it for me?"

I blinked. "What?"

"I love you, Peta, but you've a habit of bringing trouble. I don't know what it is about you."

Stunned by that statement, I strode from the pool, thoroughly annoyed with everyone. "I'm finished here." I flung water at him. "You just said you wished to live in peace, and then you attack me!"

He appeared chagrinned. "I should've kept it to myself. I'm not attacking you."

I donned the skirt, tying it at my waist. "You think I'm some sort of bad omen."

"You said that," murmured Leota. "We didn't."

"You're not, Peta. Stop this. Come back." Enwan rose from the water, wetness glistening off his muscled chest. "Never mind what I said. I'm an idiot."

"No, now I know your true thoughts." How had everyone turned against me, even those I loved? "I want to be alone. Bring my son up when he's done." I stalked away angry, feeling a host of unwanted emotions. I could hardly be blamed for everyone's misfortune, or could I?

Twenty-Eight

"Bondo, do you think everyone would be happier if I wasn't here?"

He sat by the fire scraping stones together. "What?"

"If I took my children and left?"

"Ah, no." He shook his head, a lazy grin emerging. "Why would you think that?"

"Everyone hates me. They blame me for Ronan's death."

"That was hardly your fault."

"But it is my fault, because we had to leave. I forced him to flee. I knew … I knew Greggor would come."

"It's not your fault. Stop this nonsense talk. Leota complains about everything. Nothing's ever good enough for that woman. I all but beg to mate her, and then she's never up for it. Don't take what she says to heart. It matters not."

I had to giggle at that, feeling a little better. "I fear nothing will be as it was before."

"Nothing ever is. The river of life always changes. It never looks the same at any given point. You've traveled it well. You're still here. You've two beautiful children and one on the way. You'll probably have many more. That's where your concern should be. Don't mind the talk of silly women."

I thought about that. "Women do cause trouble, don't they?"

"What do you mean?"

"The way I left Greggor. That wasn't by choice. I'm ashamed to admit it, but I would've stayed with him. Perhaps I should have. Then Ronan would still be alive and Leota would be happy. Greggor's wife and her friend conspired to get rid of me. I left at their urging." Why could I not let go of this? Leota's words had torn the scab off old wounds, provoking me to question the past again. "Oh, never mind. It doesn't matter."

"Indeed." He scraped stone away. "It truly doesn't matter."

I felt a tightening in my belly, the feeling lasting a moment. "If it doesn't matter, then why are we still talking about it?" For days now we had gone back and forth on the subject, with no solution in sight.

"Are you feeling well?" He eyed me.

"Now that you ask, I do believe I might be in labor. I thought it the other day, but the feeling stopped. I feel it again now. They're getting stronger."

A smile emerged. "I wish you the best of luck, Peta."

Earlier, I beat all the pelts, sweeping the cave and arranging things neatly in baskets. It was obvious now, the nesting instinct that drove me to make everything ready. The only thing I dreaded happening was the pain.

"I hope this goes easier. I don't want to die."

"You're a strong woman. You had Bannon alone. You won't be alone now. We'll help you."

My belly tightened then. "I … should eat something now. I'll eat and try to sleep. I might be … I might be at this all night."

As the day progressed, so did my labor. I prepared as much as I could, slicing strips of leather into smaller pieces to use for the baby. Despite being upset with me, Leota hovered about, making a tea for the pain and arranging the pelts for my comfort. I felt gratitude for this, relieved not to have the baby all alone.

"You should walk," said Saffron. "It might hasten the

labor."

I breathed through another contraction, this one feeling far more intense than the ones before. "I can try."

Enwan helped me to my feet. "I'll walk with you."

"You don't have to do that. None of you need make a fuss. I'm fine. I've been through this before." I ventured around the cave, my feet delighting in the feel of soft pelt. Every bit of the room had a nice, thick pelt for comfort. The fire in the center crackled, Bondo cooking meat. "It's not so bad—" The contraction proved formidable, my body aching with pain. "Oh! Oh!"

"Perhaps she should sit," said Leota. "Before she falls."

Enwan grasped me. "All right. This wasn't the best idea."

"She's further along than I thought." Leota frowned. "We could have this baby soon. I should check you. Do you feel the need to push?"

"Not yet," I grated, lowering to the pelt. I got on my hands and knees, the relief instant. Sighing, I delighted in not having the pressure strictly on my lower back. My belly hung before me, hard and round. "I'm better now."

"Give her more tea," said Saffron.

"Is my mamma dying?" asked Silla.

"No, my dear." Leota shook her head. "Your mother's having a baby."

"Oh."

"And no more tea. It slows labor. I'm sure Peta wants to have this child tonight. Let me check you."

I sat back, opening my legs. "It's too soon to push."

"I'll determine that."

I felt her fingers at my entrance, but due to the pressure in that region, I did not feel anything else. "Is there any water?" I licked parched lips.

Enwan handed me a bladder. "Here you are."

"Thank you."

"You're nearly there," said Leota. "You could push soon, even now, if you wish."

"I'll wait a little." I remembered Sungir's teachings, and how a woman should never push before her body was fully ready. "I'll just … lay here a little while." I offered a weak smile. "Someone play something. Isn't there a bone around? I'd like a distraction."

Enwan dug through a basket. "I'll provide the amusements for this evening. You ladies relax."

I laughed at that, "Oh, certainly. *This* is relaxing." I grimaced, enduring another sharp contraction. "Blasted stars!"

Silla watched over Poppy, playing with carved pieces of wood, helping Bannon build them up, although he knocked them down straight away. The sounds of their voices filled the cave, rising above the snapping branches in the fire, the room nice and warm.

Leota knelt by my side, placing a wet piece of leather on my forehead. "How's that?"

"You needn't be nice to me. I know you don't like me."

She sighed heavily. "Must you be difficult? Even in great pain, you wish to fight?" An eyebrow lifted.

"But you hate me."

"I don't hate you."

"Yes, you do."

"I lashed out at you in grief. I wanted Ronan to return so badly. I would've shared him with you, but now that's not possible."

"I said I was sorry. If I could take it back, I would." I gritted my teeth, suffering another contraction. "Oh, it's terrible. I can't wait for this to end." The dog began to bark, the sound shattering the peace of the night. "Why must this hurt so? I curse the gods. I truly mean it this time. They're not happy unless we all suffer, women especially."

Leota laughed at that. "This should be amusing. I can only imagine the things you'll say when you're fully in labor." She eyed the cave entrance. "Do hush, you stupid animal!"

The pretty music stopped, Enwan getting to his feet, as did Bondo. They grasped their spears, sensing some sort of danger. Darting to the opening, they disappeared behind the thorny barrier, but we could hear them.

"Men come!" Enwan shouted.

In the grips of another contraction, I ignored them, realizing I was of no use in this matter. If a hostile clan chose to attack, I would die alongside my children. In my condition, I could not hold a weapon, or could I?

"You might want to get on your hands and knees. It'll help move the babe down."

I shook my head. "No."

"Do you know who they are?" asked Saffron. "Should we hide the children?"

"They carry torches. I suspect it's Greggor and his men again."

That name rattled around in my mind, but I cast it away, oblivious to anything but the pain. "Oooohhhh … I don't like this one bit."

"It'll soon be over."

I grasped her hand, surprising her. "If I die, please take care of Bannon and Silla, please."

"Don't be stupid. You're not going to die. You're in your prime. You'll have this babe any moment."

Voices rang out by the entrance, men speaking loudly. One rose above the rest, the timbre familiar.

"Stand aside," he commanded. "I've come for my woman. I knew she'd return."

"You may enter if you refrain from killing us all," said Bondo.

Laughter rang out. "I could've done so the last time. I'm no foe. I merely wish to fetch Peta."

"You're going to have to wait then," said Enwan.

"I wait for no one."

"She's in labor. She's hardly in any condition to travel."

"Move aside!" he bellowed.

Leota and I watched his arrival, the man striding into the chamber, an authoritative air about him. Dark eyes blazed with anger, his posture tense. Wearing several pelts, he tossed a spear and a leather pouch to the floor.

"Peta?"

"Hello … Greggor." I grimaced, suffering another contraction.

I had forgotten how broad his shoulders were, how he filled a chamber just by entering it. Scars in various stages of healing adorned bulging muscles. My attention lingered on his face, seeing a thick beard that had grown too long. He approached slowly, stepping over pelts, the look of anger still evident.

"I should strangle you with my bare hands, woman."

Leota backed away from him, her look wary. She picked up her baby, holding the infant close.

"You can kill me after I have this babe," I muttered, feeling a strong urge to push. "Oh!"

In an instant, the anger evaporated. He knelt by me, his eyes the color of night, his skin tanned from the sun. He smelled musky, the man having traveled for some time. I gazed at him, while a host of emotions bubbled up, the feeling of relief so great; I wanted to cry.

"Gods' teeth," he whispered. "You're beautiful. You're worth every bit of aggravation. I'm the greatest fool who ever lived, but I regret nothing."

"I regret everything."

Twenty-Nine

"Like Peta said, if you wish to murder us, you'll have to wait until after the babe comes." Leota handed Tartar, her son, to Saffron, while the men lingered by the fire, tired and hungry from travel. Bondo gave them fresh meat. "You can push. There's nothing stopping you, even this brute." She eyed Greggor.

"I will." With the next contraction I pushed, the feeling so odd, the baby sliding downward slowly.

"Good girl. Keep doing that."

With the next cramp, I pushed a little harder, the head suddenly breaching. I experienced a sharp stab of pain, but it lessened at once. "This is so much faster than before." I smiled, knowing the agony would soon be over.

A look of concern flared in Greggor's eyes. Perhaps, he had never seen a birthing before. He sat beside me, his hand on my arm, the feeling possessive, yet secure. I took comfort in it, gladdened to be with him again—stunned actually, but the birthing process proved distracting. The urge to push gripped me, the head breaching, with pain flaring. Crying out, I gritted my teeth, pushing, wishing to have the torture end. The babe slid free completely, landing in Leota's hands.

"You've done it!" She beamed, her smile bright. "It's a girl!"

My head fell to the pelt, eyeing the indentations in the rocky ceiling. "That wasn't fun," I muttered. "It didn't hurt as badly as before, but I'd rather not do it again—ever."

Leota cleared mucus from the babe's mouth, using a finger. A newborn's cries filled the cavern, the sound a welcome one. After wiping the infant dry, she handed the girl to me, the babe sporting a thick patch of dark hair. I reached for her, startled by her appearance. I expected a light-haired infant with eyes as blue as Ronan's. The baby cried, her mouth tiny and pink, each of her fingers and toes perfect.

"You should feed her," encouraged Leota. "That'll put her to sleep."

I held the babe to my breast, pushing a nipple into her mouth. She latched on immediately. Exhausted, I lay upon several pelts, glad the labor and delivery had gone so well.

"My daughter's beautiful, just like her mother." Greggor stroked the infant's cheek. "She'll grow to be strong and kind and capable." He smiled, which softened his features. "Like her mother."

"What makes you think this is your child?"

"Look at her."

I had so wanted the baby to be Ronan's, but I knew in my heart that she wasn't. "You've no claim to us."

His gaze sharpened. "Indeed I do. You're *my* disobedient wife. You've just had *my* child." He nodded towards Bannon. "I consider that boy mine too, although I'm not his birth father."

"People can't be owned."

"Whatever insanity made you run from me, it's over. I've been searching for you far too long. Once you've recovered and you're well enough to walk, we leave."

"What if I don't wish to go with you?"

"You know as well as I where you belong."

"Let the poor woman rest," said Enwan. "She's only just returned. She's grieving for her man. She's been through enough."

"This Ronan person," he said darkly. "What of him?"

"He was killed," I whispered. "I don't wish to discuss it." The babe fell asleep at my breast, her look peaceful in repose. "Can we not argue for one night?"

"If he were here, would you have killed him?" asked Enwan.

Leota gave me a bladder filled with water. "Drink."

"Thank you."

"If he'd given me reason to, I would've."

I sat up, annoyed by everyone. "Shush. Let's not speak on the subject this night." I drank eagerly, the water cool and refreshing. "I need to … relieve myself. I doubt I can stand just yet." I left my baby bundled in a swath of leather.

A rough-feeling hand grasped mine. "I'll help you." Greggor lifted me to my feet, an arm around my back. "How's that?"

"Easier than I thought." He led me to the doorway, the night air cold against my skin. Feeling weak and unsteady, Greggor's support guided me along a path to the latrine. "Thank you." After finishing my business, I faced him, the man bathed in moonlight. From this vantage point, the sky loomed, littered by many, tiny flashing lights. I presumed those were a great distance away, more than I could ever fathom.

"Why did you run from me?"

"Oh, for pity's sake. Must we?"

"I need to know. We were so happy. I know I made you happy. I've never been more content than I was with you. Why did you do it? Why did you ruin something so perfect?"

I swallowed through the constriction of my throat, my heart beating almost painfully. "I … I was going to stay. I'm weak where you're concerned. I didn't want to go." I had to admit the truth. I could not lie.

"Then what happened?"

"Shay and Wildre—"

"I knew it! Blast it! Damn those interfering wenches!"

Unsteady, I leaned into him, feeling him tense with anger. "They … convinced me to go. You'd left to hunt. They prepared everything for me. I thought about Ronan and how he'd never met his son. I thought about the life he promised me. I … do love him."

"I knew they had something to do with it. The conniving, scheming wenches." He held me close. "No more. I'll not have others meddling with my life again. We will not be separated, Peta. Is that understood?"

"You mean to take me from my home."

"Your home is wherever I am."

I sighed, knowing I did not have the strength to deny him at the moment. "I'm tired."

"Let's go back to the cave, where there's light. I desire to look upon my daughter and my wife. I can hardly see you." He gripped me tightly, his mouth by my ear. "I've missed you beyond words, beyond reason. You torment me, Peta."

"I didn't mean to." I'd felt just as lost and empty without him. "Take me inside."

"Yes, my love."

***

I fell asleep within layers of soft fur and an arm securely about me. When the babe woke, I fed her, the infant so tiny and perfect. Waking with the sun, I watched the men prepare to hunt, Greggor's men readying to procure meat. I recognized Frendo, his master's guard. He had watched over me in the past, when I had been Greggor's captive. They left a moment later, although their leader stayed behind, his soft snores resonating.

Needing fresh air, I sat at the entrance of the cave with Leota, the children having gone down to bathe with Saffron.

"How are you feeling?"

"I'm fine." I offered a smile. "I'll heal soon enough."

"We all expected him to return. He's the determined sort. I knew that from the last time I met him. He fears little."

"No."

"The babe's his."

"Yes."

"She looks just like him. You make beautiful babies, Peta. I'm envious."

"Tartar is beautiful. You've a lovely boy."

She ignored that, saying, "You'll leave soon."

"No."

"I think yes. He won't let you stay, and you're too weak to resist him."

"Must we discuss this?"

"What shall you name the babe?"

"I've been pondering it." Glancing at the heavens, I smiled. "I like the name … Skye."

"Oh, that's nice." She nodded. "Good choice, but will he like it?"

"It's my baby. I shall name her what I wish."

"Your man might have other ideas."

"He's not my man."

Laughter rang out. "He is." Then her smile faded. "You should've stayed with him. You never should've come back. Ronan would still be alive."

A familiar pain registered. "I had to return. I love Ronan. I love him just as much as …. " I tossed a stone. "I don't want to discuss it." Why was she so determined to remind me of the past? "Yes, he should still be with us, but he isn't. I can't help it."

"It was wrong of me to bring it up. I'm sorry."

"What about me?"

"What do you mean?"

"I return from a long and arduous journey to find my

man with another woman. How do you think I felt about that? Do you think that pleased me? I know he thought I might never come back, but it wounded me that he'd found another so quickly." I glared at her, challenging her to deny this. "It wasn't easy, knowing I'd have to share my man. If he had lived, you and I would've been his wives."

She pursed her lips, not having a response.

"I'm going in. I've had enough air." A baby cried. "My daughter needs me."

Thirty

Feeding Skye, I held her in my arms, eyeing the man who slept beside me. I hadn't seen Greggor for some time, fleeing his encampment on a chilly morning long ago. Memories of that day returned, along with the turmoil I felt, how torn I had been. If it hadn't been for Shay and Wildre and their coaxing, I would have stayed with him and the clan by the water.

Leader to many, he had earned the respect of his people, the communities loyal to him. I once feared and hated him, having witnessed his brutality towards the dark-skinned ones as a child. I vowed to hate him for all he did that day, but now, those feelings weren't the same. So much had changed over the seasons.

Greggor's black hair fanned out over the fur of a pelt, his lashes casting shadows over tanned cheeks. Weathered by the elements, his skin sported various small scars, with a larger one across his neck. Most of his torso remained hidden beneath the covers, while an arm draped across his chest, littered with black hair and scars.

A hand suddenly closed about my wrist. "Oh!"

"I feel your appraisal, woman," he murmured in a gravelly voice.

"I haven't seen you … in a long time."

He cracked open an eyelid. "Have I changed much?"

"No. You're still as boorish as I remember." I could not help antagonizing him.

Laughter rumbled in his chest. "I've missed your feistiness. It's refreshing. My men wouldn't dare insult me in such a way, nor would my woman."

"I'm not your woman." I tried to free myself, but the

grip remained firm.

"You are. This is one argument that's long settled. I've been searching for you for ages. I'm glad it's over."

"What if you hadn't found me?"

"I would've kept looking." He pulled me close, an arm secure about my back.

I snuggled into the heat of his chest. "I'm hardly worth all the trouble, Greggor."

"You are." His lips grazed my forehead. "That and more. I care not."

"Are you ill?"

"Why do you ask?"

"You're not hunting with the men. They left some time ago."

"The last time I hunted, you went missing. Forgive me for not trusting you. You're not leaving my sight, Peta."

"This is my home. I've no plans to run from it."

"Oh, you will. When you're recovered enough, you'll come with me."

"I don't want to live where you live. It's better here."

"I tire of the argument. Your place is with me. My people grew to accept you—to like you. When you left, you betrayed them as badly as you betrayed me."

"All the more reason to stay away. They'll hate me."

"You shall ask for forgiveness. It will be given. If not, then you'll have to earn it back."

I doubted it would be that easy. "What of Shay and Wildre?"

He sighed, clearly aggravated by the mention of their names. "I shall deal with them. I'm not pleased in the least with their meddling." He suddenly tossed aside the pelt, sitting. He ran his fingers through his hair, which hung past his shoulders. "I'd like a bath."

"The water's delicious." I glimpsed various scars, my attention drifting, admiring the way muscles rippled beneath the surface of his skin. "Your hair is wild. You look like a woodland creature."

Dangerous … compelling …
How will I resist him?

"I've not groomed in some time. You may attend to my needs later." His gaze skimmed over me. "You look … ravishing." Heat flared in his eyes, their meaning clear.

A warm, pleasurable sensation drifted over me. "I'm tired, Greggor. I doubt I look anything but tired."

"You're just as I remember; a woman kissed by the light of the gods. I'll never forget your eyes. I long to see them soft with love, the way you looked at me when we were together before."

"What do they look like now?"

"Unsure."

"I am … not certain about anything."

"I'll have to remind you of what we had."

"Mamma?" Bannon interrupted the moment, having woken.

"Yes?" I smiled at him.

"Me tired." He tossed the pelt over his head, disappearing.

I glanced at Saffron, who slept. Leota wove a basket, having heard our discussion, no doubt. "Let's bathe then. Bannon can't sleep if we make noise."

Greggor got to his feet, reaching for a spear. "Lead the way."

***

The path wound down to the base of the mountain, the bushes on either side rustling in the wind. I followed Greggor, walking in the shadow of his broad shoulders, a leather skirt hiding firm buttocks. Not feeling nearly as weak as the night before, I breathed in the fresh air, clearing the smell of campfire deep in my lungs.

"I'll admit," he said. "This is a pretty view."

"I like it."

"We came here in the evening, many moons ago. I set out to find you as soon as you went missing. I followed your trail easily enough."

"I know." Reaching the bottom of the hill, another path led to the heated pool, the smell wrinkling my nose. "I saw you."

"You weren't here. How could you see us?"

"I had a dream you were coming. I made Ronan leave the next morning. We went to that mountain." I pointed to the range across the valley, the tips white. "We climbed halfway up and made camp. I saw your torches."

"Ah, now I understand." Untying the leather skirt, it fell to the ground. "You weren't that far after all."

"No."

Wading into the water, his buttocks bulged, the muscles taut. "This is wondrous." A smile lit his face, as he fell backwards, disappearing beneath the surface. When he emerged, he grinned. "I see why you like it."

I waded in, where I lowered and sat upon slick rocks. "It's how I imagine the gods bathe. They must have warm water."

"Surely."

"And we're just as lucky, I suppose."

"It smells horrid, yet it leaves the skin clean and odor free."

"It does."

He scrubbed his face, running fingers through tangled hair, massaging the scalp.

"You can use this." Leota or Saffron had left a lump of wood ash and oils. "It looks terrible, but it's useful."

He took it. "Thank you." Foam bubbled soon and coated his skin, until he rinsed it off. "Do my hair."

My feet sank into the slickened bottom of the pool. "If you wish. You'll have to lower. I can't reach." He squatted before me, whereby I lathered the hair, scrubbing vigorously. "Rinse now." After cleaning, we floated together, with parts of leaves and small bubbles drifting around. I soaped my hands and face, cleaning myself. He took hold of me then, pulling me near. "Yes?"

A smile toyed around the edges of his mouth. "I've missed you dreadfully. I feared never seeing you again. When they said you'd gone from the cave, we went to the valley, although there wasn't a trail to follow. They'd sent us the wrong way."

"They did."

"We didn't think to look over the mountain. I don't know why. I assumed you'd not want to cross the river. It was quite high then."

"We crossed anyhow."

"Of course you did. You were determined to get away from me."

"I had to try." I thought of how Ronan and I escaped. "There are other clans that way, some not friendly in the least. We found piles of bones—human bones."

"I've heard of clans that eat their own."

"Do you think that's what we found?"

"Possibly. Who can say? Maybe they were attacked and eaten by cats."

"We found marks on the bones, marks made by spears."

"Victims of a clan attack then." He shrugged. "It hardly matters."

"Until they attack us, yes. Then it matters very much."

"I fear nothing, Peta. My men and I are capable. We've made quick work of hostiles."

"I know. I remember." I frowned.

He noted my expression. "I've not harmed any of the dark ones since you begged me not to."

"I'm glad."

"I won't attack unless provoked. I made you that promise. I intend to keep it."

"Good."

"I know I frightened you long ago, and I'm sorry. I was … younger. I followed what our healer preached, wanting to please him. Ripa warned of the inferior races and how we shouldn't breed them. I know now that his teachings weren't entirely true. I've met Bondo. I consider him a good man."

"He is."

"Yes, and a part of your clan."

"Where I belong." I waited for the response I expected, not disappointed in the least. His grip about me tightened.

"You must come with me, Peta."

"Even if it's against my will?"

"Please don't make me tie you up and throw you over my shoulder. I've been gone far too long. I must return to my people soon. I pray you're able to travel in the next day or so. I really must go, but I refuse to leave without you and my children."

I hated having to make this choice, but … I knew I would never be happy without him, long buried feeling surfacing. "Will your people hate me?"

"They don't hate you. You'll atone for … leaving. They'll know what Wildre and Shay did. Given time, they'll accept you again." A hint of fear flickered in his eyes, but it vanished then. "Peta?"

He worried I would deny him; I could see it. "I've only just arrived. I … hate to leave. I adore this place." Tears filled my eyes, knowing what I had to do. "But … I love you—you terrible brute. I shouldn't feel this way, especially after everything's that's happened, but I do."

"You'll go with me?"

"Yes, of course."

Although I adored Enwan and Bondo, I did not love them as I did this man. They could never stir my anger or spark the passion I felt, the emotion unlike anything I had ever known. Ronan would always hold a special place in my heart, the man father to Bannon, but he no longer lived. I had to find safety and shelter for my children. No one provided that better than Greggor.

He held my face, his lips nearing. "Kiss me, Peta."

I wrapped my arms around his neck, where I found myself crushed against him. "Yes, my Lord." I savored the kiss, his lips feeling soft. He held himself in check, kissing me with retrained lust, pushing me away a moment later.

"No more. Not now, or else I'll take you over that rock. You're in no condition for such a thing."

I giggled, "You've command of your baser needs?" Most men did not.

"For now," he grumbled, annoyed at the prospect of not getting his way. "I desire you like no other, wench, but I'll wait."

I giggled, "Then how will we spend our time?"

"You'll groom me."

I eyed him, smiling. "Can I do what I want?"

"Please explain."

"You're hairy."

"I'm well aware."

"You require a good deal of grooming."

"You may do whatever you like, Peta. If it makes you happy to see me bald, then so be it." He grasped my face, his look unexpectedly severe. "How I long to mate you, to feel your softness around me. It's taking every last bit of restraint … but I shall wait."

I shivered, my body more than aware of his current state. "I'm quite eager too." Leaning my forehead against his shoulder, I could not look at him. "Yes, we should groom. It's something to keep our thoughts … on safer things."

Thirty-One

While feeding Skye, I observed Silla and Poppy playing, the girl mothering the toddler, encouraging her to babble happily. I stayed behind to recover from birthing, while Saffron and Leota foraged. Leota's baby slept in a nearby basket. I fed him as well, having more than enough milk for both infants. Whenever I held Tartar, I was reminded that this was Ronan's son too, though he would never meet him. It saddened me to think of his loss, although I could not imagine what might have happened had he lived, and how Greggor would have reacted.

It's in the past now, Peta.

I know, but I still wonder. Greggor and Ronan would have fought for me, and they might have killed one another.

"I want to speak to you."

Stunned someone had returned, I saw Enwan with a young stag over his shoulders. "You're back."

Tossing the carcass to the floor, he nodded. "I've been waiting to catch you alone."

"I'm surrounded by children. I'm hardly alone." I grinned. "What is it?"

"Do you really wish to leave with this man?" An earnest expression appeared. "I've heard him talking. They're going soon."

"Yes."

"And you're going to live with him?"

I sighed, placing Skye over a shoulder to burp her. "I

agreed to go."

"But do you want to?" He neared, kneeling before me. "You've only just returned. You had a babe three days ago. You're in no condition to travel. Why do this? Is he forcing you?"

"I've agreed because I want to. He's leader to many clans, Enwan. He's been gone too long as it is. I've seen his home. I'll be comfortable there. He'll take care of me."

"Then we may never see one another again. This might ... be the last time. You won't be coming back."

I nodded. "But I'll be well. You won't have to worry about me. I know you'll be happy here. You've Saffron to love. Leota will find another mate. I don't know how things would've been had Ronan lived, but ... Skye is Greggor's. He loves Bannon as his own. He's a good man."

"But you fear him."

"I feared him as a child, yes." I smiled, feeling a wistful sort of sadness. "That's long in the past. I'm sorry about everything. I'm sorry about Ronan. You lost a friend who was like a brother."

"I did. There will never be another like him."

"You'll be happy here."

"It's the perfect place to make a home, but I always thought you'd be here."

"It's not meant to happen that way, I suppose."

"Are you strong enough for travel?"

"Yes. I'll be fine. Greggor assures me they'll walk slowly."

"With three children in tow."

"I've spoken to Silla about it. She says she wishes to stay here."

He eyed the girls playing, nodding. "She's grown close to Poppy. They're inseparable."

"And Saffron says she'll love her as her own. I'd rather not drag her on another journey. The child's been through enough. She witnessed the slaughter of her parents and her tribe. I know bad dreams plague her. I can hear her in the night. She needs to be settled. Walking for great distances will remind her of fleeing the clan. She's happy here. I don't wish to distress her."

"You needn't convince me, Peta. Children shouldn't roam around the wilderness. They should be sheltered and safe."

"Then it's agreed."

"Except I'll never see you again."

"You've been such a good friend." I touched his cheek. "I'll always think of you fondly. You and Ronan will be forever in my heart."

"I almost wish it was just the three of us."

"What do you mean?"

"You, me, and Ronan. When you first came here. I miss those times. Everything's changed now. It was simpler. It was easier then." He grinned. "All we did was mate."

"And it'll change over and over with the passing of time. Nothing stays the same."

"I curse the day you were taken while hunting. The men who took you belonged to Greggor."

"And they're dead." A stark memory returned. "The gods have a plan. It may not be what you or I want, but they're determined to see it out. For some reason, they want me with Greggor. I can't fathom why."

"You love him. Anyone can see that. He's strong. His men are strong. I'd not win a battle with them. I know you'll be safe. I just ... I'll miss seeing you. You'll always be my little smelly Peta."

"I wish you and Saffron the best, Enwan. You deserve happiness. I know you'll have a good life here in the cave of the wind. It's where you belong."

He kissed my cheek. "I adore you. Please take care. I pray you'll be safe. I pray your children will thrive. You'll always be in my heart."

I hugged him. "And you in mine."

***

"We'll take turns carrying the boy," said Greggor.

Having said goodbye a day ago, the farewell emotional, I thought of what I had left behind. I would never see these people again. With a heavy heart, I gathered my possessions and my children, bracing myself for an exhausting walk. Greggor and Frendo shared carrying Bannon, the boy sitting upon their shoulders. I slung Skye over my chest with leather tied around my hip.

"Let's stop here." Greggor set Bannon on his feet, the boy happy to be free for the moment.

"Don't go far," I warned, eyeing the forest with concern.

The men fanned out to secure the area, Sal remaining. He glanced at us. "Are we making camp already?"

"No, we're just letting the … " he smiled at me, "my wife rest."

Sal nodded, his look pragmatic. "The going is slow."

"With good reason. She's hardly healed from having the babe." He touched Skye's cheek, the infant asleep. "My daughter. Have you ever seen anything more beautiful?"

"No, and I've never seen you so besotted, my Lord."

"Aye, that I am."

"I'm fine. I can walk. We needn't stop for long." Despite not sleeping well the night before, I felt strong enough for this trek, desiring to reach the encampment by the great body of water sooner than later. I recalled the walk lasted three days, although at this pace, we might have to add another day or two. "We can go faster."

"We'll arrive when we arrive." Greggor untied the leather at my hip. "You should wash up in the creek. The water's clean enough to drink." He held the baby, his hands appearing enormous against the tiny body. "I can manage Skye."

"I better find Bannon. He's run off." Hurrying into the forest, I heard men talking, hearing the sound of my son's voice. I found Bannon near a stream with Nesco and Brayer, Frendo scouting in the distance. "There you are."

"Mamma!" He appeared wet.

"Please don't go far." I dropped to my knees to wash my face and hands, the water cold and refreshing. When I appeared clean enough, I took his hand. "Come along."

"I play, Mamma," he protested.

"We can't right now. We must go. We've a long walk, son. We're going to a new home."

Frendo approached, having killed a small woodland creature. He grinned. "A snack for supper. I'll tuck it away for later."

The men of Greggor's clan used bows as well as spears, my bow being among the weapons I carried. "I look forward to it." Dried meat filled several leather pouches, and we ate berries and mushrooms as we found them.

Greggor waited for us holding Skye, while everyone gathered. "Rest for a while. Sit," he said. "Please sit, Peta." The baby fussed, her cries carrying.

"Let me feed her." I held out my hands. "She's too noisy." He gave me the babe. "Thank you." I sat, leaning against the rough bark of a tree, my hair the only protection. "Shush, little one." Traveling with infants presented several challenges, but she quieted the moment she attached to my nipple. "That's better."

Greggor took a sip of water from a bladder. "Rest for now. When the babe's done feeding, we shall go."

The angle of the sun revealed the time of day, the shadows in the forest expanding. We departed soon enough, trudging onward in a single line. I let my mind wander from thought to thought, but was always alert for any unusual sounds. A small clearing appeared with what looked like a cooking fire. A pile of discarded bones littered the ground.

"Was that one of ours?" asked Sal. "We came this way."

Greggor shook his head, having felt the ashes, his fingers black. "No. Three people were here." He pointed to the prints on the ground. "Three men. The ashes are cold."

"It could be anyone," said Frendo. "I wouldn't be concerned. They're travelers. A small party."

"Let's keep an eye open for a good place to rest for the night," said Greggor. "The day is waning."

"I can walk still. Please don't stop because of me."

He wiped his fingers on a patch of grass. "I'm aware of your health, my love." A smile appeared. "I can see you're able."

"I am."

Glancing at the trees, he motioned. "A way's further, men."

"We can make torches and walk in the dark," said Brayer. "It's too early to stop now."

"No. No night walking, not with women and children. There's no rush in hurrying. Keep an eye out. I doubt anyone is about, but you never know."

"Yes, my Lord."

He nodded at me. "A little further, then we rest."

"I can walk at night."

A smile appeared. "I don't doubt it, my brave girl. You need your rest. I can see how tired you are. You've circles beneath your eyes."

"But—"

He held up a hand. "We rest soon. I command it."

Thirty-Two

Traveling with men offered superior comfort, the warmth of a thick pelt providing softness and heat. Greggor lay beside me, his arm over my belly, while Bannon slept on his other side and Skye between us. The low murmur of conversation woke me, the men sharing a laugh. Far more exhausted than I thought, I went to bed with the children directly after supper, with Greggor joining us a short while later.

"Do you think your woman will recognize you?" asked Sal. "Perhaps she's gone off with another man."

"I told her I'd be back, and I will."

Hidden beneath the pelt, I listened to Sal and Nesco speaking, the other men asleep, including Greggor.

"What if she's gone?"

"She won't be."

"It's been too long since we've been home. I fear … nothing will be the same again."

"How so?"

"Owen's hungry for power. He's leader in Greggor's absence. I reckon he assumes we perished. He did the last time. I fear a fight."

"Bah, I fear nothing."

"I wouldn't be so sure of it. There's always something to fear, whether it's the weather or predators or man."

"I can battle all three."

Laughter rang out. "We'll see how brave you are, Sal. You'll be challenged one of these days."

"Every day we're challenged." A branch snapped in the distance, the sound echoing. "Shush! Where's that?"

I tensed, worried about what might be in the forest, knowing the dangers that lurked. What if the hostile group of half-breeds attacked us? How would we protect ourselves? Pushing aside the pelt, I sat up, seeing the men sitting by the fire, their hands on their weapons. They waited several breathless moments, nothing else making noise besides the crackling of the wood.

Sal got to his feet, gripping a spear. "I'm having a look."

"I'll stay." Nesco noted me. "Go back to sleep. It's nothing."

Crawling from the comfort of the pelt, I approached the fire, as Sal disappeared into the foliage. "I can't sleep. Is there any meat?"

"Of course." He handed over a pouch. "Have as much as you like."

"Thank you." I chewed, eyeing the trees warily, the night silent except for noisy insects and owls. "What do you think it was?"

"It could be anything." He chewed a piece of meat, his jaw working. His eyes drifted over me. "You're a handsome woman."

I hadn't expected to be complimented. "Thank you."

"I can see why Greggor chased after you, although it's foolish."

Continuing to eat, I pondered that.

"It's one thing to hunt an enemy or take in another clan, but … " he shrugged, "chasing after a woman shows weakness. He could have any woman he wants."

"Does he know you insult him behind his back?"

He sat with his arms over his knees, saying nothing.

"You should speak your concerns to him."

"We've done so. It matters not. He was determined to find you."

"And now you return to your land."

"After being gone far too long."

"You're worried, I can see it."

He shook his head, a look of annoyance appearing. "Yes, I'm worried. My life is good. I've a wife and child. I thought the days of endless wandering were behind me."

"I think that often too, but then I'm in the wilderness again with nothing but a strip of leather."

He nodded. "Women don't survive alone—not for long anyhow."

"I've managed to. Most of my life I've been alone." Although that wasn't entirely true, it felt that way often enough. "I can find your encampment. I know the way. I sought it out a while ago to take my son back after you attacked a dark clan."

"I'm well aware of your ability. You boldly challenged our lord. You impressed him. You taunt him. You're not afraid." His lips thinned. "You're practiced in the art of seduction."

I had never heard of such a thing before. "What?"

"You blind a man with your beauty."

I nearly bit my tongue chewing. "I do what?"

"You know what I speak of." He sounded irritated, an angry gleam in his eye.

"Seduction?" I had never heard that word before. "Is that an illness?"

Sal approached, carrying a spear. "It's nothing. All is quiet." He sat next to Nesco. "Why is she awake?"

"You speak so loud. You woke me." Chewing on meat, I mulled over what Nesco said, still not understanding what he meant. "What is seduction, Sal? What does that mean?"

"Seduction?" He grinned. "It's … one of the ways to get someone to mate with, I reckon. You entice them in a way. Why are we speaking about this?"

Appalled, I glared at Nesco. "You think I did that

with Greggor?"

"Indeed." He dared me to deny it, his look bold, challenging.

"I hated the man. I won't mate with someone I hate."

"You had a child with him. How do you explain that?"

"Only after a while." I felt a twinge of unease. "My feelings grew. I suppose, I weakened towards him. If anything, he seduced me."

"I can explain it better." Nesco got to his feet. "You worked your feminine wiles, until he bent to your will. I've never seen a man so love-struck." He grimaced. "I just pray this silly chase hasn't cost me my family."

"Ah, don't be so hard on the girl. It's not her fault. All will be well. In a day or so, we'll be home." Sal grinned. "No harm done."

Nesco stalked away, muttering, "I doubt it."

***

The odd conversation with Nesco continued to plague me, my mind wrapping around the idea that a woman could sway a man with what he called seduction. I had hated Greggor for his many misdeeds, planning on killing him on sight, but … circumstances prevented it. He had my son, whom he refused to relinquish. He forced me to stay with him for some time, whereby I observed his behavior—his kindness towards Bannon and I. The hate I felt so acutely began to fall away. Then we mated … and I could not deny him. Everything changed then.

Sliding beneath the pelt, I moved Skye, placing her next to Bannon. Waking, Greggor drew me to him, his arms around me.

"There you are," he murmured.

"Yes," I breathed, feeling a little out of sorts, yet eager for his touch. The conversation about seduction brought back memories of mating. I had always enjoyed being with Greggor in that way. My lips grazed his neck. "You're so warm."

He stiffened for a moment, a hand drifting down my back, the fingers rough. "I am." A hand cupped my buttocks, pulling me closer. "I can make you … warmer."

His manhood pressed to my belly. "I … don't doubt it."

A low chuckle escaped him. "Is there something you desire, my love? If there is, you should take it."

I shivered at the thought, kissing him with an urgency I hadn't anticipated, my teeth nibbling his plump bottom lip. When I pushed at his chest, he fell fully onto his back, where I flung a leg over him. Grasping at the pelt, I brought it above our heads, providing some privacy, Sal and Nesco still awake. I did not want an audience.

"Something's gotten into you, Peta." He held my waist, his face in darkness. "Are you ready to mate so soon?"

"I don't wish to speak now." Kissing him, I devoured his mouth, my tongue delving into silken wetness.

"As you wish," he chuckled. His fingers tangled in my hair, holding me close. "I've dreamt of this—of you. You never disappoint."

"Shush." I bit gently on an earlobe, tasting the salty quality of his skin.

"You're the only woman I've ever wanted."

My hand closed over his mouth, whereby he licked me. I giggled, kissing his throat, the shorn beard scratching me. Having groomed him thoroughly, he wasn't nearly as hairy as before.

His hands drifted down my back. "You may have whatever you wish," he murmured. "Anything … "

I could not have what I truly wanted, Ronan alive and Kia and Ara and Maggi with me. I would never see my family again or the cave of the wind. I had to put it behind me, along with all the other people I would never see again. The gods, for some odd reason, had directed me to Greggor.

"What do you want, Peta?" His heated breath fanned across my cheek. "Tell me."

"This." I took him boldly, feeling the length of him slide within me, the sensation utterly pleasurable. "I'll take this."

Thirty-Three

"You will never run from me again."

I rested my cheek against Greggor's chest. "I won't?" His arm tightened about my back.

"No, you won't. I forbid it."

I hadn't wanted to leave the cave, but the choice had been made. "I'm with you, Greggor."

"You are, but you're sly. I fear you'll disappear again some day."

"I'm with you, although I wasn't given much choice."

"You belong to me, Peta. You're my wife. You'll stand by my side, you'll help me rule. It's how it should be."

I did not wish to see Shay and Wildre again, my feelings torn where they were concerned. "Not all your people will be happy about that."

"I care not. They'll do as I say."

"They listen to the healer, don't they?"

"He'll do as I say."

"All healers I've ever known make their own rules."

"Ripa will do as I say."

"I hope so."

"None of this should concern you. It's my worry." His lips grazed my forehead. "You should try to sleep, my love. It's nearly dawn."

I yawned, feeling tired, yet happy, the man by my side warm. "You too."

"I've a great deal to think about."

"Rest, Greggor." Skye would wake soon enough, demanding to be fed. "We should all sleep."

"Aye," he murmured.

I drifted for a while, hearing the noisy call of birds a while later, the pelt beside me empty. Skye's cries rang out, the babe demanding to be fed. I pulled her near, offering a nipple, which quickly quieted her. Gazing at the cooking fire, I saw Frendo sitting there, his look tired.

"Where is everyone?"

"Washing up."

Rolled up pelts littered the ground. "When do we leave?"

"As soon as you're up." He picked at his teeth with a stick. "We've been waiting."

Annoyed, I sat, holding Skye to my chest. I gazed upon Bannon, the boy still asleep. "You should've woken me."

"Greggor said not to."

I searched for the sun, the rays struggling to stream through the branches. "It's early still."

"It is." He tossed the twig into the fire. "Would you like some water?"

"In a moment." I needed to change Skye and wake Bannon. Flinging hair over a shoulder, I got to my feet. "I'll be ready soon enough." Greggor appeared in the distance, followed by Brayer and Sal. "I know everyone's eager to return. I don't wish to delay you further."

"It's far too late for that." He snorted.

I hurried to ready myself, waking my son, who protested unhappily, grumbling. I tied fur to his feet, securing it with leather strips. Gathering my things, I rolled the pelt and tied it, leaving it with the others.

Greggor approached, a smile on his face. "You're awake."

"You shouldn't have let me sleep so long."

He shrugged, his hair appearing wet. "It's no worry.

We can go whenever you're ready."

"I'm ready." I knew his men were eager to return home, although it would take another day or two. "We can leave now."

"In good time." He picked Bannon up, holding him close. "Hello there, little fellow."

"Dadda!"

"I've missed you. It's good you remember me. I worried you might've forgotten." He kissed his cheek, Bannon wrapping his arms around his neck. "You're a good boy." He held him tightly. "You're a strong boy."

A host of conflicting emotions drifted through me, Greggor having the advantage here, spending time with Bannon early on, while Ronan met him later. The bond that formed was far stronger than I had realized.

"I'll wash up." Grasping a spear, I nodded. "Then we can go."

"You'll find Nesco by the water. The area's secure."

***

With Skye draped over my chest, I held a spear, using it as a walking stick. The bow and arrows hung from a shoulder, while Greggor carried the rolled pelts. Bannon traveled upon Sal's shoulders, the boy often grasping at the branches above his head. We stopped every so often to assess our progress, the men finding various footprints belonging to man or animal. At times they knelt before a print to assess its freshness. We encountered the body of a man a while later, some animal having gotten to him, the corpse ripped to pieces and eaten by bugs.

Bannon made a face. "Dead man." He held a hand to his nose. "Smelly."

I pulled him away. "Yes, something killed him." I cast a worried glance towards Greggor.

He scratched his chin. "It could be anything."

"It looks like a dark fella," said Sal. "Look at the color of the skin, what's left of it."

"I see only one set of prints," said Brayer. "He traveled alone."

Nesco nodded. "Which is dangerous."

"Go on," urged Greggor. "It smells. There's nothing we can do for him." He stalked towards me. "How are you?"

"I'm fine." I offered a smile. "You don't have to worry about me."

"You've just had a baby. I've every reason to worry."

"My legs are sturdy enough."

A grin appeared. "Indeed." He swatted my butt.

"Ouch!" I giggled.

"Let's move. I don't want to linger here." He glanced at Frendo. "It looks like a cat attack. I'd rather not encounter the creatures. Their den might be near here."

"Onward," called Sal, taking the lead. "We'll find a better place to rest later. Let's clear these woods."

Carrying Bannon on his shoulders, Greggor walked behind me, his presence a comfort. I wasn't nearly as fearful being in the forest with him and his men, because they provided ample protection to whatever danger we might face.

When we stopped later, finding a small clearing with sunshine, I sat with Bannon and Skye, the babe suckling at my breast. I lifted my chin to the sun, closing my eyes, the light warming my face. I felt eyes upon me, every man glancing in my direction. Being the only woman in the group, I intuitively knew what they thought—what they wanted, my senses prickling. Draping Skye over a shoulder, patting her back, I hid myself from them, anticipating Greggor to return, as he had left to find water.

"She looks better every day," murmured Brayer.

Sal cleared his throat. "Do you think he'd share her? We've another night or two."

"You can ask him," said Nesco.

"Or we could … stage a rebellion." Frendo tore off a piece of dried meat. "Kill him, and take her."

I gasped. "You wouldn't."

A smile appeared on Frendo's face. "No, but … it's tempting."

Would they really do such a thing? Were these the thoughts that occupied them? I reached for the bow, suddenly fearful over my welfare and terrified for Greggor. Would his own men murder him?

"For pity's sake," muttered Sal. "She's ready to kill us all. We're only teasing—mostly."

I glared at Frendo. "You'd kill your leader?"

"In jest." He shrugged. "We've been too long without women." He tapped his head. "It's on my mind. What's worse is watching you feed your child. You look …far too good."

"She does," agreed Sal, nodding.

Nesco lowered his head. "Let's not speak of this again. My only wish is to return home. I've been too long without my wife and child. I'm sick of travel."

"We mean you no harm, Peta," said Frendo. "You may put the weapon down."

I glimpsed Greggor in the distance, emerging from the trees, relief washing over me. "We can go soon."

Frendo got to his feet. "Ah, he returns."

Greggor's men behaved like every other man I had ever known, their baser needs never far from their minds. It would not be the first time I had been shared among a group. Would Greggor offer me up in such a manner?

"Are you rested?" he asked, nearing. He had filled two bladders of water.

"I am."

"Good." He grinned. "Shall we continue?"

I nodded.

"Are you unwell?" His smile faltered.

"I'm ... perfectly fine."

He eyed his men. "This is *my* woman. I know what's happening here. I'm not stupid. She looks like a cornered wolf. Her weapon's by her side." A hard gleam entered his eye. "You'll not lay one hand on her; is that understood? I share my woman with no one."

Stunned, I gaped at him.

"I shall kill any man who touches her. Do not try me."

Thirty-Four

They killed a stag for supper, the aroma of grilled meat filling the air. I sat on a pelt with Bannon and Skye, the baby at my breast. Following Greggor's angry outburst earlier in the day, the men behaved respectfully towards me, often lowering their gaze in my presence. I marveled at the difference, relieved to no longer be the object of their particular fascinations.

Skye fell asleep, bundled in a strip of leather. I left her on the pelt, getting to my feet. Greggor sharpened a spear tip, his attention suddenly on me. "Where are you going?"

"The forest." The men ate, speaking among themselves, while Nesco and Sal sharpened weapons.

"I'll go with you." He stood, grasping the spear. The light of the fire illuminated the planes of his face. He nodded. "This way."

"I don't need a guide. I can do it myself."

"Yes, but I wish a word with you." His lips neared my ear. "Alone."

Privacy was a luxury rarely afforded us. "All right."

"Watch my children."

"Yes, my Lord," said Frendo. "They're in good hands."

I felt the men's appraisal, my spine tingling. "What is it?"

Stepping into the trees, his hand fell to my back. "I don't want you to feel ill at ease with my men."

"I don't."

"But they've been bolder lately. I guessed it earlier today. I'm right, am I not?"

"A little." I stopped walking, gazing at the bright orb visible between the branches of a tree. "I except as much, Greggor. They're men after all. You've not been with a clan in some time."

"Too long."

"And they're … wanting a woman."

"But they can't have you."

"I'm gladdened to hear it."

His hands landed on my shoulders. "You're mine, Peta."

"I know that." As he drew me near, I melted into the embrace, the feeling warm and secure. "I don't want any other man."

"Over my cold, dead body. That's the only way you'll be with another man."

I lifted my chin to look at him, although we stood in shadow. "How much longer?"

"Tomorrow. We're close. Tomorrow we'll come upon the first of the clans. Then we'll approach the great water where I live—where *we* live."

"I want to settle for once, to stay in a place a long time. I want my children to know a home as their own."

"That will come."

"I'd prefer the cave, but I'll make the best of it wherever you are."

"We can heat water in skins for warm baths, Peta. It can be done. I know you love the heated pool."

"I do."

"You'll lack for nothing, my love. You'll never need to forage. Food will be brought to you whenever you wish it." He kissed my forehead. "I'll teach my son to hunt soon enough. You'll give me more sons and daughters. This is all I've ever wanted."

"It sounds like a dream." I closed my eyes, imagining

such a life, looking forward to it. "After everything's that's happened, I'm relieved to finally have a place to live forever." And a strong, capable man to share it.

"This is what I promise you."

He could provide everything, but … I still felt as if something was missing. Pushing the impression aside, I lifted to my toes to kiss him, his arms going around me. He groaned into my mouth, suddenly grasping my hips and turning me away from him.

"Greggor?"

"Hold onto the tree."

Roughened bark grazed my palms, while he flung aside the leather skirt, positioning himself behind me. One arm wound around my belly to offer support, while an errant hand skimmed over my buttocks, drifting lower to my inner thigh. Knowing what he meant to do, I shivered with anticipation.

"Is there something you want, my Lord?"

"Aye," he breathed, the hard, heated length of him entering me. "There is."

Gasping, I trembled, leaning further into the tree. "Oh!"

"Hold on."

Tonight he took all that he desired, just as I had used him the previous eve. Despite the unexpected nature of the mating, we both sought our pleasure moments later, the sound of his guttural cry echoing in the silent forest.

***

A kiss landed on my neck. "Wake, my love. We go soon."

Drowsy from sleep and lost in the sweetness of a dream, the image faded far too quickly, I muttered, "No."

"I'd let you sleep, but we've a great deal of walking today. I desire to reach home tonight."

Stretching arms over my head, I yawned. "I … as you wish." Skye's cries rang out. "She needs to be fed."

"See to our daughter." He flung back the pelt. "I'll pack our things and bring you some meat." The aroma of smoke lingered, the smell embedded in the pelt.

"Mamma!" Bannon's face gazed down at me, the boy smiling. "Get up, Mamma."

"I'll take him." Greggor grasped the child. "Come along. Time to wash up." He flung him over his shoulder, Bannon giggling. "You're in need of a bath, son."

I smiled at the two of them, reaching for Skye. I let her feed, the infant suckling hungrily, nearly choking on a sudden rush of milk. The last of the dried wood burned, the fire feeling warm against my skin, despite the chilly morning. My hair provided a barrier to the cool air at my back, the tresses hanging past my hips. As I fed my daughter, I glimpsed several men striding towards camp, Sal and Brayer walking with Frendo. They had rolled their pelts and gathered their things already, everyone waiting on me. If they felt annoyance at the delay, they did not show it.

"Good day," said Frendo, a smile appearing.

"I'm sorry I'm keeping you." Traveling with children wasn't an easy task. "She'll be done soon."

"It's early still," said Sal. Being the taller of the men, he towered over Brayer. "Would you care for some meat?"

"Yes."

"And a bladder of water?"

"I would. Thank you." These things came my way. "Thank you," I repeated.

"It's our pleasure, Lord Lady." Sal bowed his head slightly.

"I've never been addressed so." I marveled at the change in the men, although it pleased me. I tore off a chunk of meat, chewing heartily.

Once Bannon and Greggor returned, we set off,

walking through the forest with a hint of mist in the air, the fur on my feet damp from the newness of the grass. With Skye draped across my chest in a leather sling, Bannon tried his best to keep up with the men, although he grew tired often, needing to be carried.

When the warmth of the sun broke through the branches, I secured my hair on top of my head with leather twine. I felt stronger each day, the muscles in my thighs and calves not aching as they had before. After stopping to eat by a brook, I sat with Greggor and shared a thick strip of meat, Bannon playing in the water.

"Catch a fish," encouraged Greggor. "There are some little ones."

He thrust his hands beneath the surface, although he came up with nothing. "Fish! I want fish!"

"Keep trying," I said. "You'll get one."

The men sat nearby watching him, Nesco chewing on meat. "He's a sturdy boy, a good walker."

My son's blond hair hung to his shoulders. "Fish!" He tried again, losing his footing and falling into the water. He landed on his belly, spluttering.

Laughter rang out, Greggor smiling. "Not so sturdy after all, eh?"

"He'll learn in time," I said, placing Skye over a shoulder to pat her back. "I hope he doesn't drown." Bannon splashed around, his hair wet. "It must be cold."

"It doesn't seem to bother him."

I smiled, admiring Greggor's profile, despite all the scars that littered his skin. The nose appeared slightly crooked as well, having been broken more than once. He sat with his legs before him, the muscles in the thighs rippling each time he moved. There was nothing small about the man, his shoulders impossibly broad, with wrists twice the size of mine, if not bigger.

He cast a sidelong glance my way. "Yes?"

"Are all northern people so … big?"

A smile appeared. "Big?"

"You're bigger than most men."

"Because it takes more meat on the bone to ward off the chill, I suppose. My younger brother, Geon, looked just like me."

"And he's dead?"

"He is, as are the rest of my family."

"Did you have sisters?"

"I did. They're gone too."

"I'm sorry."

"I'm the last one, although not any longer. Skye will endure. She'll grow strong and sure and have many children to carry on."

"I pray it's so." His hand touched my back.

"You'll give me sons. We'll have a large family."

"I'll try my best." Such a task seemed monumental. "You're rather demanding."

"I've wanted you from the moment you walked into camp. You're the answer to my prayers. Together we shall rule my people and raise our family." A shadow passed over his face. "Don't run from me again."

"I had my reasons."

"And prodding from Wildre and Shay. I plan to scold them for their part in this, but it won't happen again."

"In time you'll trust me." I bundled Skye in leather, the babe asleep. Getting to my knees, I wrapped my arms around his neck, inhaling the musky scent of him, his hair smelling of wind and sun. "I'm where the gods wish me to be. I know that now. There's nothing left for me anywhere else."

He grasped my face, kissing me. "You're mine, Peta."

"I am."

"Never leave me, never."

"No."

Thirty-Five

Before dusk, we emerged from the forest finding a settlement of crudely made huts, all of them with active cooking fires. A small group of men approached, brandishing weapons.

Greggor lifted his spear. "Good people, it is I, your leader. I've returned. People gathered, a low murmur spreading, as news filtered through to the inhabitants.

Several men broke from the crowd, women and children parting to let them pass. I held Skye in my arms, while Bannon stood by my side, the boy chewing on a strip of meat.

"Do you not remember your own leader?" Greggor grinned. "I've returned."

A shorter man with long dark hair came to stand before him. A thick collection of bead necklaces hung around his neck. "Lord Greggor?"

"Aye, it is I. We're on our way home."

"They said you perished."

"Clearly, I have not."

"We've a new lord. Lord Owen. We're beholden to him now."

Greggor's mouth formed a thin line. "He's done well in my absence, but I've returned." His attention scanned the crowd. "Things look peaceful."

"We've had little trouble. We manage." An uneasy smile appeared. "I … welcome you to my fire this eve, if you wish. You may sup with me and my healer."

"We're passing through. I'm determined to reach home by nightfall."

Frendo glanced at Greggor. "Owen's taken your place. What will you do?"

"Take back what's mine. I suspected this might happen."

People lingered to access us, although they lost interest quickly enough, desiring to return to their supper, meat roasting over open flames. I felt the appraisal of many, some women casting dubious glances my way. I assumed they knew Greggor left to find me, which he had.

"The welcoming is … somewhat lacking," murmured Nesco. "Something's amiss."

"We go on," commanded Greggor, an annoyed frown upon his face. "I'd prefer to reach the encampment sooner than later. We've another clan or two to pass through until then."

The leader of this group nodded. "Safe travels, my Lord."

"Thank you."

No one said another word, the people paying us little mind as we ventured through to slip into the forest, finding a path. I remembered this trek from when I first came to Greggor's land. This would eventually lead to the encampment by the water.

"What will happen?" I asked, concerned about the unknown.

"My people await me. They'll celebrate my return. They think me dead, but I shall show them otherwise. They'll rejoice in my children. They'll know their new lady." His gaze drifted over me, a smile emerging. "Have cheer, Peta. You've nothing to worry about."

"But that man said everyone thinks you're dead."

"Undoubtedly. I've been gone too long. I'd assume the same. They'll know soon enough that I'm alive and well. They'll greet me with open arms." He patted my back. "There's nothing to fear, my love. All is well."

***

Tired from days of travel, I held onto the notion that we might sleep well tonight, remembering the comfort of Greggor's hut, with its sturdy walls and pelt-strewn floor. The men made torches after sunset, wrapping kindling and leather around thick sticks and lighting them. I fed Skye to quiet her cries, the men waiting for me to finish. We continued, hearing the faint sounds of dogs barking a while later.

"We're nearly there," said Frendo. "I wonder if the place is much changed?"

"There's no reason for any change," said Greggor. "I anticipate a great welcoming." Torchlight illuminated his face, a spear in the other hand.

Bannon walked by my side, while men strode ahead and behind. I glimpsed an opening in the trees, seeing the flames from a cooking fire. "There." I pointed.

"Ah, we've arrived." A dog darted towards us barking. "Hold it there, fellow," warned Greggor. "You bite me, I'll kill you." He thrust the spear before him. The animal cowered, slinking away as men appeared.

"Who goes there?" called a man. "Who are you?"

"This is a fine start to the evening," said Greggor. "You don't recognize your leader?"

Nesco and Sal stood close, their torches offering light, while Brayer and Frendo brought up the rear. The men approached, and I recognized the one named Owen, having met him before. Their healer, Ripa, came as well, the man scowling. I felt an inkling of unease then, grasping onto Bannon's hand tightly.

"Greggor?" asked Owen, the man waving a torch before him. "Ah, it is you." Several people came forward, having heard the commotion. "Back from your journey, I see." He eyed me. "You found her."

"Clearly." Greggor grinned. "It's good to be home. I was gone longer than expected."

"The little bitch gave you good chase." Owen failed to smile, his chin lifting fractionally. "We feared you dead. All of you."

"Well, as you can see, I'm alive."

Owen stood with his legs apart, a leather skirt at his hips. "You were gone too long."

"Which could not be helped."

The healer nodded, saying, "Welcome back, Lord Greggor. I'm pleased to see you in good health. We prayed for your survival."

"That's kind of you." Greggor pointed to the baby in my arms. "That's my daughter, Skye. She's my blood through and through."

"Congratulations," murmured Owen, the statement sounding flat.

"Thank you. You'll remember my son, Bannon. He's a good, strong boy. He travels well."

"Your children appear healthy enough." Owen glanced at me. "As does … your wife."

"My men would like to be reunited with their families. There's no reason to linger. I desire a warm meal. It's been a trying journey."

"There have been some changes," said Owen. "It falls to me to impart the news, I suppose."

"What news?" Greggor frowned. "Has there been trouble?"

"Not in the least. I've taken care of the clans readily enough. They see me as their leader, Greggor. I've … been named leader by all—all the clans."

"Which has served you well in my absence."

"And after. I've no intention of relinquishing the … title. I'm known as Lord Owen. You and your men are now under *my* power."

Greggor shot Ripa a look. "This will be undone."

"I've declared it so, I'm afraid. You were missing too long. There was some strife, which had to be handled. Owen's proven to be a fine, firm leader. He's taken Wildre to wife. She's … carrying his child."

"Which is a dangerous thing," countered Greggor. "She'll die. She nearly died birthing the last one, which was born dead." An angry gleam flared in his eyes. "You think you can usurp me? You should've known I'd return and claim what's rightfully mine. I've no intention of giving up everything I've fought so hard for."

"Then you should've thought of that before you went running after this … this woman. She's not of our clan or any of the clans in the area. She means nothing to us." He took a step nearer. "The way you behaved, like a raving madman, they say she's bewitched you. You've lost your senses to this one."

"What I do or don't do is my own business. I'll not explain myself to anyone. I don't need to. I left to find my woman, and I have. Wildre and Shay had a hand in her leaving. They coaxed her into running. She'd still be here, if they hadn't interfered."

"None of that matters," said Ripa. "We won't have her back, none of us will." He pointed to me. "She's a sorceress. She's bad luck."

Laughter filled the air. "The only madness I hear are your words. What rubbish you utter. Peta's no sorceress. She's but a woman. She's a bit of a healer as well."

"Which only proves her guilt," said Ripa. "She'll not be received in any way." He glared at Greggor. "Nor will you."

"We shall let the people decide. They'll know they're true leader when they see him." He pushed past Ripa, the man nearly falling to the ground. "I tire of this argument. I'm leader, and I will take my rightful place." He waved to us. "Come along."

Thirty-Six

Greggor strode into the encampment with his head held high. People gathered to see what the commotion was about, inquisitive eyes staring at us. Owen and his men closed in, all of them holding spears, their presence threatening. I swallowed the lump in my throat, grasping at the bow by my side, although using it with Skye in my arms would prove difficult.

"Good people," called Greggor. "I've returned! I'm certain you'll all remember your leader." A murmur drifted through the crowd, a woman coming forward. I recognized her. "Wildre. How kind of you to greet me." A hint of distain laced his tone. "You and Shay are responsible for Peta's flight."

"She left on her own." Her belly bulged with child. "I'm glad you're well, but … you're no longer leader here."

"So I've been told." All humor vanished from his face. "What sort of greeting is this?" He eyed the people, all of them fearing to come any nearer. Women held their children, while men stood awkwardly, most gripping spears. "I'm your leader! I've been leader of the northern clans for ages. I've kept the peace. I've kept you all safe."

"And now it's my turn." Owen lifted his chin. "The matter was settled some time ago. There's nothing left to discuss. If any of your men wish to stay, they may, but you're not welcome." He eyed me. "Or your witch woman and her spawn. You cannot stay."

Nesco broke rank, hurrying for a woman and her child, hugging them. "I wish to stay."

Being outnumbered, Greggor glared at Owen. "You dare challenge me? I say we fight then. The winner shall be leader. It's how it's always been done."

He smiled coldly. "I don't fight old men."

"You're my age, you thieving, lying bastard. You mean to steal all I've worked for. You take my home. I relied on you to watch over things in my absence, not rob my life from beneath me."

"And such it is." Owen glanced about. "You failed to return. We declared you dead. Now we move on. I've proven my worth to these people. They trust me far more than they trust you."

"Lift your spear and fight me!" Greggor thundered. "Fight now!"

"I think not." Owen glanced at his men. "Escort them out. I assume Sal, Brayer, and Frendo will accompany you."

Greggor lunged at him, the spear nearly piercing his forehead. Owen jumped back, just as four men pounced on Greggor, knocking him to the ground. Terrified they would kill him, I screamed, lifting the bow despite having Skye slung across my chest. A hand darted out to knock the weapon away, the bow landing in the dust by my feet.

"No, girl," said the man.

Sal and Brayer held their spears defensively, standing with legs parted, while Frendo whirled at those around him, his eyes glinting in the firelight.

"You're too few," said Owen. "If you'd brought more men, perhaps this might've ended differently. As I've said, you're not welcome here. If I let you stay, you'll undermine all I've accomplished. I won't do it. You'll have to leave. I'm letting you go with your life. You may take these men and this witch of yours, but go you must."

Greggor held his ground, a hard gleam in his eyes. "I've known you my entire life. We were friends from boyhood. It shocks me—it wounds me to be treated this way. You and everyone I've ever known has benefited from all I've done. I've given my life to all of you. These are my people."

"And you deserted them to chase after a sorceress." Ripa nodded solemnly. "We thank you for the service, Lord Greggor, but … it's no longer needed. Lord Owen shall be leader now, as he's been since you left. It's a hard, bitter truth to swallow, but you'll survive it."

Owen said, "Escort them out. Make sure they're far. I don't want them making camp anywhere near here."

"Mamma?"

I squeezed Bannon's hand. "It's all right."

"What's wrong, Mamma?"

I released the breath I held. "We're … we're going to walk a little more."

"You'll rue this, Owen. You'll regret it."

"I'd leave now. I've thought of … killing you all, if you must know. If I were wise, I would. You might return one day and cause trouble."

"Hear me, people," called Greggor. "Speak now or hold your peace forever. If I leave, you shall never see me again. I was a good, fair leader to you. You prospered under my protection. You cannot deny it. If you wish me to stay, say something. Speak now!"

The only sound came from a barking dog across camp, the people chillingly silent.

***

"Mamma, me tired."

"I'm tired too. It won't be long now." Someone closely followed me, his spear pointed at my back. A contingent of Owen's men surrounded us, holding spears and torches, the flickering flames leaping into the air. Exhausted from the long walk, I longed to make camp.

"This is far enough," said Greggor.

"We've been told to take you further," said one of the men.

"You know me, Galdo. We've known one another

since boyhood and before. Our mothers were friends."

Regret flickered in the man's eyes. "I'm … following orders, Lord Greggor. I'm … sorry."

"I've hardly been gone long enough to warrant banishment. How did this come to pass?"

"It doesn't matter."

"I assume someone's words poisoned my good name. Who was it?"

"We thought you dead. Owen became leader, and we've grown to accept him."

"I'm being exiled from my own clan by a man who pretended to be a friend. That thieving, conniving … wretch!" Greggor's anger flared again, his posture rigid. "I curse you all. Damn you to whatever hell the gods have in store for you. You shall burn there."

Sal and Brayer nodded, Sal saying, "It's a sad day indeed, being cast out by your own people."

"You needn't have come," said Greggor. "It's not you they wish gone, it's me. It's Peta. You and Brayer and Frendo didn't have to come. You could've stayed and lived in comfort."

"Owen might not know what loyalty is," said Frendo. "But I do. I've no intention of leaving your side, my Lord."

"Nor I," said Sal.

Brayer nodded. "Or I."

"We'll find a place to make camp." Greggor glanced at me. "I know you're tired. I'm sorry, Peta. This isn't what I was expecting."

"You don't have to apologize. It's not your fault. It seems to be my fault. I'm the … witch."

A smile appeared. "You're not a witch." Owen's men stopped walking. "Is this far enough?"

"We leave you now," said Galdo. "I wish you … safe travels, my Lord."

"I wish you luck. Without my guidance, you're going

to need it. I won't be back. It's a sad day when a man is banished from his people for no reason other than he was gone for a while." He spat. "None of you deserve me."

Galdo lowered his head, stepping away. "We shall go. You may camp here, but leave at first light."

It looked as if Greggor wanted to say something more, but he held his tongue.

"Let's make camp," said Brayer. "It's late."

Greggor stared absently into the darkness, his expression morose. I touched his arm. "What will we do?"

"Survive."

"Can we go back to the cave?"

"I … believe so."

"Truly?"

He caressed my face. "It's what you want. You'll get your wish, my love."

"I'm sorry your people were … so awful. I didn't think they'd cast you out."

"I should've guessed it with Owen. He tried once before to take my place. I foolishly forgave him for the grievance. I shouldn't have."

Choosing a spot in a small clearing, Frendo lit a fire using the sap from a tree that would burn for a good time. Our pelts lay scattered around the heat source, Bannon sleeping with Skye. Weary from the long day of travel, I lay on my side eyeing the fire, listening to the men.

"What do you suggest?" asked Greggor.

"It's your choice, my Lord," said Sal.

"No. No, it's not. I'm … not your leader any longer. You've equal say in the matter. I'm taking Peta to the cave. It's where she wishes to be. You may go wherever you desire or you may come along."

Frendo chewed a piece of meat, his attention on the fire. "It's not a bad shelter. It's the biggest cave I've ever seen. There's water and game. The valley's fertile. The river's full of fish. I can't say I'm saddened to return. The only concern is the lack of women."

"Yes," said Brayer. "That's a problem."

Sal beamed. "Leota looked good to me. I could mate her."

Frendo grinned. "She wasn't all that friendly, but perhaps you can persuade her."

"She'll come around. She's without a mate. Every woman needs a mate. I'll convince her some way."

"With your charm and wit, no doubt."

He threw a small rock at him. "Shut up!"

"What will you do?" asked Greggor, his eyes on Sal.

"We're with you, my Lord."

"You needn't call me that any longer."

"But it's your name."

"My name's Greggor."

"Yes, my Lord."

He sighed. "It'll take time, but I'm hoping you'll see me more as a friend than a leader." He stared into the flames. "You could've stayed with the clan. You didn't have to leave. I'm humbled by the gesture. I expected you all to stay. Is everyone coming to the cave then?"

"I am," said Frendo. "If you're not leader, then there's nothing for me with the clan. I've never been fond of Owen."

"Yes," agreed Sal. "I don't like him either."

"Indeed." Brayer nodded. "I'm not taking orders from Owen. There's only one leader I'll ever follow, and that's you."

Greggor sighed, his expression chagrinned. "Then it's settled. Let's pray there aren't any more unpleasant surprises tomorrow. I'm weary enough as it is." He touched my arm. "What say you, my sweet?"

"I'm happy to go home." I hated having to walk again for days, but the journey would be worth it. "I love the cave. I never want to leave it again."

"Then that's what we'll do."

Thirty-Seven

Greggor stayed awake talking with his men for some time, crawling into the pelt with me a while later. I turned, finding myself in his arms.

"I didn't mean to wake you," he murmured.

"It's fine."

"We were supposed to be in my hut tonight, surrounded by soft pelts and a watertight roof. The homecoming wasn't what I expected."

"No."

"I'm stunned still. I … tried to hide my emotions. I didn't want them to see how … how dreadful I feel about being cast out of my own clan."

I touched his face, feeling a rough beard. "Greggor."

"After everything I've done for those people. I've liberated clans from evil leaders to have them join us and live in freedom. Some of those people knew nothing but pain and slavery. They flourished under my command. They lived better lives. This is how they treat me. I go away for barely a season, and they cast me aside like a bundle of refuse."

"I'm sorry." I felt a measure of guilt in this. "If I'd stayed, you'd still be leader."

"It's not your fault."

"But it is."

"It matters little now, Peta. By all rights, I should've returned and taken my due place. My family has always ruled as far as I can remember. My father was leader before me and his before him. It's in the blood."

"Perhaps Enwan and Bondo will let you be leader at the cave."

"I don't want it anymore."

"Are you certain? You just said it was in your blood."

"Being leader's not brought me the happiness I crave." His hand stroked my shoulder. "I'd rather be … husband to you and father to our children. I prefer that to anything else."

Considering the power this man wielded not so long ago, that statement staggered me. "Goodness."

"What I say is, I'm not going to fight the will of the gods. It's clear to me where they wish me to go. I'm to be with you."

"That was more your choice than the gods."

"But they interfered, as they always do. They brought you to me and then took you away. I find I cannot live without you." He was silent for a moment. "Did you think of me at all while we were apart?"

"Yes."

"When you were with Ronan?"

"I tried not to."

"But you did."

"Of course."

"If I'd not come after you, what would you have done?"

"Lived the rest of my life at the cave, I suppose."

"You wouldn't have come to me?"

"I don't know. I can't say what I might've done. I thought only to have the baby and not much further than that."

"I understand."

"I knew you searched for me. I suspected you'd return, and you did."

"I wasn't going to stop until I found you."

"No."

"And now it's all new. We'll have a fresh start."

"Two more days of walking. It feels like a lifetime, but I know it's not very long."

"Then let's sleep, my love. The sooner we sleep, the sooner it'll be sunrise. Then it'll only be another day."

I closed my eyes, feeling blissful and secure, saying a little prayer to the gods to guide the way … the journey nearly over.

***

I fed Skye, the baby swaddled in a strip of leather. "Can you watch her? I want to take Bannon to the stream."

Greggor nodded, having a drink from a bladder. "Don't stray too far."

The men had already washed, Sal and Frendo sharpening spear tips. "We won't be long." I slung the bow over a shoulder, taking the sack of arrows. The sun hadn't appeared yet, the forest grey with mist. "Come along." I took Bannon's hand. "We go find water."

He wore nothing on his feet, protesting stepping on something sharp. "Ouch, Mamma."

"You'll have to harden up that skin of yours. A few rocks won't kill you." We ventured towards a nearby brook. The sugary odor of pine needles lingered in the air. This wasn't a broad river, but a small meandering water source, littered with tiny stones along its banks. "We don't have time to play. You need to wash up." I led him to the edge, the boy wading in. "It's a little cold."

"Me not dirty, Mamma."

"Oh, yes you are." I grinned, glancing at a flattened expanse of mud nearby, seeing tracks. I froze, recognizing the paw prints. "Come here, Bannon! Come out now!" The prints looked fresh—far too newly made for comfort.

"Why, Mamma?"

I took his hand, dragging him from the water just as a low, rumbling growl resonated, a predator close. It had been ages since I had faced this sort of danger. Being alone with my son, the men nowhere to be found, I swallowed the fear that threatened to paralyze me. Spying movement out of the corner of my eye, I had no time to secure Bannon, the danger upon us. Affixing an arrow to the bow and pulling back on leather twine, I held my breath, knowing we had been seen.

"Mamma?"

"Keep silent!"

I stared into the bushes, seeing something brown moving behind the leaves. Letting the arrow fly, I prayed it hit its mark. If the creature wished to attack, Bannon and I would not survive. I had to kill it first. Reaching for another arrow, I prepared to shoot again, listening for any sound. A raspy growl came, followed by an angry howl. Had it been wounded?

The thunder of heavy feet distracted me, Greggor appearing with a spear. "Where is it?" He had heard the sound. Sal and Brayer followed, with Frendo behind them.

"In the bushes."

Bannon stood upon the rocks. "What's wrong, Mamma?"

"A bad animal. He was about to attack us."

"A cat?"

"Yes, my love."

His eyes widened. "That's a bad animal."

"Go see if it's dead," directed Greggor. He approached with the weapon before him, his eyes scanning the forest. "There might be more. We might be surrounded."

Sal and Brayer cut a path through the bushes on either side of the stream, while Frendo brought up the rear, his eyes wide, searching for trouble.

Greggor nodded at me. "Stay where you are, Peta."

"I hit it."

"That remains to be seen."

"I know I did." I could protect myself, having done

so in the past. "Go see for yourself."

Brayer called out, "She got it, but it's still alive."

Sal drove his spear downward. "Not now. I'm looking forward to a fine meal. This'll make a proper supper."

"She's a good shot."

That hadn't been the first time I had killed a cat, relief washing over me, but I worried still. "They hunt in packs."

"It might've been the odd one out," said Greggor. "Have you washed?"

"Not yet."

"You should, so we can go."

Sal stepped through a bush with the cat draped over his shoulders. "A fine meal we'll have this eve." He grinned, tossing a bloodied arrow my way. "Here you are."

"Thank you."

"She's capable," said Frendo.

Greggor pressed a finger to his mouth to indicate silence. We stood still listening to the wind through the branches and the sound of trickling water. "I thought … there might be something else." A slight frown appeared.

"What did you hear?" asked Frendo.

Sal glanced his way. "Another cat? I don't hear anything."

"No, not a cat." Greggor stood still waiting. "Something else, but perhaps it was nothing."

"Shall we go on?" Brayer nodded at me. "Where's your baby?"

With all of us at the stream, no one stayed to watch over Skye! My daughter was alone at the camp! I gasped, feeling ill to my stomach at the thought that something might have happened to her. Had the animal distracted us so another might take her away?

"Oh, no!" I bounded out of the water, tearing through the bushes to run back to the where I had left Skye, terrified she might be missing—taken by the jaws of a hungry cat. "How could we leave her?"

Greggor held Bannon, running past me. "She's fine, Peta. Please don't worry."

"You were supposed to look after her. I trusted you!" Drawing back an arrow, I prepared to defend my baby, although she would not survive being mauled. We burst through the trees a moment later, finding an empty camp with pelts strewn upon the ground. Sal, Brayer, and Frendo arrived the next instant. "Skye?" One of the pelts bulged slightly. "Skye?"

Greggor drew it back, revealing my daughter, who slept peacefully. "All is well, my love. Our daughter's perfectly fine."

I fell to my knees, feeling shattered, yet relieved. "Oh … that was … " tears flooded, blurring my sight, "awful. I truly feared the worst."

"She's as healthy as ever." He picked her up, holding her to his chest. "I shouldn't have left her, but I heard the growl and ran. It was instinctual. I'm sorry. I worried you and Bannon might be killed."

"You hid her under the pelt."

"They would've sniffed her out," said Frendo. "We were lucky."

Sal tossed the carcass to the ground, the cat landing with a thud. "We should remain vigilant today. There's a den nearby."

I reached for Skye, feeling relieved she hadn't been harmed. "Give her to me."

Greggor failed to smile, handing the baby my way. "Let's gather our things. I … don't like these woods. They feel … off."

"Off?" Sal shrugged. "They're like any other."

"I don't know. I'm ill at ease here. I wish to clear this place before we stop for the midday meal."

"You heard him," said Brayer, rolling a pelt. "Let's not stay a moment longer."

Thirty-Eight

Everyone seemed anxious, the men scanning the forest as they walked. No one engaged in lighthearted banter, the men listening to the noises of the wilderness. I felt the tension, worried over the lack of birdcalls. When we stopped for water, I overheard the men speaking, while I leaned against a tree to feed Skye.

"We didn't come this way," said Sal.

Greggor nodded. "No. I don't recall the area. There are no open places to hunt. There was no reason to be here."

"That, and the cats," said Brayer. "I don't like seeing their droppings. We passed a pile or two not long ago. It bodes ill."

"And I've this odd feeling of being … watched." Frendo glanced at me. "I can't explain it, but it feels … less than welcoming."

Greggor's hands went to his hips. "Someone needs to climb a tree. Tell me what you see."

Sal got to his feet. "I'll do it." Reaching for a branch, he pulled himself up. Then he grasped another.

"We could go back the way we came." Frendo gazed at Sal, the man making quick work of the climb.

"We cannot." Then Greggor seemed to reconsider those words. "I'm not leader any longer. Everyone has a say in the decision. I shouldn't dictate it." He grinned. "An old habit."

"No, you're right," said Brayer. "Whatever it is, we

walk through it."

"I see smoke." Sal balanced on an upper branch. "More than one plume. There's some sort of camp over there. We're heading straight for it."

"I'd avoid it entirely," said Brayer. "They may be hostile."

"Or they may be peaceful." Greggor frowned, his look thoughtful. "Come on down, Sal. Thank you." He eyed me. "I've my family to consider."

Climbing quickly, Sal dropped to the ground. "It's not a big camp, but there are at least four cooking fires from what I can see."

"How far do you think?"

"We'll reach it by nightfall."

Greggor did not like this idea, the frown on his face deepening. "I don't wish to meet people in the dark. We can't make a fire then to cook this meat, which will spoil."

"We walk on then," said Frendo. "Take another direction."

"Which will add an extra day to the journey. Peta's tired. We were supposed to be safely ensconced at home, comfortable in our huts, but instead, we're stranded in the wild."

"I'm fine. I'm not tired. You're not walking all that fast anyhow."

"We could approach the camp and observe them," said Sal. "If they look friendly, we offer some of our meat. If they're … hostile, we carry on."

"They might see us." Frendo held a spear, staring at the tip. "They could attack. We've few men and far too many children."

"Then what do we do?" asked Greggor.

Frendo shrugged. "What do you recommend?"

"I like Sal's idea, but it's risky."

"Peta could stay behind," said Brayer. "We run ahead and see what we can see. When it's safe, we come get her."

"I don't wish to be left alone." I hated that idea. "I've my bow. I can protect myself, but I prefer not to."

"She did kill the cat." Sal grinned. "She's better able than I thought."

"But she's got babies to protect," said Greggor. "And I must watch over her." He scratched his chin. "No decision has been made."

Having finished feeding Skye, I hung her over my chest in the leather. "Let's go on. Sal can climb another tree in a while. If he sees trouble, we skirt around them."

"We risk life and limb that way," said Greggor. "But … the idea is as good as any. I don't want to spend an extra night in the woods. I want this to be the last night."

Brayer bundled a pelt. "That's the decision then. I like it."

"All right." Greggor's look betrayed doubt, but he masked it a moment later. "We continue on. Let's hope the gods are smiling on us today; although, I feel the cat attack was more of a warning than a welcome."

***

I marveled at how well Bannon traveled, the boy walking more and more and asking to be carried less. He wore soft fur on his feet, as did the other men, the boy carrying his own spear, made especially for him. When he grew tired of walking, Greggor and Sal took turns with him, Bannon often sitting on Sal's shoulders.

"She has to feed the baby," said Greggor.

Skye cried, the sound carrying. I sat by the base of a tree, the infant quickly latching onto a nipple. I worried about the crying, knowing someone might hear it.

"I'll climb again," said Sal. "We should be close."

Greggor scanned the forest, his look stark. "You do that."

Brayer and Frendo ventured out, walking in a large

circle, their attention on the ground. They searched for prints or animal scat or evidence of human or animal occupation.

I smiled at Greggor. "What do you think?"

He sighed. "I don't want to alarm you."

"You may speak your mind. If I were alone, I'd feel … worried. It's too quiet."

"Yes."

"If there's a clan, I don't hear any dogs."

"There's little game from what I've seen. They've probably eaten their dogs." He shrugged. "I don't know." He glanced at the cat carcass. "We need to cook that meat or it'll spoil. I hoped for a hearty fire tonight."

"I pray we have one." I lifted my chin to see Sal, who stood upon a high branch staring into the distance. He said nothing, climbing down a moment later. "What did you see?"

"I didn't want to shout, but there's a clan nearby." He pointed. "Over there."

"How far?"

"A little further than a large field. It's not far."

"Are they in a clearing?"

He nodded. "My sight isn't the best, Greggor. I … saw several cooking fires and … people."

"What sort of people?"

"The dark ones, but … others too."

"A mixed clan?"

He nodded.

"That's unusual."

"We should approach carefully. I'd leave her here, my Lord. Only the men should go."

"I can fend for myself."

Greggor ignored that, asking, "How many men did you see?"

"Many."

He sighed. "If something goes amiss, she's alone."

"I've managed alone well enough." I felt the weight of their conversation, wondering at what Sal did not say. I sensed trouble. "I'll be fine."

Frendo and Brayer returned, Bannon following them. "We found prints," said Brayer. "Animal and man."

"Aye," murmured Greggor. "There's a clan nearby. Dark ones and white ones mixed together."

The men exchanged a glance, Frendo saying, "That's odd."

"I propose we get a little closer and have a look. Peta will stay here with the children."

Placing Skye over a shoulder, I got to my feet. "I'll manage."

"We could just go around," said Sal. "We needn't alert them to our presence. They need not know we're here."

"That might be the best course of action." Frendo eyed the forest. "The light's waning as we speak. I want to find a safe place to cook this meat."

"The dark ones are always hostile. We shouldn't risk it. We don't have enough men."

Greggor sighed. "If they'd been a white clan I would've taken the chance, but Brayer's right. It might be wise to skirt around them and find a place to make camp downwind."

I felt a measure of relief, releasing a deep breath. "Yes. I like that."

"Are we ready?" Greggor offered a smile, the tension in his face lessening. "Let's give them a wide berth. I don't wish to alert them to our presence. We must be utterly quiet."

Sal nodded. "Let's go. I've a hunger for some cat meat."

Brayer reached for Bannon, placing the boy upon his shoulders. Bannon protested. "Me wanna walk."

"I'll let you down once we're further away."

I hurried after Greggor, with Brayer and Sal behind and Frendo up ahead. We spoke little, moving as silently as possible in a wide circle around the clearing where the clan made camp. The faint smell of fire lingered, along with the stench of a latrine, the pit in the vicinity. Each step brought the possibility of discovery, my footfalls careful. Few insects or birdcalls sounded, the air oddly oppressive.

When we had gone far enough, Greggor motioned to me. "We should still be as quiet as we can," he whispered.

I patted Skye, relieved she slept soundly, the babe resting against my chest. "Let's not stop here."

"No."

Some other smell wrinkled my nose, the pungent odor of rotting meat. "The air is foul here."

"The stench of death," murmured Sal.

"Aye." Greggor's lips formed a thin line. "We're getting closer to whatever it is." Gripping the spear with both hands, he waved to Brayer and Frendo. "Be aware."

I glanced at Bannon on Brayer's shoulders, the boy kicking his feet, blissfully unconcerned with the danger that surrounded us. "You should give him to me," I murmured.

He let him down, the child giggling happily, darting forward, heedless of the noise he made. Greggor grabbed him, hoisting him into arms, while he screeched with laughter, thinking this to be play. A hand closed about his mouth, silencing him at once.

"Shush!"

My eyes flew to the forest, staring at every rock and tree, looking for a sign that we had been heard. I gathered my hair in one hand, winding it about my neck. If the wind blew, it might be seen, the color not one to easily blend in. Brayer and Sal crouched in the bushes, while Greggor and Frendo stood behind threes, all of us having taken cover. We waited for a glimpse of someone approaching, the woods eerily silent.

"They didn't hear it," whispered Sal.

"Or they're hiding." Greggor gazed stonily around, his eyes missing nothing. "Why is it so … still?"

"Perhaps the animals are afraid of us," said Brayer.

Greggor shook his head. "No, but it doesn't matter. We need to leave this place. Let's go." He waved. "Onward, but quietly."

"We should've long since passed the camp," said Sal.

"But trouble lurks." Greggor smiled faintly. "I can feel it."

Thirty-Nine

We had not gone far when we came upon what stank, a pile of bones discarded in a heap, with a dead animal rotting nearby. Holding a hand to my nose, I encouraged Bannon to keep going.

"Smelly, Mamma."

"I know." The animal appeared to be some sort of woodland creature, its hide black with fur. "Don't stop."

Greggor motioned for us to follow, Sal and Brayer behind me. Nearly dusk, the shadows beneath the trees grew, the air cool. I longed to rest, but we had not gone far enough to make a fire yet. I worried I might have to feed Skye again, the baby waking and making little noises. She stared at me with eyes wide open. Greggor and Fendo suddenly gripped their spears protectively, Sal and Brayer doing the same. Something had spooked them, but I knew not if the trouble came from animal or a man.

"Look," said Sal, pointing. "That's not … natural."

We neared what looked like a man, his skin dark, with an oddly protruding forehead. He hung from a tree, his wrists bound by twine and tied higher on a branch. Injured and bloodied, someone had left him here to die. Stunned, I tried to shield the sight from Bannon's eyes, but the boy had seen him.

"Look, Mamma!"

I took him in my arms, stepping away from the man, who moved then, moaning. "Oh, he's alive."

Greggor's mouth widened, his expression one of

horror. "Someone's done this to him. He's been … he's missing his … manhood." He pointed.

"For the love of the gods," muttered Frendo. "Who'd do that?"

"He's not going to live long," said Sal.

The man appeared to drift in and out of consciousness, suddenly realizing he wasn't alone. He lifted his head, his eyes white against the dark skin. A glazed sort of look dulled his expression. He spoke, the language familiar to me, although I had not heard it in a long time.

"What's he saying?" asked Greggor. "He's saying something."

I listened, catching a word here or there. "He says … to be aware. He's been cast out for some misdeed."

Frendo glanced at me. "You understand it?"

"I've lived with the dark ones before. I learned to speak their language."

"What else is he saying?" asked Greggor. "He's muttering something."

I approached, leaving Bannon behind me. "Who are your people?" I asked, hoping I remembered the dialect correctly. He blinked away a trickle of blood, his skin gleaming with perspiration. "How many are there? Why'd they do this to you?"

"The chief banished me for mating his woman," he murmured. "He … tore out my manhood. He wants all the women to himself."

"How many men are there?"

"More than what you have," he rasped, hanging his head.

"What does he say?" Greggor waited on my reply, his expression concerned.

"It was a disagreement over women. They have more men than we have."

Sal shook his head, appearing disgusted. "What sort

of clan does this to their own people?"

"The leader wants to mate the women." I shrugged. "I'm not sure. I can try to ask him again."

"We should carry on," said Brayer. "I don't want to get too close to these barbaric people."

A hard gleam appeared in Greggor's eyes. "I've dealt with dark clans before. I've always attacked first, as Peta knows too well. If I had more men, I'd … I might do it."

But I had begged him not to treat people in such a way. I waited on what he would say, feeling anxious and concerned.

"Ask him something else. Ask him about the women?"

I glanced at the wounded man, his face hidden by long, blood drenched hair. "What of your women and children? Are they safe?"

Lifting his head, he grimaced. "They are property of the chief. If they please him, he offers food."

"What did he say?"

I glanced at Greggor. "He said the chief feeds the women if they please him."

"What does that mean?"

"I don't know." I shrugged, disturbed by the conversation. "Is there anything we can do for him?"

"He's bleeding to death." Sal spat. "We should go before it's dark. I've a belly to fill with cat meat."

"Something's off here," said Frendo. "I can't tell you what to do, but I wonder if the women are slaves."

I frowned. "Slaves?"

"They've more than likely been captured or rescued."

"But they're provided for. It sounds as if they're being fed at least." I struggled to understand what he meant.

"At what cost?" Greggor frowned. "I've little desire to interfere, especially with so few men."

"Are the women slaves?" I asked the man, who had

fallen into a stupor again. Touching his shoulder, he woke, gasping. I took a step back, horrified by the extent of his injuries, the wound between his legs bleeding profusely. "Are the women slaves?"

"We're all slaves," he uttered, his head falling one last time.

"He says they're all slaves."

"I think he's gone," said Sal. "Poor man. That must've hurt badly. I can't imagine having my—"

"We must decide now," said Greggor. "I'll not do this alone. We either carry on or we inspect this clan." He glanced at the men. "What say you?"

Frendo grimaced. "We should bury him. He's gone."

"There's no time. Darkness comes." Greggor waited for a response, his hands at his hips.

"Being darker is better," said Sal. "We can observe them without being seen. That'll give us some insight into who they are."

"I wish to cook this meat," grumbled Brayer. "What of our meal?"

"We shall have it later," said Greggor. "I like your idea, Sal. We'll wait until it's fully dark, then we approach."

Panic drifted through me. "But, you said you'd stay away. We don't need to get any closer."

"You won't. We'll find a safe place for you and the children." Greggor, his mind made up, nodded. "Let's look for it. Something hidden. We've enough daylight still to make a shelter."

I wanted to protest, fearing for his welfare, but I had little choice in the matter. We ventured further away from the dead man, leaving behind the horrible stench of blood and decay. In a copse some distance off, Sal and Brayer sliced free several large branches, creating a leafy hut, where they tossed down the pelts. Bannon crawled over them, happy to not be walking at the moment.

"Here's some meat." Greggor gave me a small leather

pouch. "Eat, my love."

Skye slept peacefully in her swaddling. I wrapped my arms around his neck, pressing myself to him. "Please don't go."

He kissed my cheek, holding me close. "You've nothing to worry about."

"That's a lie. If you don't come back, I'll have to fend for myself again."

"That will not happen."

I held him tighter, suddenly feeling weak and fearful, terrified at the prospect of losing him. "No. Please don't go." Sal and the men waited, standing in near darkness.

"You rest, my love. There's nothing to fear. We're having a look. If nothing's wrong, we'll be back."

"Please don't go."

He held my face, his lips brushing mine. "I fear very little, Peta. I know you'll protect our children. You've mastered the bow. You're hidden well beneath the branches. They can't find you."

"What if you perish?"

"I won't." He drew back, smiling. "I've faced far worse. I must leave now. I won't be gone long."

I hated feeling so emotional—so needy. I could not bear to lose him, the man occupying my soul so completely. "May the gods bring you back to me. I … please don't die."

A chuckle escaped him. "That's the last thing I plan to do. I've never lost a battle in my life. I won't now." He touched my face. "My beautiful girl."

Bannon listened to the conversation, the boy sitting cross-legged. "Dadda. Stay."

"I'll be right back." Warmth flared in his eyes. "You're a good boy. You watch over your mother."

Grasping a smaller version of a spear, he held it firm. "Yes, Dadda."

"You see," he chuckled. "You're in good hands."

I wanted to leave the children in the hut to help them, but I could not. Skye might cry and draw attention. "I don't like this. We should just go on."

"And we might still."

"Let's go," said Frendo. "There's no reason to delay further."

I kissed him, tasting the salty quality of his lips. "You'd best return in one piece. I shall never forgive you if you die."

"I won't die." He squeezed me. "I'll be back before you know it, my love. Then we'll have a nice fire and a fine meal." He drew away, backing out of the makeshift hut and getting to his feet.

I watched him from the doorway, seeing the men in shadow. They all gripped spears.

"Are we ready?"

"We are," said Frendo.

"Does anyone object to this?"

"It's been decided," said Brayer. "We watch from a distance and count the men. If something's amiss there, we step in. If it's just another clan, we leave them be."

"This is no ordinary clan. No leader I've ever known punishes his people by cutting out their … male parts. It's cruel."

"Indeed, Sal. I couldn't agree more," said Greggor. "Let's go then. I want to put this behind me. Then I wish to eat a fine meal and bed my wife." He strode away, his feet crunching over dried leaves.

Forty

After feeding Skye, Bannon and I picked up dried branches in the dark, finding them with our feet. With the baby across my chest, I listened to any sound on the wind, worried over the men. They had been gone quite a while now. Bannon and I would wait to make a fire, not wanting to alert anyone to our campsite.

"Mamma?"

I could hardly see his face. "We've gotten as much as we can. I can't see anything."

"Dadda come back?"

"Soon." But doubt plagued me. If they did not return before dawn, I had to assume the worst. "Let's settle in for bed."

"Me not tired."

"You are, you just don't know it." Escorting him to the shelter, I ushered him inside, scraping my forehead on a branch. "Ouch."

"What?"

"Nothing. Try not to poke your eye out. This isn't the best hut." Untying the leather around my waist, I held Skye in my arms, the baby asleep. "She's such a good girl. She hardly ever cries."

"She funny, Mamma."

"Why would you say that?"

"Funny face."

"She's a baby. You looked like that too when you were little."

"Smelly."

"I have to change her." Working in the darkness, I fumbled around for a leather strip, discarding the soiled one a moment later. "She should smell better now."

"When dadda come?"

I sighed. "I don't know."

"Want to eat cat."

The carcass laid nearby, the men not having cut it open yet. "So do I, but it's dangerous to make a fire now."

"Why?"

"Because someone might see the light. We don't want bad men to come, do we?"

"No."

"You always have to be careful, Bannon. There's danger everywhere."

"Like cats?"

"And bad men."

"Why man bleed?"

"Because he was hurt." I did not want to discuss this with him. "Why don't you try to sleep a little? If you sleep, the night will go by faster. Then your father will be here."

"Me not tired." He shuffled around, settling on a pelt.

Skye fussed then, and I patted her back. "Shush, my love. You'll have to be quiet tonight." I stared out the doorway of the branches, seeing nothing other than darkness and the black outlines of trees.

What if he doesn't come back?
People disappear like this.
They go away and … vanish into the air.
Greggor has to come back to me.

Sitting here waiting renewed feelings of fear and the distinct impression of loneliness. I lived with these emotions far too long as it was, hating them.

"Where are you?" I whispered, reaching for the bow.
Maybe you should go and see where they are?
I'd like to, but I can't leave my children. I can't.

What if the men … what if everyone's dead?

I brushed that notion away, a chill drifting through me. Sitting with my legs drawn up and my arms around the ankles, I rested my chin on my knees. A memory from long ago returned, when I had been a child. I remember the dark-skinned men that took us in so long ago, my mother falling in love with their leader, Magnon. It hadn't been a large clan, with only five men and a handful of women. My mother and sister and I lived with them peacefully for a season, until the morning Greggor and his men arrived.

I had seen them from a distance, eyeing their approach. What we did not know was that they would attack entirely unprovoked, slaying all the men. Hiding in a hole in the wall with other children, I had seen the violence, horrified at the sight. Greggor had been younger then, his body thinner, yet still muscled like today. I hated to think about the past; not wishing to relive it, but the memory gave me an odd sense of hope. Greggor's men possessed skill with their weapons and physical strength; they had proved victorious.

"He's strong," I whispered to myself. "I've seen him fight. All the men are strong." I listened to the wind, suddenly aware of a noise, the sound of … voices. Getting to my feet, I burst free of the shelter, gripping a spear.

Something came at a distance, branches snapping loudly and a baby crying. Shocked, I held my breath, worried over what approached. With any luck, they would pass without seeing the shelter, because it looked like a bush. No one would know I stood here, unless … the men returned.

***

"Peta?"

I recognized Greggor's voice, sighing with relief. My

children asleep, I crawled from the hiding place, seeing the outlines of a group of people in the dark, stunned by how many there were. "You're back!" I flung myself at him, relieved they returned. "You're wet."

"It's blood." He kissed the side of my face, pushing me away gently. "You'll be covered in it. Be careful." He turned around. "Make a fire."

"I gathered wood, as much as I could."

"Thank you, my love."

"What happened?"

Someone rubbed sticks together, kneeling over where I tossed the wood. I surrounded it with rocks, although it wasn't the best fire pit I had ever made. It would have to do.

"We came upon a clan of dark men," said Brayer. "Most of them were mixed breed."

As the fire took, engulfing the branches, I saw the men better, startled to find the faces of women and children, most of whom appeared far too thin. "You took the women?"

Brayer bent over the carcass of the cat. "Freed, would be a better word. They were captives."

"Captives?"

"Aye," said Greggor with a hint of bitterness. "They were bound, even the children. It's no way to live. I know you made me promise never to harm the dark ones, but … I … we could not let this stand. They were hostile, Peta. They attacked first. We tried to make contact, but they wouldn't have it. I was forced to … we were forced to kill them." His look betrayed worry, fearing I would now rebuff him. "Peta?"

I eyed the women, seeing them better in the firelight. They appeared to be a mixture of both races, all of them far too thin, their expressions dull. "Cook the meat and eat. They need to eat."

"Which is what I'm doing," said Brayer. "We need

more wood."

"I'll get it." Sal strode into the forest, disappearing at once.

"You're not angry?" Greggor seemed to hold his breath.

"If it's as you say, then you did something good for these poor women." I offered a tentative smile, wondering where everyone would sleep. "How many are there?"

"Quite a few," said Frendo. He glanced at them. "Please don't be afraid. Come sit by the fire."

A woman stepped forward, her hair hiding most of her face. "We thank you," she whispered. Thin and pale, she held out a hand. "Are you a god?"

"W-what?"

"I prayed for a spirit to help me. The gods listened."

"I'm not a god. What's your name?"

"Lelana."

"Who are the other women?"

"My friends, even the dark ones. They speak our language."

"Well then, please come sit." Brayer tossed strips of meat onto a flattened rock in the center of the pit, the meat sizzling at once. The aroma drifted, making my belly rumble. "We're eating soon."

"You are kind." She nearly fell sideways then, suddenly off-balance. "Food … would be good."

I grasped her arm, feeling how thin she was, merely skin and bones. "Gods' teeth, you're in dreadful shape. Are you all this way?"

"Mostly," she murmured, lowering to the ground, her shoulders hunched over.

Greggor and I exchanged a glance. "Are the children like this too?"

"They're all … hungry." He motioned. "Come, sit. We mean you no harm. Warm yourself by the fire. Have some food."

Sal returned with an armful of branches, tossing them on the ground. "I can get more, if need be." He eyed the group. "They smell."

"A bath will be in order at first light," said Greggor. "Please have food, but eat slowly. It looks like they've not had any in quite a while. Too much could make them sick."

"What sort of clan was this?" I saw another woman, a dark-skinned one, who looked no bigger than a few sticks tied together. "Gracious, how awful." She cast a glance at me, her eyes sunken into her head. "Please sit here, please." I reached for her hand, but she pulled away. "I'm not going to harm you."

"Here's meat." Brayer gave a piece to a woman. "We've a bladder of water as well."

One by one, the group sat by the fire, all of them filthy and tired, their bodies shockingly frail. I chewed on a fingernail, thinking about what this meant, how it might delay our return to the cave.

"Are you angry?" Greggor's knee touched mine.

"No."

"I … did what I promised I wouldn't."

"You had to kill them. I've never seen women and children so … so thin."

"I think they suffer from some sort of fever. When one goes without food for long, it weakens the mind."

The dark women huddled together, one of them with a young boy, the baby frail from lack of nourishment. They ate slowly, as if they hadn't tasted food in a season or more, not quite knowing what to do with it.

"What happens now?"

"We can't leave them. They're too weak to fend for themselves. I propose we feed them to health and take them with us. We needed more women anyhow." He grinned, surprising me. "In a way, our prayers have been answered. There are enough women now to please everyone, wouldn't you say?"

"What if they don't wish to go with us?"

"It'll be their choice." His hand touched my back. "If they desire to eat well and be safe, then they should join us."

We spoke loud enough to be overheard, and yet no one said anything. The women ate, their fingers dripping with the juice of the meat. The dark group sat alone together, none of them speaking. Something struck me as familiar about them, but I could not place it.

"Things will look clearer at dawn," I mused.

"Yes." He tore off a chunk of meat. "Have some food, Peta. Eat. There's plenty. Then I need to wash. I've dried blood all over me."

I glanced at the dark women again, pondering the situation.

Forty-One

"They weren't our prisoners," said Greggor. "There's nothing to be done about it."

I sat up, moving hair from my eyes, feeling groggy from sleep. I listened to the men, Greggor having left the shelter. Bannon and Sky continued to sleep, although the baby woke twice during the night.

"They're hardly strong enough to venture on their own," said Sal. "I don't understand it."

"It's their choice."

Scrambling from the shelter, I eyed the men, Brayer cooking the last of the meat. "What happened?" I did not see the women from the night before, the area clear. "Where'd they go?"

Greggor shrugged. "They left."

"But why?" I sat next to him, my hand on his thigh. "Did something happen?"

"Nothing from what I can tell."

I wondered at my mood and why I felt so badly about this. "I thought they might come with us. They're without protection. Most of those women can barely stand."

Frendo cleared his throat. "They ate quite a bit of meat. That should give them some nourishment."

"That's a shame. We needed women." I flung a small stick in the fire. "This means we leave soon, doesn't it?"

"There's no reason to delay." Greggor touched my hand, a grin appearing. "We'll make good time. If we're lucky, we'll be at the cave by nightfall."

I desired greatly to be home, the thought appealing. "I'm going to wash up. Is there a stream nearby?"

"I'll take you." Greggor helped me to my feet, his hand on my back. "You look lovely first thing in the day, Peta."

His endearment skimmed down my backbone in a pleasing little tingle. "You flatter me, my Lord. I look a sight. I feel dreadful. I'm dying for a bath."

"Which you'll have tomorrow."

We slipped through the trees, the ground feeling moist with dew. "I'm eager for it." Eyeing the forest, I asked, "Where's the stream?"

"Some ways."

"You didn't bring a weapon."

"I'll take the risk."

Was that wise?

"We've cleared the place of the unwanted. All the predators are feasting as we speak. There's plenty of meat to go around. They won't be coming after us."

I shuddered at the thought. "Let's not turn in that direction."

"No, we won't. It's not a pretty sight."

Glancing at him, I spied small marks on his arms, cuts from the skirmish. "You're hurt."

"Hardly. A few scratches."

"You should clean them."

"Which is why we're bathing, my love." A grin emerged. "The danger's passed. I sensed it yesterday, but we've taken care of it."

"I should've known you'd be victorious, even with so few men."

"And in the dark." He continued to beam, flashing strong, even teeth. "It wasn't my intension to dispatch all the men, but they left us no choice."

"You needn't explain. From what I saw of those women, you did them a favor. You freed them. Now they're off … somewhere. With meat in their bellies, they should do well." We followed the sound of water. Venturing down a small embankment, I untied the skirt at my hips, letting it fall. "I hate it cold, but I've no choice."

Greggor waded in, emerging to his ankles. "It's not deep."

Shivering, I muttered, "Gods' teeth. It's cold."

I sat in the deepest part, the bottom hidden by small rocks. The ends of my hair floated around me, although the top portion remained dry. I hurried to finish, jumping to my feet a moment later, wrapping the leather skirt around my hips. Greggor donned his, taking my hand, leading me back to the shelter, although I heard voices now—many voices.

As we approached, a group of women sat by the fire, the dark ones amongst themselves while the others formed their own group, a few children running about. The meat from the night before had done them wonders, no doubt.

"Look at that," said Greggor, his smile revealing surprise. "They didn't leave after all."

They appeared freshly bathed, their faces and hands clean, many with damp hair still. "No." I smiled brightly, because they stared at me. "Good day. We thought you might've run away."

The woman named Lelana spoke. "We needed to wash. We foraged a little. It's been an age since we've walked this much." She lifted her hands, where dark red circles appeared at the wrists. "We were bound for a long time." Holding her foot up, the same wounds occurred there around the ankle. "Walking feels so odd. I'm as feeble as a newborn stag."

My eyes drifted over the group, resting on the three women huddled together with a baby, who looked to be Bannon's age. "What are your names?"

The white women spoke first. "Seffa." She held a baby in her arms.

"Shanny," said a younger girl.

"Silva."

"Marry."

"Maggi," said a dark-skinned girl. She lowered her head, a messy bundle of hair falling in her face.

"Ara," said the next woman. "This my son, Bunder."

It felt as if someone stole the air from my lungs, my chest thumping. I waited breathlessly, knowing the name I would hear next.

"Kia."

"Bless the stars!" I cried. "It's you! I've finally found you!"

Greggor's look revealed confusion. "You know these people?"

"They're my family!" Tears formed in my eyes. "I've found them! It's me, Peta! You do remember me, don't you?" I ran to them, dropping to my knees. "Peta!"

A glimmer of recognition flickered in Kia's eyes. "Peta?"

"Yes, it's me! I've been so worried about you. I can't believe I found you." I wondered at her hesitation, her thin shoulders trembling. "It's me. You're safe now. We should never be parted again. You must come to my home."

Kia reached out to touch my face. "Peta?"

"Yes, it's me."

She smiled sadly. "My child Peta."

"But I'm not a child anymore, Mamma." I hugged her, alarmed by how bony she felt. "I'm your daughter. You're safe now. I'm going to take care of you."

***

With so many women weak, we could not embark on a journey, despite my desire to do so. I settled in next to my family, where I shared strips of cooked meat. Bannon ambled over, lowering into my lap.

A wet glimmer shone in Kia's eyes. "He looks like Ronan. Exactly like him." She touched his pale colored hair. "So beautiful." She sniffed, her eyes straying to Greggor. "I remember him too. Men like him attacked the clan, as you know. They killed all the men. They took Bannon."

"I came back to get him. I saw the carnage. I assumed the worst. There weren't any women and children among the dead. It gave me hope you were alive."

Ara listened, her gaze straying to Greggor. "He looks ... he looks like someone I've seen before."

Greggor sat at a distance with Sal and Frendo. He held Skye in his arms, the babe sleeping.

"I remember him well." Kia frowned. "A long time ago. He and his men attacked our clan. They killed the men and let the women go, but they took the white ones." Her look became questioning. "He's your enemy, Peta. What are you doing with him?"

"I went looking for you. I found the camp and all the bodies. A woman there said the white men took my son. I went after him. Greggor took him."

"This horrible man," murmured Kia. "He murdered Magnon and the others."

"Yes."

"And he had your son."

"I ... lived with him for a while. I then ran away with Bannon. It's a long story, Mamma. I don't know how to explain it all to you."

"That babe he holds," said Maggi. "Is that yours?"

"It's my little girl, Skye."

Kia nodded. "He bred you."

I sighed, knowing how deeply she hated Greggor for ruining her happiness all those seasons ago. "Yes." I touched her hand. "He's not as bad as we think. I can't make excuses for what he's done, but ... he's promised not to kill the dark ones without reason. He said you and the women were held against your will. The half-breeds weren't friendly in the least. They … they did what they had to. You're free now."

"He's the reason we fled in the first place," said Ara. "We were without a clan for a good while, until these heathens came upon us. They …" she shook her head, as if warding off an unpleasant memory. "I've no wish to relive what's happened." Her eyes shone with tears. "I thought I'd die. I thought we'd all die. I'm tired of the suffering, Peta. I lost my man. Bunder's without a father. So much has happened … that he can be blamed for."

"How does he treat you?" asked Kia, her attention on me. "You look healthy. Your children look healthy."

I cast a glance at Greggor, who gently tossed Skye over a shoulder, the baby crying. She needed to be fed. "He's not the monster I thought, although he's done … bad things."

Kia's hand touched my shoulder. "Where's Ronan? Why aren't you with Ronan?"

Forty-Two

I ran from Greggor and found Ronan and Enwan. I knew he'd follow me. I feared for Ronan's safety, so I made him leave. We hid alone for a while. Then we found a clan to stay with, but half-breeds attacked us. It was … horrible. Almost no one escaped. I thought Ronan dead. I found him wounded." Memories flooded, the feeling of loss cutting deep. "He died from his wound. I tried to heal him, but I failed."

Maggi chewed a piece of meat. "Half-breeds attacked? The men we were with liked to do that. We moved camp many times. Whenever they found strangers, they'd kill the men and take the women."

"I don't know if it was those men," I said. "But, that's what happened to Ronan. I returned to the cave to have Skye. Then Greggor found me."

Kia took a sip from a bladder, wiping her mouth with the back of her hand. "I've thought a great deal about things, Peta. Being bound as a slave with nothing to do, I … thought of many, many things." She handed the bladder to Ara. "You begged me to go with you—to live with you. I refused."

"I remember."

"You've not had peace either, my child. It seems as if we've been running around in circles, losing and finding one another."

"Yes." I smiled weakly. "I'm tired of it. Greggor's taking me home. I love the cave. It's where I feel my best.

It's where I've had my children. It's where I wish my life to be."

Kia glanced at Greggor. "And I see the choice I must make. Do I search for another dark clan or do I go with you?"

"I want you to come home with me, but I know you hate Greggor. I know."

"You need a strong man to protect you. With so few men, he still killed everyone in that horrible clan. I can't say I'll miss any of them. We've freedom now, but for how long?"

"What do you mean?"

"If Ara and Maggi and I venture off again, we risk capture by others." Her shoulders slumped. "I can't do it. I'd rather live without a man than … live with animals. The half-breeds are no better than animals."

"I want to go with Peta," said Maggi. "I don't know anything about this Greggor person, but they're feeding us. They haven't beaten anyone. They haven't forced us to do other things either."

I smiled sadly at my younger sister, her features much like Kia and Ara's. I touched her hair, feeling the coarseness of it. "I do hope you'll come live with me."

"And is Enwan alive still?" asked Ara.

"From what I know, yes."

"How many others live there?"

"A few women and a half-breed, but he's harmless."

"We've little choice," said Kia. "Like I said, I'm tired. I long for a comfortable shelter and … a measure of peace. These last few seasons have not been kind. We've survived things … " clouds reflected in her eyes, "that are too awful to mention. Since the day men took us from the stream near Sungir's hut, nothing's been peaceful. I always worry, and I'm tired of it." She eyed Greggor. "I know not what to think about that man. I swore him to damnation and back for killing Magnon, but he's freed us from peril.

We would've died with the half-breeds. They didn't think to feed us. A woman or child died every few days as it was. They never buried the dead either. They just ... they ate them." A shudder rippled through her. "Let's not speak of it. It's over."

***

I hardly knew how to react after finding my family again. A great many things had happened, from Ronan's death to meeting my birth family, and now this blissful reunion. I offered the shelter to Kia, Ara, and Maggi, introducing them to my new baby.

"This is Skye."

Kia held the infant, her features softening. "She's young. She looks no older than a few days."

"She's a bit older, but not much." I shrugged, eyeing the fire. Women sat together in groups, while Greggor left to hunt with his men, although Sal remained behind. "I went with Greggor to return to his people, although they didn't want him. He'd been searching for me too long. Another took over his clan. Many clans. He was leader to many, many people."

"White heathens," murmured Ara.

"I called them that too. I hated him for many seasons for what he did. I don't blame you for not liking him. He's promised never to kill the dark ones again, unless there's good reason, unless they attack first."

"This is his babe." Kia touched Skye's cheek, the infant sleeping. "She's a sweet little thing."

"Yes."

"And he really is kind to you?" asked Maggi.

"He's ... good and kind to me and Bannon. He thinks of Bannon as his own. I know you hate him, but you needn't worry over me. If he was the sort to harm a woman or child, I would ... kill him." I eyed the bow, my weapon nearby.

"I don't doubt that," said Kia. "You've given me plenty to think on." She held the babe close, hugging her. "Such a precious little thing. I thought never to see you or Bannon again. The terror we felt when Greggor's men attacked." She closed her eyes. "I thought that was the worst of it, but I know now the … horror was only beginning."

"You don't have to speak about it."

"There's no safety with my kind of people. They're either not strong or skilled enough to fight back or they're half-breeds and insane. It's just no good."

"Then I hope you come with me."

"I want to," said Maggi. "I'm scared, Mamma. I know you hate the white men, but they're strong. They freed us from the animal men. I'd rather live with the white people and be safe than fear all the time with our own kind."

Kia sighed. "I want to learn to forgive Greggor for what he's done. I remember the anger and hatred you held for him. I told you to let it go. The gods wanted you to meet again. I know not why they would kill Ronan, but who are we to question them? I've given up. I just don't wish to starve anymore. I don't want to be beaten. I'm tired of sleeping in the cold and wet like a dog. I'll do whatever I must to see Ara and Maggi and Bunder safe and happy. I care not about finding a mate. I've had my one love."

Tears formed in her eyes.

"I wasn't supposed to be happy for long. I hold those memories within, so very close to my soul. That's where Magnon lives. My time with him was a gift. He gave me Maggi. It's all I can ask for in this life." She smiled at Maggi. "You remind me of your father every day."

"Don't cry, Mamma."

"I cry not just because I'm sad, but I'm happy too. I have all my girls together and this one." She hugged the baby. "This one too. I want to be mother to you all. I'm grateful to be with you. We shouldn't separate again."

Relief washed over me. "Then you'll come to the cave?"

"Yes, Peta. I will."

"Even though you hate Greggor?"

"I shall forgive him in my time. Once I know more of what sort of man he is, perhaps I might call him friend. I know nothing about him. I can't promise anything just yet. I owe him for freeing us. In a way, he's redeemed himself, I suppose. He killed Magnon, but he's given us our freedom. We would've died, Peta. Things were not good."

"I can see that. You're terribly thin."

"Yes." She placed the baby on a pelt next to Bannon, who played with animals carved out of wood. She ruffled his hair. "I've missed this one. Being with my family means more to me than anything."

"I'm so happy we're together again." A burst of emotion drifted through me. "I'm sorry you've suffered so, but no more! I won't let it happen again. We're going to live the peace we deserve. This was how it's meant to be."

Men returned with game, their voices resonating. Greggor appeared in the doorway, leaning in to look at us. "Are you hungry?"

"They can eat." I scrambled to my feet, moving aside a branch to face him. "They're coming home with us."

"Is that what they want?"

"Yes."

"I've discussed it with Brayer and Frendo. Sal agrees too. We've the makings of a new clan with these women, but they must come willingly. I know not what the white ones have to say." He eyed them, as they sat by the fire. "They're a sorry sight."

Frendo cut off a portion of meat from a stag, tossing it onto a rock where it sizzled. "We can eat soon." He eyed one woman in particular. "You may have this piece, if you want."

She scooted nearer, taking it. "Thank you."

"See, you've nothing to fear from us. There's no reason to be afraid any longer."

"They've been mistreated," I murmured, chewing on my lip.

"Are you hungry?"

The low tenor of his voice drifted over me. "No."

He took my hand. "I wish a word with you."

"All right." Leading me towards the trees, I glanced over my shoulder. "But I've left Bannon and Skye."

"Your family's with them."

I liked the sound of that, smiling. "Yes, they are." Standing amongst the trees, he turned to face me, his hands on my shoulders. "What is it?"

"I've history with your family that's unpleasant."

"You killed my mother's one true love."

He sighed. "Yes, that. Are you sure she wishes to live with … me? I'm not just providing safe passage to the cave. I plan to live there as well."

"I'd hoped so." I smiled at the thought.

"And yet your family … hates me."

"My mother believes in forgiveness."

"You've forgiven me."

"Because you promised not to kill the dark ones."

"But that's exactly what I just did."

"To free women and children. They were starving. They would've died. You've atoned now, Greggor. It's over and done with, as far as I'm concerned. I don't want to rehash it all."

"No?"

"No."

He drew me to him, his lips by my ear. "I adore you, Peta. I've been waiting for a moment alone with you."

A tingly shiver raced down my back. "You have?"

Grasping my face, he kissed me, his lips soft, yet

urgent. "Yes. I desire to mate you."

"Now?"

"There's no better time." He dropped to a knee and then sat, drawing me onto his lap.

"What if we're seen?" I inhaled the scent of him, all pine and wind with a hint of musk.

"I care less." He kissed me, his tongue invading. "No more talk. I'd rather you use that mouth in a ... more pleasurable way."

The firmness of his manhood pressed into my buttocks. "I see." I eagerly returned the kiss, wrapping my arms around his neck. Then I nibbled on an earlobe, which elicited a manly groan.

"Oh," he murmured. "Peta." Emboldened, I pushed against his chest until he fell to his back. "What do you intend now?" He held his hands behind his head, a certain heat glimmering in his eyes.

"I see something I want." Giggling, I shoved aside the leather, which revealed his anatomy. "Will you stop me?"

"You may have whatever you desire, my love."

I flung a leg over his belly. "I want this."

Forty-Three

Brayer and the men built three more shelters, cutting branches and affixing them in such a way to provide a barrier to the rain and cold. Although weak and timid at first, the former captives gradually recovered their health. Greggor and his men waited, knowing they needed strength and stamina for the journey to the cave.

My mother and sisters kept their distance from Greggor, sleeping in a shelter on their own. I foraged with them, the four of us picking nuts and berries where we found them, the feeling familiar.

"I've missed this." I held a basket, with Skye sleeping against my chest. "Oh, how I've missed this."

Kia ate a berry. "It's like the old days." A ray of sunlight fell over her face, as she stood between two trees. "I never thought we'd be together like this again."

"Nor I."

"Remember the time in the woods when the water came?" said Ara. "We sat in a tree for days."

"I can't forget," I murmured, frowning at the memory. "So many of our clan perished."

"It was the beginning of everything." Kia sighed, her gaze straying into the distance. "Much happened after. I met Magnon then."

"And that cat killed Bena," said Ara.

I nodded, remembering the horror—the fear. "And then we met Sungir."

"Where we lived for many seasons in peace. I had

Maggi there. He was a good man."

"But it didn't last." Ara bent to pick mushrooms. "It never seems to last."

"I know you don't like Greggor, but he's strong. His men can protect us like no other. Once we're at the cave, you'll see how wonderful it is. It's large, big enough to hold many families. I know we'll be happy. The valley's fertile. The game's good. It's safe."

"No place is ever safe," said Kia.

"True. We do have cats, but Ronan and Enwan and Bondo killed some. I killed one too. We must always be wary, but once we're established, we can set traps like Sungir did. He made those deep holes around his hut, remember?"

"The one you fell into?" Ara grinned. "You broke your leg. You couldn't walk for a long time."

"I should be lame. Sungir was a great healer. I wish I was more like him."

"We're out of practice. I've forgotten what he taught me too."

"When was the last time you used a bow?" Sungir taught us the weapon, a skill I favored.

"The elders of the last clan took it from me. They tossed it in the fire thinking it was an evil talisman. They weren't free-thinking in the least. They were more like beasts."

"We'll find some wood and make you one. You need a weapon."

"The tree is hard to come by."

I nodded. "Yes, true, but it's around. I'll keep an eye out for it."

"Can we go back now?" asked Maggi. "We've enough. The other women are foraging too."

I smiled at my younger sister, delighting in having her near. "Yes." A rumble echoed overhead, bad weather approaching. "We should hurry or we'll be wet."

Maggi darted into the foliage. "I'm not getting wet!"

I giggled, "Nor am I."

Kia and Ara followed, the three of us arriving at camp a moment later, where cooking fires burned and women sat together. Bannon hunted with Greggor today, the men returning a short while later. I grinned at the sight of them, Bannon sitting upon Greggor's shoulders, the boy's blond hair falling into his face. Frendo tossed the carcass of a stag to the ground, several women scooting nearer to help carve out the meat.

"There you are, you little hellion." Greggor grasped Bannon, setting him on his feet. Go to your mother. She's waiting for you."

Having fed Skye, the babe asleep in my arms, I smiled at my son, the boy wearing a leather skirt. "Did you help in the kill?"

"No, Mamma. Me too small to kill a stag."

Greggor glanced at Kia and Ara, nodding at them. "I'm washing up. I'll be back."

Getting to my feet, I handed Skye to my mother. "Watch her for me, please."

She held the baby, her harsh features softening. "I adore this little one."

"Watch Bannon. I'll be back." I hurried after Greggor, although he knew I approached, having waited for me. "The women are healthier."

His gaze drifted over me. "So they are."

"Can we go home?"

He touched my face. "Are they ready for travel?"

"Yes."

"I know you're eager, but there are some weak ones in the bunch. I worry over this. I fear too much labor might harm them."

"We can walk slow, until they build up their strength. Everyone forages, even the sick ones. I've done what I can. I made Seffa a tea for her bad belly. The wounds

Marry and Silva had are healing. All can walk."

He drew me near. "I'll speak to the men. I'm sure they're ready to go on. I'd like to find a better settlement. The cave will do nicely."

"It will." He felt slick, his skin coated with dust and perspiration. "You need a bath."

"Let's wash up, shall we? It's been a long day."

"Were there any signs of other clans?" They hunted in a wide parameter, often venturing quite far.

"We came upon a corpse, but it looked like the odd one out. It was someone traveling alone."

We strolled towards the stream. "That's always dangerous. You'd survive alone. You're strong."

"I am, but I prefer company." A grin appeared. "I especially like your company, Peta."

"I've thought about some things lately. You gave up your clan for me. Do you realize that?"

"Aye, I'm aware." The sound of trickling water revealed the stream. Dropping the leather at his hip, he waded in and sat, splashing his face and neck clean. "I gave up a great deal for ... you."

"And do you regret it?"

He scrubbed his face. "I regret nothing, Peta. It is as it should be. We begin anew now. We'll make it better."

I sat upon the gravel near the edge. "How?"

"We've the makings of a new clan—a mixed clan. It won't matter what anyone looks like or where they've come from. We shall live together as one."

"I've been in mixed clans before. People tend to stay with their own."

"Yes, but in time that'll change. When dark children play with the light ones, friendships will build and last." He got to his feet. "When Bannon's your age, he'll have both dark and light friends, perhaps even a dark mate."

"And you'll let him?"

"If that's what he wishes, yes."

"Your healer taught you to believe the dark ones are lesser. They should all be killed."

He sighed, tying the leather to his waist. "Yes, I'm aware. I believed him because I thought him wise. I'm deciding more things for myself." He reached for my hand, drawing me into the forest. "I've been watching you with your family. I know how much you love them. They adore you as well and your children, even Skye. Kia knows the babe's mine, but she cares not about that."

"This pleases me," I murmured, my heart swelling. "I've never known a man to change his thinking before."

His lips grazed my cheek. "It makes you happy to be with your family. I can see that. You desire us to live together. It's not impossible. The men are warming to the idea. My only wish is to make you happy, Peta. I've caused you and your family pain—great, great pain. I'll do what I can to make it right for them. I'll give you whatever you wish, anything." He grasped my face, staring at me intently. "I adore you. I'd breathe my last breath, if it meant life for you."

"I believe it," I murmured.

His lips crushed mine, a tongue invading. I melted into his arms, shivering with several emotions, until they faded away to only the sensation of arousal.

"These moments alone are precious."

"We'll have our own pelts in the cave." As it was, we shared the shelter with my children and Maggi and Bunder. One pelt hardly covered us all, the little ones always sleeping close. "But this is nice." I felt the tension in him, the kisses growing urgent. "What do you intend, my Lord?"

"To pleasure us both." He lifted me into his arms, lowering to the ground, where soft grass cushioned my back. "Like this."

I closed my eyes. "Oh!"

"We have a little time." Leaning over, he kissed me,

the feeling languid and sweet, but it soon became urgent, our tongues battling.

Pleasure rippled through me. "Oh, yes."

"I think only of mating you."

"Truly? Even when you're hunting?"

"Yes, especially then, because I'd rather mate than hunt any day."

"I'd rather mate than forage."

"I'd rather kiss you than eat."

I giggled at that. "Then you'd starve."

"No, you fulfill me in every way, Peta." His mouth closed over mine, the force clinking our teeth together. "Gods' mercy, I want you."

"Then take me, my dearest. I'm yours."

Forty-Four

"Are they able enough to travel?" asked Sal, his expression doubtful. Standing with his hands on his hips, he eyed the women. "They've improved, but some are still weak."

"Peta says they'll manage."

I sat with Kia and Ara, while Bannon played with Bunder, the boys sharing a carved wooden toy.

"I tire of waiting." Frendo tossed a bone into the fire. "We've meat for days. We smoked the rest. It should keep us."

Greggor nodded. "What do you say?" He glanced at the women. "Are you ready to go on? Can you leave come daybreak?"

Anapia, one of the dark women said, "We can." She spoke with a heavy accent, the white language difficult for her.

"How long must we walk?" Seffa appeared worried, holding her baby. "I'm not as strong as I wish to be, but I can try."

"It's a good day's walk," said Brayer. "It might take two, though. I say we go and hope for the best. I tire of this camp. There aren't enough huts or pelts for comfort."

"Are there any objections?" Greggor glanced at me. "Peta?"

"I can't see any. I'd like to go."

"We go then," said Shanny. "I want to see this cave. Peta's spoken about it often enough. It sounds like paradise. I'll walk forever, if I must. I don't care. There's nothing left here. This wasn't my home anyhow. They stole me from my home like so many of the women. We owe you our lives, Lord Greggor."

A hint of a frown appeared. "You needn't call me that. It's just Greggor."

Kia chewed on a stick, her eyes straying to me. "I'm ready to walk."

"So am I," said Maggi. "I don't like this place."

"It's settled then." I grinned. "We needn't stay any longer."

"Good." Greggor sat next to me, resting his arms on his knees.

I hugged him, kissing his cheek. "You're hairy again."

"I need grooming, but not until we reach the cave." His grin softened. "You can groom me all you want then."

"For the love of the gods," muttered Brayer. "I can't listen to another moment of this." He got to his feet, hiding a smile. "All you speak are love words, and it's … disgusting." Casting a sideways glance at Shanny, he motioned for the woods. "I'm off to do my business." Disappearing into the foliage, the white woman soon got up after him.

"Where are you going, Shanny?" asked Ara, although she knew the answer to that question, a teasing glimmer in her eye.

"To … to see to … to relieve myself. It's really none of your business." She hurried to avoid having to answer more questions.

"Oh, indeed."

"Are they mating again?" asked Maggi bluntly. "I saw them mating earlier."

"Shush, child," admonished Kia. Then she laughed, "It's none of our concern."

Greggor rubbed his beard. "It'll happen." He exchanged a look with Sal. "Eh? How else will the next generation come to be?"

Seffa and Silva giggled, the women casting sly glances around the camp.

"I anticipate a batch of babies with the change of season," said Frendo.

Greggor's hand stroked my shoulder, the touch intimate and possessive. "Without a doubt."

***

I truly wished to arrive at the cave by nightfall, but that was not to be. We made camp in a secluded copse, the trees and bushes growing in a wide circle. Frendo and Sal tended the fire, while Greggor and Brayer hunted a stag, returning a short while later with the carcass. I sat with my family, while Bunder and Bannon played.

"Are you well?" I asked my mother.

She offered a smile. "I'm as well as can be hoped for, Peta. I'm sorry we didn't reach the cave. I know you wanted that badly."

"We made good progress. I've seen some of the marks I've left on trees long ago to guide the way. They tell me we're getting closer."

"I'm happy to hear it. I'm glad we're not lost."

"No, of course not. Even without the marks, Greggor knows the way."

"He's good with you." She eyed my man, who sat with Skye in his arms, the baby making noises. "He's devoted to that one."

Seeing a man of his strength with a tiny infant, it appeared odd, yet it warmed my heart. "I won't excuse what he's done in the past, but I've every hope he'll grow from that."

"As long as he's good to you and your children, that's all I care about." She drank from a bladder, water dribbling to her chin. "I'm tired of the anger and pain of days gone by. Thinking on them does nothing. Ara and Maggi and I have our freedom now. That's my only concern. I never want to be prisoner again." A shudder went through her. "Let's speak of other things."

I hugged her, wanting to offer solace. "I'm so sorry, Mamma."

"It's not your fault, child. You asked us to come with you, and I stupidly refused. All of this didn't have to happen. I see that now. If I'd just gone with you, we would've lived in peace and comfort with Enwan."

"You had your reasons."

"Selfish, stupid reasons. I wanted to stay to mate men of my own kind. Ara had Lowe, but they slaughtered him in cold blood." She made a face. "It's too awful to think on."

"Then don't. You'll have another mate, Mamma, so will Ara and Maggi. We might even meet some men on this journey and invite them to live with us. That's how I met Bondo. He's a half-breed, but he's a good man. He's kind. He's like you, but his hair's light and his eyes are like the sky. He looks like nothing I've ever seen before."

She patted my arm. "I'm going to trust you on this. I'm putting my life in your hands." She gazed at the men. "And them. They're a strong bunch, the strongest men I've ever met. My way's not worked. I've got to think of Ara and Maggi and their children's welfare first. I've been selfish."

"Stop that," I admonished, pushing her gently. "You're not selfish. We all want mates. I prefer to mate men of my kind. That doesn't make me selfish. You and Ara and Maggi deserve every happiness. You'll have another lover, I know you will."

"Supper's done," said Sal, holding up strips of sizzling meat.

Kia smiled. "I've missed what it feels like to have a full belly every night."

"Oh, Mamma." I frowned at that, feeling sad for her suffering.

"And your company. You're a smart girl, you always have been."

"I'm smart because my mamma's smart."

"You're smart because Sungir taught you to think for yourself."

"I've made some poor choices too. Ronan and I should've stayed at the cave and not run off. He'd be alive now."

"But then he'd have to deal with Greggor. I don't know how that would've ended, Peta. That man wants you. He's given up his clan for you. He might've killed Ronan."

I thought of how Ronan had shared me with other men. "Or … we might've lived together. I don't know. It's the unknown. I'll always feel a bit empty inside where he should be. He was such a sweet, kind man."

"He and Enwan spoiled you as a child."

I smiled at the memory. "Yes, they did."

"Even when you gave them the bugs in the hair, they spoiled you."

"Those were happy memories."

"Until the flood." She frowned. "But, let's not dwell on it. That was so many seasons ago. It seems like another life."

"It was."

"And now we've the prospect of tomorrow. It's a new day for us with strong men for protection."

I eyed the bow resting against a tree trunk. "And women. Ara and I will hunt as well. With some practice, her skill will be like mine."

"Mamma!" Bannon ambled over. "Meat!"

I smiled at my son. "Yes, I'll eat."

"Here." He gave it to me. "For you."

"Thank you, my love." Greggor gazed my way, Skye

beginning to fuss. "My daughter's hungry." He got to his feet, striding over.

Settling in by my side, he asked, "Are you tired?" He handed Skye to me.

"I'm fine." The baby latched on, suckling happily. "The women are tired, but I'm fine." Bannon, each fist filled with grilled meat, sat on Greggor's lap. "We should reach the cave tomorrow."

"Indeed. I've seen your markings."

"I left those long ago to guide the way. Do you think they're too obvious? Should I have hidden them better?"

"I'll have Brayer and Frendo scratch them out as we go."

"Yes, do that."

He glanced at Kia. "How are you?"

"I'm well."

"And your daughters?"

"They're tired, but well. We'll be ready to walk come sunrise."

His attention drifted over the cloistered group, the sound of soft female chatter filling the air. "I never thought I'd be leader to a clan of women. It's odd." A smile lingered. "We might have too many women."

I giggled at that. "Isn't that what most men want?"

That caught his notice, his look sobering. "No. I only need you, Peta. I knew that the moment you set foot in my camp. You were so angry with me, so bold. I knew then that I'd have you—no matter the cost."

A tingle of warmth drifted down my spine.

"I get what I want. I keep what's mine. I share with no one."

Forty-Five

Seeing the small X carved beneath a branch brought a smile to my face. I made those marks to help guide me back to the cave, if I ever lost my way.

"Scratch that out," said Greggor. "We don't need to light the path for anyone."

"How will we grow our clan then?" I asked, as Sal scraped away my handiwork.

"We'll find people, if need be." He glanced over his shoulder at the line of women. "That's the least of my concerns now." A frown appeared. "Should we rest?"

Seffa overheard that. "How much further?" Her baby slept across her chest in a leather strap.

"It's a while still," I murmured for Greggor's ears only.

"I know." He said loudly, "Is anyone about to fall over? Can you go a little further?"

Anapia held up a stick. "Go. We go on."

"Don't stop because of us," said Kia.

Greggor waved. "Onward then."

I fell into step behind him, while Frendo walked at the end of the line, with Brayer in the middle. Sal scouted out the path, disappearing behind the trees. We stopped for the midday meal a while later, sitting around the banks of a stream, the water clear. I nibbled on a piece of dried meat while feeding Skye. Bunder and Bannon splashed and played, the boys giggling.

Ara washed her face, kneeling on small, round rocks.

I smiled at the sight, pleased to have my family with me. Kia and Maggi ate, Maggi picking at a scab on her knee. Leaning against a tree, Brayer eyed the forest, his fingers wrapped around a sturdy spear.

Despite the tedium of the trek, I found a measure of peace in it, feeling that, with each step, I came closer to reaching the final destination in a journey that had lasted a lifetime.

"What are your thoughts?" Greggor knelt next to me. "It must be a good thought, because you're smiling."

"I … think I'm … happy."

"Happy?"

"It's such an odd feeling. I'm not sure I've ever felt it like this before. I hope nothing ruins it."

"Why should that happen?"

"Good things are always ruined."

He touched Skye's cheek, the baby asleep. "Not this time, Peta, not while you're with me. I'll watch over you. I'll protect you and our children. You've nothing to fear."

I sighed, wanting to believe him. "What do you fear?"

"Not much … losing you."

"I won't run again. I'm home now."

"We will be soon enough. From what I recall, there's a patch of grassland to cross until we reach the hillside where the cave is. It's more of a mountain, I suppose. It was dark the first time we came upon it."

"I saw your torches."

A rueful smile emerged. "To think you were across the way watching us from a hiding place. You were so close. I knew it. I could feel it."

I met his gaze. "That was a long time ago, Greggor."

"Yes. I forgive you for being disobedient. You did what you felt you must."

"I worried you'd kill Ronan."

"I was angry then, so very angry. I honestly cannot say if I would've killed him. He was an important person in your life. I've heard you speaking about him often enough. You've history."

"We had history. I knew him from when I was a child."

"After I destroyed your peace of mind and ruined the happiness of your mother."

I touched his hand. "I forgive you too."

"Do you?"

"Yes, of course. When I think back on it, I don't feel the hatred anymore. I don't know where it went, but I don't feel the same about any of it."

"What about your family?" He glanced at Kia and Ara, the women sitting nearby. They had more than likely overheard a good portion of this conversation.

"They're grateful to you for freeing them. They owe you their lives. They would've died with those horrible men. Whatever's happened is … like the water in the stream. It's moved on."

"I'd like a new beginning. I've a family now. We're building a new clan. I don't want to be leader any longer. Managing all those clans and the day-to-day problems of people exhausted me. Ripa managed a great deal too, but I carried the weight of the burden." A finger touched Skye's nose. "She's the most beautiful thing I've ever seen, almost as beautiful as her mother."

"I agree."

"My only wish is to take care of you and our children. I'd lay down my spear for any of you. Your health and happiness is all I desire, that and … " he grinned, "you in my bed."

"Oh, I see." Wrapping an arm around his neck, I hugged him. "That's my dream too. I thought I'd have that with Ronan and Enwan, but it wasn't meant to be." I pulled away, suddenly alarmed by a thought. "You won't be angry with Enwan, will you?"

"No, why would I?"

"Because he lied to you. He was friend to Ronan."

"That's all water down the stream, as you say. I care not. As long as you're with me, the rest doesn't matter."

"Then I'm happy."

His lips touched mine. "Me too." He stood, eyeing the women. "Are we ready to press on? We should reach the cave before nightfall, if we're lucky."

***

A wide swath of grassland stretched into the distance, a familiar-looking mountain behind it. I gazed at the sight I feared I might never see again, my heart swelling with emotion. Cradling Skye against my chest, the baby asleep, we set out to cross it, walking in a long line with men at the front and back and middle. I held the bow, alert for any sign of cats, the animals preferring to hunt out in the open.

"Are we close?" asked Maggi. "I'm tired."

"We are. Just a little ways more."

"Then a comfortable bed?"

I ruffled her dark, messy hair. "Yes. A bed and a fine meal." Sending out a prayer, I hoped Enwan and Bondo were well, along with the women and children. How would they react to our arrival? Leota blamed me for Ronan's death. I had ruined her happiness, but, then again, Ronan had been *my* man. How would everyone get along?

"Are you tired, Peta?" asked Greggor. He carried Bannon on his shoulders, the boy having cried earlier, all the children exhausted.

"I'm fine. We're nearly there."

"Worried?"

"About what?"

"It's a strange homecoming arriving with your sworn enemy and a passel of women and children."

"We needed more people."

"And now you'll have them."

"And then some," I laughed, feeling a growing sense of excitement. "It's not long now." Nearly to the other side of the field, I inhaled a hint of the heated pool, smelling slightly foul air. "The hot spring."

"One would never think such a thing would be so wonderful, soaking in water that smells rotten."

"But it leaves the skin nice and soft. Oh, how I've missed it."

"We can bathe alone tonight," he murmured, his meaning clear.

I grinned. "I would like that."

"We're getting close," said Frendo. "I remember that smell."

"Onward!" called Greggor. "We're nearly there."

"They won't be pleased with the last bit of climb," I said.

"No, but it must be done."

We passed the pool a short while later, the water hidden by tall reeds, a path emerging. This wound around to the bottom of the mountain, where a rocky path led to the cave entrance. From the smell of a cooking fire, I knew the shelter to be occupied. Glancing up at the hill, I saw a man on the ledge, another standing behind him. They held spears, watching us.

I grinned, feeling elated to see my friends again. "That's Enwan and Bondo."

Kia and Ara saw him too. "Oh, Enwan," murmured Kia. "I never thought I'd see him again."

"Enwan!" I shouted. "It's Peta!" The sound carried.

He disappeared down the path, with the dog hard on his heels, leaving Bondo standing by the cave. Two women joined him, with a little girl I assumed was Saffron's daughter, Poppy.

Enwan, having run down the side of the mountain, appeared then. "Peta!" His gaze strayed to Greggor and his men, a flicker of alarm in his eyes. "Are you well? I thought never to see you again." The dog sniffed us, the mangy creature wagging his tail.

"It's a long story, but I've good news. We're all going to live here now."

The women came in behind us, having climbed slower. "Who ... who are all these people?" He glanced at Kia. "Mother of the gods," he murmured, clearly shocked to see her again. "You too?" He grinned broadly. "And Ara? I'm ... speechless."

"It's good to see you, Enwan," said Kia. "You look exactly as I remember."

Ara said, "We're tired, Enwan. I pray you've some food."

"How many are you?"

"Myself and my men and a passel of women," said Greggor. "I wanted to return to my clan, but they've taken another leader. Peta would rather live here anyhow. We came across her kin on the journey, and more women." He picked Bannon up, the boy having walked for a short while. "I've no desire to be leader any longer. I'd like to live with my family in peace for once. The cave's more than big enough for all of us."

An array of emotions drifted over Enwan's face. "I hardly know what to make of this. I ... you may all live here, if you wish. We've meat aplenty and pelts for comfort. You look tired." He grinned. "You smell."

"I'm aware," murmured Greggor, his bland stare transforming into a smile. "Carry on. It's a little ways further. Food awaits!" He touched my back. "Shall we?"

I nodded. "What do you think of this, Enwan? You wanted a bigger clan." I moved to pass him, Kia and Ara and Maggi coming up behind me.

Enwan stood aside, glancing at all the women. He shook his head in disbelief. "I've ... no words."

Forty-Six

I worried about a chilly reception from Leota, who blamed me for Ronan's death, but her attitude seemed changed, the woman scurrying around to provide pelts for the everyone, making people as comfortable as possible. We sat around the fire, which burned brightly in the center of the cavern, the flames flickering around thick, broken branches.

"Here you are." Bondo offered meat to Kia, a smile on his face.

She stared at him, taking the meat. "Thank you."

"It's my pleasure." He grinned, flashing yellow teeth.

"He's happy," I murmured, placing Skye over a shoulder. She had just fed. "All these women." The sound of chatter filled the cavern, some of the women having eaten already and sleeping, exhausted from the journey. I held out a piece of meat to the dog. "Here, Putty. Take it." He ate the treat from my fingers. "Good boy." Bunder and Bannon chased the animal around earlier, the boys delighting in having a new playmate. They sat now eating, having exhausted themselves.

Greggor took a long pull from a bladder, wiping his mouth with the back of his hand. He sat cross-legged before the fire, his men surrounding him. I noted his stare. "You needn't be so far away."

"I'll join you in a moment."

"We're fine," said Kia. "This is a most … " she gazed around, "glorious cave. I've never seen anything like it.

Even with all these people, it's still large."

"It goes back some distance. But we prefer to be around the fire."

"I can see why you like it."

"I don't want to leave." Ara sat upon a thick pelt. "We'll never be cold here."

Maggi petted the dog. "He's a friendly thing."

"I'm glad you find the shelter to your liking."

"Where's the latrine?" asked Kia. "It smells far too fresh in here. Where do you go?"

"Outside around the side. You'll smell it there."

"Smart."

"Only heathens soil their own homes." I frowned, thinking of how my family had lived with the half-breeds. "Let's not dwell on that."

"No, no more bad memories," said Ara. "I can't wait to explore and see what's here."

"There's a river in the valley where the men fish. Game's plenty everywhere. There are cats too, so we must always be careful."

"We killed the den," said Enwan, having overheard that. "There are a few pelts waiting to be scraped."

"Are they all dead?" This was good news indeed.

"Yes. I can't say more won't come, but the den is gone."

"I'm glad you survived it."

"I'm glad you returned, Peta." He knelt beside me, casting a glance over his shoulder at Greggor. "Are you well? Is he treating you well? You must tell me the truth."

"I'm very happy, Enwan. I only wished to come home. I never want to leave again."

He eyed Skye, the baby asleep in my arms. "She looks bigger."

"All she does is eat."

He chuckled, "Indeed."

"I'm putting her to bed. I wish to bathe with my

husband."

"I'll take her." Kia reached out her hands. "Give her to me."

"Thank you, Mamma."

Bondo tossed another branch into the fire. "There's plenty of meat. You may have more." He glanced at the darker women, who sat together. He spoke to them in their language, the sound so odd, yet I understood every word. He said, "Please feel welcome. You may help yourself to food, if you wish."

"It's not often I hear that language," said Kia.

"They speak our tongue, Bondo." I smiled at him. "That's kind of you, but they know what we're saying."

"I want them to feel welcome." He eyed Kia, a bright smile remaining in place. "So, this is your mother?"

"Yes, this is Kia and my sisters Ara and Maggi."

"I'm happy to meet you." He held out a piece of meat. "Would you like more?"

Kia took it. "Thank you."

"Might I sit with you?"

"It's your cave. Sit where you like."

He settled in next to her, his knees up. "Shall I make the fire bigger?"

She glanced at the flames. "It's hearty already." She leaned in murmuring, "He's so odd-looking. I've never seen light hair on a man of our kind before."

"He's a good person, Mamma. I found him on one of my travels. He's always been kind." I knew Bondo could hear that. "You should consider him for a mate."

She grunted. "I don't need a mate. I'm too old for such things."

I giggled, finding that ridiculous. "Nonsense. I don't believe that for one moment." Despite this denial, she cast a sideways glance at the man.

Greggor got to his feet. "Peta?"

"Yes?"

"Let's take a walk."

I longed to have a bath. "Will you watch over Skye, please?"

"Of course."

Skye slept wrapped in a thin blanket of leather. "I'll be back."

"Take your time."

Enwan, who sat with Saffron and Leota, watched our exit. Leota offered a genuine smile, which then fell upon Sal, who sat nearby. I once heard him speaking about finding Leota to his liking, and one had to wonder if anything might come of that.

Greggor's hand pressed to my back, guiding me through groups of people. "The women look happy."

We stood before the cavern, the cooking fire filling the space with a yellowish light. "They're happy to rest. I can't blame them." I gazed at the twinkling of lights in the sky, marveling at how many of them there were. "We should be very happy here."

He touched my shoulder. "Will you be happy?"

I nodded, emotion suddenly getting the better of me.

"Peta?"

"It's been such a long journey. As a child, Ronan spoke often about finding paradise, a place of warmth and beauty, where the hunting was good. It sounded so promising. Then when the flood separated us, I feared I'd never see him again, but I always remembered what he said about the land where the mountains were."

"It is special."

"I feel a little guilty for living his dream without him."

"He'd want you to be happy, Peta. He'd want his child protected. I can offer you all that and more."

"I know. You and your men would never let anything bad happen. You're far stronger than most. I like that."

His arm went around me. "You and Skye and Bannon are what matters to me. I shall die keeping you safe."

"I'd do the same for you." I leaned into him, inhaling his musky scent. "I don't want to leave again."

"Why would you?"

"I don't know, but I don't wish to journey so far. I want to stay right here."

"Yes, my love."

"Will you be happy with such a small clan? You were leader to many clans. You were raised to be leader."

"And now I shall share the power. I'll be leader to my family. That's all I want."

"Does it pain you still to be cast out?"

"It angered me at first, but not now." He kissed my cheek. "I've so much more than I could've ever imagined. You didn't know me before. I wasn't a happy man, Peta. I didn't love my wife. I wanted a family. I felt the gods had forsaken me. Everything changed the moment I met you."

I sighed, wrapping my arms around his neck. "I wanted to hate you."

"I know."

"I loved Ronan."

"I know."

"I love you too."

"It would upset me if you didn't. I love you."

I wrinkled my nose. "You smell."

His laughter filled my ear. "Indeed. I'm weary and rank from travel."

I took his hand, feeling the rough quality of his fingers. "Then shall we bathe?"

"I'd love nothing more."

Also by Avery Kloss

Caveman
Caveman 2
Caveman 3

Clan of the Wolf
Chamber of Bears
Cave of the Wind

Made in the USA
Middletown, DE
16 July 2020

12383622R00179